S🍷NERGY

A Brooks Family Values Novel

Printed in the United States of America

ISBN-978-0-9913426-2-4

Library of Congress Control Number: 2014918933

SIRI ENTERPRISES
RICHMOND, VIRGINIA
www.sirient.com

www.irisbolling.net

Books By Iris Bolling

The Heart Series
Once You've Touched The Heart
The Heart of Him
Look Into My Heart
A Heart Divided
A Lost Heart
The Heart

Night of Seduction Series
Night of Seduction/Heaven's Gate
The Pendleton Rule

Gems and Gents Series
Teach Me
The Book of Joshua I – Trust
The Book of Joshua II – Believe

Brooks Family Values Series
Sinergy

Prologue

Friday
Manhattan, New York

Somewhere along the line, Nicole Brooks was certain her friend Alicia Robinson had lost her mind. She listened as Alicia attempted to persuade her to, not only buy a ticket, but to participate in the charity event. The more details Alicia shared, the more Nicole was certain participation was not in the cards for her.

"I will be more than happy to buy a ticket to donate to the cause. However, I draw the line at buying a man, even for charity." Nicole smiled at her friend, "You cannot believe I'm that desperate."

"I do believe you are in need of a man. I mean a real man. Not a, 'I'm just too fine to work man,' whom you have a way of attracting. I am talking about a man's man. However, this is not about being desperate or needing a man. This is about raising money to build a recreation center for the Highland Park area in Richmond. The city has closed every center for after school and summer programs. It baffles me when politicians have the nerve to wonder why kids are hanging on the corners or stuck in front of an electronic babysitter. It is going to take money, and lots of it, to get that center built. Let's not forget furnishing it with equipment and computers to keep the kids occupied. Nikki, you know what it is like. The kids need a place to go to stay out of trouble. How can you turn your back on that?"

Nicole knew Alicia was right. The area of Richmond the center would serve, was in need of some revitalization. Her brother James and his wife Ashley had a home in the Richmond metropolitan area. Of course at the moment, their home was in Fairfax, Virginia. Her brother, James, Political Advisor for the President of the United States, JD Harrison, was also the President's brother-in-law. One of the campaign promises was to improve education and after school programs for children across the country. Highland Park was one of the areas President Harrison mentioned was in desperate need of assistance. They wanted to find ways to reduce gang activity in that area. The President's belief was that in order to eliminate the gangs we must find alternatives for the kids, otherwise the gangs would just resurrect themselves.

What Nicole was not clear on was why she had to be the savior. "I'm sure Richmond has plenty of people who will attend the event and be very generous. The function will not fail if I'm not there, and Brooks International is already considering a proposal for the community center. Besides, you know your sorority sisters aren't particularly fond of me. And if I remember correctly, some of them aren't too thrilled with you, either."

With hands on her slender hips, Alicia smiled. "Well, maybe you should not have called them a group of 'wannabes', when we were in college."

Arms folded over her chest, Nicole countered, "Well, maybe they should not have shunned me because my skin was a little darker than theirs."

"Maybe you should not have told them you were going to have your daddy kidnap them and have all of their asses shipped back to Africa, to learn about their real roots."

They both laughed. "That did kind of piss them off, didn't it?" Nicole smiled. "I don't mind supporting your event, but I'm not too crazy about being around your *sisters*. Can't I just give a donation and be done with it?"

"Any other time I would say yes," Alicia agreed relaxing her stance. "However, as you said, some of my *sisters* aren't very loving towards me these days. You know I've been on shaky ground with them since I walked out during pledge week, because they voted you out." Taking a moment to push the guilt button, Alicia continued. "If I remember correctly, Shirley Ann wasn't too happy either."

Nicole exhaled. "Yeah, your mom was pretty pissed."

Pissed wasn't the word Alicia would have used, ballistic was more like it. Alicia's mother expressed her displeasure in very direct language. *'Nicole's father has enough money to buy her a sorority if she wanted one, your father and I do not. You will go back to school, young lady, and apologize, beg, grovel and anything else you have to do to cross the line. It is a legacy in our family and you will not break it.'* Alicia was sure her mother would have broken every bone in her body if she had not become a soror. "To this day, seven years later, she will not let me forget it. I'm not trying to make you feel guilty or anything, but you do owe me."

"Cut the crap, Alicia, that's exactly what you are doing."

Alicia rose from her seat in front of Nicole's desk and walked over to the window that overlooked Central Park. "You know there are thousands of people in New York City. At least one-fourth of them are men. You have been here for two years, sitting behind that desk trying to impress a group of old men who run the Real Estate world. What you and I both know is that they will never accept you, or I, into their inner circle no matter how good we are at what we do." She turned and looked down at her friend, who was seated at her desk. "You, my friend, have three things going against you. One-you are Black."

"No, say it ain't so. Say it ain't so." Nicole looked at her friend with astonishment.

Alicia smirked. "Two, you are a female and you know females have no place in this male dominated career. Then last, but certainly not least, you are young. There is no way the men who run the Real Estate business in New York are going to accept you. They don't care that your daddy is one of the richest African-Americans in this country. You sitting around, working twelve hour days and not having a social life is not going to change their minds." She sighed. "I just want you to have some fun, at least for one weekend, with a man that does not feel it's a crime to have a job. I'm not asking you to fall head over heels in love or anything close to that. Just have fun, get your little groove on."

Nicole smiled at Alicia, appalled. "You want me to buy a man to have sex with for a weekend? A man I don't know anything about and who is willing to strut across a stage for money."

"Nikki, it isn't like that." Alicia became excited. "These men are all business owners or partners. They are donating their time and the cost of the weekend package. You get to see their bio and what they have planned for the weekend before you bid. If you don't like the way they look or what they have planned, you don't bid. It's that simple. From what I'm told, the bachelors participating represent the cream of the crop of African-American men from across the Commonwealth of Virginia. We always say the good looking ones are in jail, not working or on the down-low." She stopped and looked at Nicole's reaction. "I'm not judging. I'm just saying, this is your opportunity to meet some honest to goodness hard-working brothers, especially since you refuse to come to the other side."

The look that Alicia had become accustomed to since she declared her sexual preference to Nicole during college was immediately evident on her friend's face. "I love you and always will, but that is your preference, not mine." A small smile crept on to her face. "I like the solid feel of a brother between my legs."

"You have made it clear that is your choice. However, don't knock what you don't know. Okay?" Alicia crossed her arms over her chest. "Although rumor has it, you've crossed over."

Nicole exhaled. "So I heard. Is that why you are so desperate for me to be seen with a man, because of the rumors?"

Alicia pouted. "I feel bad. I know the only reason the rumors started is because of our close friendship. I never meant for my openness about my sexual preference to affect you. I'm sorry."

Nicole smiled at her friend. She knew the rumors were floating around the office about her, but she was never one to concern herself with rumors. She was a firm believer that her personal business was just that—personal. It was nobody's business what she did behind closed doors. "You know, I couldn't care less what people think of me. I like who I am and I like who you are." She hugged her friend and smiled. "Don't worry about what people say, I'm not."

There was a knock on the office door. Nicole's secretary, Stacy Crane, walked in. "Umm hmm, excuse me. Ms. Brooks, your ten o'clock, Mr. Prentiss is here." She stood with a disapproving look at the two women embracing.

Nicole smiled and put her arms around Alicia's shoulder. "Would you have him wait for a moment?" She turned to Alicia and then back to Stacy. "Stacy, would you call my pilot? Have him fuel the jet." She smiled at Alicia and continued. "We will be going to Virginia for the weekend." Nicole put the brightest smile she could manage on her face for the judgmental woman standing in her doorway.

"As you wish," Stacy replied and closed the door.

Alicia looked at Nicole. "You know she is going right to the lounge and tell those heifers who work here what she just saw."

"Oh, I'm sure she will. That will only give me another reason to let her go. I have a hard time dealing with judgmental people." Nicole walked back over to her desk. "Now get out of my office so I can get some work done."

Alicia smiled. "So Virginia is on, right?"

Nicole exhaled and looked up. "I make no promises about bidding on anyone for sex. But I'll go to the event."

***

The scene was hilarious, at least it was to Xavier Davenport. He watched as two women discussed the merits of monogamous relationships with his friend Grant Hutchinson. Tapping one hand to the beat of the music in the club, Xavier lifted his drink with the other hand. The woman sitting next to him, he did not know her name, wrapped her hands around his to stop his progress.

"Why are you so quiet? You don't have anything to add to this conversation?"

Grant was shaking his head as he laughed, anticipating his friend's response to the question. "Don't do it." He chuckled.

Xavier noticed the woman had a sassy smile and a devious look in her beautiful eyes. Her hand was soft, well-manicured, and teasing. Her lips, inviting as she stared up at him. He raised the glass to finish his drink.

"I believe a conversation on monogamy is moot."

"Why is that?" the other woman, sitting next to Grant asked.

Grant lowered his head, shook it, then raised his hand for a waitress. He knew in about two minutes the night would be coming to an end.

Xavier held the woman's eyes. In his smooth baritone voice he said, "The thought of having sex with one person for the rest of my life is foreign to me. I haven't met the woman who could satisfy my every need as a man. Just as I'm certain you haven't met a man who could satisfy your every need. For if such a creature existed, you nor I, would be in this club playing the game of seek'n find. We would be home with that miraculous human being, partaking in the beautiful experience of blood pumping through our veins at an immeasurable rate. The heat in the room would be so intense buckets of ice wouldn't be able to douse it. And there would be a desire so deep, it would take touching our souls to fulfill it."

The women sat mesmerized by the response. One slowly ran her tongue across her bottom lip. "Damn. I think my panties are wet."

The woman sitting next to Xavier pulled a pen from her purse, held his hand, then wrote her address in the palm. "My door is always open to any man who can make me hot with words."

Xavier stood then dropped a few bills on the table. "With that said, ladies, I must call it a night."

"Wait," the woman who wrote the address on his hand called out. "You're leaving with an offer on the table."

Xavier and Grant glanced at each other with a knowing nod. Xavier took the woman's hand and kissed the back of it. "Thank you. However, the passion you have in your eyes is meant for someone special. That person is not me. Good night."

As the two men made their way towards the exit, they drew looks from several women, for both men were handsome and tall, each standing around six-two. Xavier, dark brown, with braids bound at the nape of his neck. His eyes were so dark brown a woman could drown in them. He was casually dressed in jeans, a polo, and a sweater. Grant, light caramel in skin tone was clean cut, and nicely dressed in dark slacks, an open collar shirt and a blazer.

All Grant could do was shake his head. "Why do you peak these women's curiosity when you know you have no intention of taking any of them home."

"I only speak the truth," Xavier said as he shrugged his shoulder.

"One day you are going to run into a woman you can't walk away from."

Xavier, with his shy smile, nodded. "I look forward to finding her."

"How do you know one of them isn't the one?"

"No sparks."

"Sparks? Give her a chance, I'm sure she will give you a spark or two." Grant laughed.

Xavier stopped before he pushed the door open, raising an eyebrow at his friend. "Along with a paternity suit."

Grant smirked as the valet pulled up with Xavier's SUV. "I'm a Hutchinson, all I have to do is look at a woman and I get hit with one."

Xavier shook his head as they pulled off. "I don't know how you put up with the lawsuits, the paternity suits, the press in your business or the women throwing themselves at you. Just because your family has money."

Grant shrugged. "You learn to not let it interfere with your life."

"I don't ever want the kind of wealth that makes people seek me out. Give me a comfortable living and I'm good."

"X-man." Grant gave him a look. "You are the architect of award winning communities. Your name is all over buildings in this city and others. I'm not in your pockets, but I'm certain you have a few zeros behind the leading digit in your bank account."

"I work for a living. You were born with the proverbial silver spoon in your mouth. The crazies seek you out."

"Yeah, well, a number of those crazies are going to be at the auction tomorrow night seeking you out, including Trish Hargrove."

"Don't remind me." Xavier huffed. "How did I let Diamond talk me into doing that auction?"

"Those big brown, puppy eyes of hers, not to mention those dimples, that should be registered as lethal weapons. Look what they did to your brother."

Xavier smiled. "Yeah, it's great to see Zack happy."

"You know, until I saw Zack and Diamond together, I didn't think that type of love existed."

"Diamond knew," Xavier stated.

"Women know," Grant said. "Men, it takes us a little longer."

Xavier thought back to his brother's relationship, then nodded. "I don't know about that. I think Zack knew, he fought it, but he knew."

"I'm not in a hurry for the love thing. I have too many plans for my future to have to succumb to thinking about someone else's happiness."

"I'm not looking for it, but I will not run when I see it coming my way."

Grant looked over at his friend and grinned. "Who knows, you might find it tomorrow night."

Xavier gave him a look of disbelief. "It's an auction. A bunch of horny women looking to get their hands on a piece of meat for the weekend. I doubt there will be one person of interest in the group."

"You never know, X-man. According to you, it only takes one."

***

"This is all you have on the Brooks'?" Isaac J. Singleton, of Singleton Enterprises, threw the folder across the conference table where four men were seated. "I gave each of you a target and this is all you bring me?"

"Mr. Singleton, you are asking for dirt on children of one of the most prominent families in the country. The oldest son is the leading criminal attorney on the East coast. His younger brother is the freaking advisor to the President of the United States. The youngest brother is in a partnership with Tyrone Pendleton. I don't have to remind you what happened when we tried to takeover the Pendleton Agency. The weakest link in the family is the daughter, Nicole, and to be honest, professionally she may be somewhat vulnerable, but that's stretching it."

"I pay you a lot of money to find vulnerabilities."

"Yes, sir, and each time, with the exception of Pendleton, we have come through for you. This Brooks family is close knit. It will not be easy to penetrate any of their businesses."

Isaac stood, looked out his twenty-sixth floor office window, fuming. He built his empire for one purpose, to destroy the so called "good name" of Avery Brooks. If he had to tear down every closet in Brooks' estate to find what he needed, that's what he would do.

"Start with the daughter." He turned back to the table. "Don't disappoint me. You will not like the consequences."

Chapter 1

Saturday
Richmond, Virginia

The Carrington Hotel in downtown Richmond was elegance personified. It had the old-fashioned style of the fifties with the grand staircases and the red carpet entrance. Upon entering the building, Nicole had to admit she could feel the excitement that accompanied the event. The attendees, however, were a little much for her. Most of them were women who believed themselves to be above others. People need to understand, money cannot buy you class or dignity. Those she recognized at the event, were wealthy with money, but had no heart. They couldn't care less about why the charity event was raising money. For them, it was a chance at grabbing a husband or possibly a fling while their husbands were out of town. *Wait, wasn't she there for the same reason?* The thought crossed her mind as she walked through the doors of the grand ballroom searching for Alicia. *No, I'm not here to find a man. I'm just here to relieve myself of a little guilt, that's all. Am I being judgmental of these women?*

"Nikki Brooks! What on earth are you doing here?"

"Hello, Patrice." Nicole turned, grateful to be pulled from her thoughts. "It's wonderful to see you." She hugged the woman she had not seen since high school. "I'm here to support Alicia. She's one of the sisters sponsoring this event."

"Alicia is here, too? It will be great to see her. How have you been? I thought you were in New York."

Nicole nodded her head, smiling as she remembered how Patrice always jumped from one topic to another, without a segue of any kind. "I am working in New York in the Real Estate division of Brooks International."

"You actually work. Hmmm, I would give anything to have your parent's kind of money. I would sit back and let my money work for me. Not you. You always worked hard. I like that about you. You always wanted to have your own." She took a sip from her wine glass. "Speaking of which, how is that fine twin brother of yours?"

They weren't speaking of Nick, she thought. "Nicolas is fine. He started his own agency here in Virginia."

"He did? Where?"

Nicole smiled, knowing Nick would kill her if she gave Patrice his actual location. "Close to home." Changing the subject, "Where did you get that drink?"

"Over there to the right. Hey, if you're bidding tonight, the table with the bachelors' profiles is next to the bar."

"Thanks." Nicole smiled. "I'll just take a drink for now." She escaped, making her way to the bar. "Chardonnay," she ordered from the bartender. Nicole scanned the room. Crowds, of women, were standing at a table that displayed photos, with a short bio and the bachelors' planned weekend beside each. The more she looked around, the more it became clear that only women were present. The only men around were the bartenders.

"You don't seem to fit in with the crowd that's here tonight. Are you sure you are in the right place?" The bartender smiled as he placed her drink on the bar.

"Why do you say that?" Nicole asked as she pulled a twenty from her purse.

"You came in alone, not with a pack. You are in business attire, rather than the 'on the prowl dress', or lack thereof. And I have yet to see you at the table trying to determine which of the men upstairs will be your next husband."

She put the twenty in the glass. "I'm here to support a friend tonight. Thank you for the drink." She walked away.

The bartender stared, shook his head and smiled. "One in a million," he said as he watched the woman in the black suit stroll away. Picking up the tray of drinks to carry upstairs to the men, he heard a burst of laughter from the group of women at the table. He grinned. "Those brothers don't know what they have gotten themselves into."

A bell sounded indicating the beginning of the event. Women pushed past Nicole, attempting to get front row seats. She stood back and waited until the crowd was through the double doors, then she followed behind. Once inside the room she noticed there was a stage, with an extended runway. Chairs were aligned on both sides which would give participants the most advantageous view of the men.

Nicole walked to the back of the room where several round tables with chairs were strategically placed. As she strode toward the tables, she felt a nervous fluttering. Her hand went to her stomach, she rubbed it in a subconscious attempt to soothe her nerves. A small frown breached her forehead. She looked around wondering why she was nervous. When she glanced up, the answer appeared. On the balcony looking down at her, was a man with the deepest, brown eyes, and the most sensuous smile she had ever seen. All she could do at that moment was stare back and smile. The man's eyes were magnetic. She couldn't pull her eyes away, she was spellbound.

"Nikki, I've been looking all over for you. Why are you back here? Come up front with me." Alicia grabbed her by the arm. Nicole turned to her friend as she dragged her off. When she looked back, the man was gone. She blinked. Maybe he was just a figment of her imagination. No one could be that fine. Yet he seemed so real.

Alicia was dressed in a skin tight red dress that screamed 'come get me'. If Nicole did not know better, she would have sworn her friend was trying to pick up a man. As they reached their seats, Nicole looked once more towards the balcony, wondering again if the man was a part of her imagination. Then she heard the annoying voice of the one and only Trish Hargrove.

"Nicole Brooks. What in the hell are you doing at an event like this?"

Nicole turned, and found herself looking directly into the eyes of the woman who'd made her high school life a living hell. Trish was one of the cruelest people she had ever met During high school, Nicole was diagnosed with dyslexia, a reading disorder. Once diagnosed, her parents spared no expense to get her the help she needed. Nicole never allowed her disability to stop her from pursuing what she wanted out of life. However, during high school, Trish had made her life a living hell, telling anyone who would listen that she was a dummy and could not read. To Trish's dismay, Nicole's self-esteem was only momentarily halted by her cruelty. Nicole went on to graduate from high school, college and law school with honors. Of course, Trish assumed and took every opportunity to tell others that Nicole's degrees were purchased by her parents.

With Trish's good looks and money, Nicole had no idea why she had it in for her or why Trish would be at an event like this. "Well, I be damned. It's Batman and his side kick Robin." Trish said to the group of women with her. "In case you two did not know, this is a male auction, as in men. If I remember correctly neither of you go that way." Trish snickered.

Alicia stepped between Nicole and Trish. "Trish, I may have on a dress, but I will beat your ass down if you don't get out of our faces."

"Now, now, ladies, this is not the place to hash out old high school rivalries." Patrice said as she stood between the two and scanned nervously around the room. "Nicole, why don't you and Alicia sit with me? Trish, why don't you and your friends take your seats down at the other end? The view will be better there anyway." She smiled. Trish began to say something. "I said," Patrice snarled through her teeth, "take a seat." Trish walked off with her friends. Patrice turned to Nicole and smiled. "Don't pay her any attention and she will fade away."

Alicia and Nicole looked at each other, both wondering what in the hell just happened. Patrice had never been one to stand up to Trish. During school, when Trish said jump, Patrice did not bother to ask how high. She just kept jumping until Trish told her to stop. But never once did Patrice ever say a cross word to or about Nicole. That seemed to be where Patrice and Trish were at odds.

"Did I miss something?" Nicole whispered to Alicia.

"Looks like we both did."

Everyone took their seats as the auction began. The commentator introduced herself and then gave the bidding rules.

"Bids must be made with the wave of your pad, which is numbered and under your seats along with a brochure of the available bachelors. Raising your pad indicates acceptance of the bid at hand. If your bid is granted, you must proceed to the cashier out front to make payment. At the end of the evening, you will have the opportunity to have dinner and a one-on-one with your date to finalize the plans for the weekend. One final rule, ladies. What happens at the auction stays at the auction! Are we ready to find a possible love connection or at the very least, a man for weekend?" The room exploded with excitement as the music began.

***

Nicole had to admit, the progression of men was impressive and the event was handled in a very tasteful manner. It was not at all what she expected. The men appeared in an array of different sizes, various complexions and noticeable styles of dress. Black brothers are a fine breed of men. Seeing them this way made her proud to be a sister. The bids started at one thousand dollars, the highest received so far was twenty-five hundred. It was going to take a lot more than that to build the recreation center. Nicole had just opened the brochure when Patrice grabbed her wrist.

"Oh my, Bobby is up next," she whispered.

"Bobby?" Nicole frowned.

"Yes, Bobby Singleton, from math class."

Nicole smiled, surprised. "I didn't know he was in this."

Patrice dropped her head and smiled. "Yes he is. What do you think? Should I bid?"

Alicia looked over at Nicole. "Bobby who?"

Nicole leaned back. "You remember Bobby who I tutored in math and he tutored me in reading." She then returned her attention to Patrice. "You two never got together?"

Patrice shook her head. "Girl, please, you know my parents wouldn't even let me go to the prom with him. Remember, he used to cut our grass."

"Yes, but Patrice you are grown now. You can go out with whomever you want," Alicia stated.

"That's right, if you like the man, go for it." Nicole smiled.

Patrice looked down the aisle to where Trish and her friends were sitting and exhaled. "I don't know. I will become the talk of the society circle if I do."

"Why do you care what they think? You have liked Bobby since the tenth grade and apparently things haven't changed."

"Nicole," Patrice lowered her head, "you don't live in Tyson's any more, the rumors and gossip don't affect you the same way it would me."

"You're right, I don't," Nicole replied. "You know over the years I had to develop a thick skin to deal with your so-called society friends. But, honey, you can't allow them to run your life. This would be a great way to spend time with him if that's what you want. If nothing else, you will have a weekend with Bobby and you can tell your friends that it was for charity."

A smile creased Patrice's face. "You think so?" Then she frowned again. "But how would Bobby feel if he found out I only bid on him for charity?"

"Patrice, you are twenty-six years old. If you want to bid on that man then do it. Wait, you do have money, don't you?" Alicia asked.

"If you don't, I will cover your bid." Nicole smiled. She liked the fact that Patrice took Bobby's feelings into consideration. "If you want Bobby, you go get him."

Patrice smiled as Bobby Singleton walked down the runway. According to the commentator, he now owned three industrial lawn care services in the Virginia area and just received the Small Business Man of the Year Award. He was dressed in a pair of black jeans with a silk black mock turtleneck shirt, with muscles that seemed to scream through the shirt.

"Damn, Bobby almost looks good enough to make me change my preference--almost." Alicia exclaimed.

Patrice gave Alicia the sista girl stare. "Bobby is mine," she declared and threw her paddle into the air at the two thousand dollar bid.

Alicia and Nicole both laughed. "You get your man girl."

"Patrice," Trish called out. "What are you doing?"

Alicia looked down the row at Trish letting her know not to interfere as the bid went to three thousand.

Nicole saw Patrice hesitate at the amount. "I have you covered Patrice," she encouraged. "If you truly want to go out with Bobby, because you like him, I have you covered."

Patrice smiled at her and yelled, "Five thousand dollars."

Nicole laughed as Alicia turned and looked down at Patrice. "Damn girl."

"I really want him." Patrice blushed.

"Five thousand going once, going twice, sold to the lady in green. Go claim your bachelor," the commentator directed.

Nicole saw the smile on Bobby's face when he recognized Patrice. She pulled her checkbook from her purse, wrote a check for five thousand dollars, and gave it to Patrice. "Take my telephone number. Call me and tell me how things turn out."

"Thank you, Nicole," Patrice said as she hugged her. "I'll pay you back," she said as she ran off.

Nicole smiled at Alicia. "Now, that felt good. I must tell Nick he doesn't have to worry about Patrice anymore." While the two friends were talking about Patrice, the bidding continued. When Patrice returned to her seat, she was still excited and began talking a mile a minute. Suddenly the fluttering began in the pit of Nicole's stomach again. She frowned and clutched her stomach, then turned back to look up at the balcony. No one was there.

"Are you okay, Nicole?" Patrice asked.

Alicia sat forward to look at her friend. There was a strange expression on her face. "Nikki?"

Nicole looked up and strutting down the runway was the man from the balcony. She was trying to listen to the commentator, but Patrice and Alicia were in her ear. "Shhh, please," she said as she stared at the man in the suit. The brother was finer than one hundred percent silk. He released the band that was holding his braids in place and removed his suit jacket. His braids fell in unison below his shoulders. The gold shirt was a wondrous sight against his dark skin tone. "Who is he?" was all Nicole could breathe out.

A small smile crept onto Alicia's face. Someone had caught Nicole's attention. She flipped open the brochure to get to his profile.

"He's Xavier Davenport and he belongs to Trish," Patrice answered before Alicia could.

"What do you mean he belongs to Trish?" Alicia commanded.

"That's the only reason she came here, was to bid on X-man."

"Well, that doesn't mean he belongs to her," Alicia argued. "It only means that's who she wants, but it doesn't mean she is going to get him."

Nicole did not hear the conversation that was going on between the two women. She was in a trance over the man's eyes again. It wasn't his tall slim, well defined frame that captured her attention. It was his exquisite eyes and his thick rich lips that seemed to take her into his custody.

"Let's start the bidding, ladies," the commentator's voice boomed.

"Five thousand dollars." came from Trish as she feigned indifference to the hush that came over the audience.

"Well, there is a five thousand dollar bid on the table, ladies. Is there anyone that will go six?"

Never breaking eye connection with the man on stage, Nicole raised her paddle. The commentator smiled. "Well, we have six thousand dollars do I hear seven thousand?"

Trish stood with her hands on her hips and turned to look down the aisle at Nicole. Her eyes sent daggers towards Nicole, who was literally undaunted by them. "Ten thousand," Trish said as if daring Nicole to challenge.

Nicole smiled slightly at the man holding her captive. Negotiation was never her strong suit. If she saw something and she wanted it, she did whatever it took to get it. She wanted the weekend, wherever it may be, with the man on the stage. She stood. "Fifty-thousand dollars," she said never taking her eyes from the man on the stage. For a moment, she saw the look of surprise, then a touch of doubt. In the background, she heard the commentator choke out, "Fifty-thousand dollars going once, fifty-thousand going twice, sold to the lady in black."

If anyone had dropped a pin, it would have been heard. The hush over the room was just that deafening, as Trish made her way towards Nicole with fire in her eyes.

"How dare you come in here spending your daddy's money? The only reason you bid on him was because I did." Trish turned to look at Xavier, turned back to Nicole and grinned devilishly. "Did you forget, you don't like men? You prefer women."

Nicole was standing in the aisle when she heard Trish's comments. She looked over the woman's shoulder, to the stage where Xavier Davenport stood. For the first time in her life, the rumors about her sexual preference embarrassed her. He looked appalled at the scene. Nicole smiled, shrugged her shoulder and turned away again. "I like this one."

"What, you think your daddy's money can buy you a decent reputation? Not only are you a lesbian, you're a dumb one at that. Can you read yet?" Trish laughed as she looked at her friends, who had joined in.

Nicole froze. All the times in high school when Trish called her a dummy came crashing back on her. She reached into her purse, pulled out her cell phone and gave them both to Alicia. "Call my brother," she said calmly as the crowd looked on.

"Nick?" Alicia questioned as Nicole turned to face Trish.

"No, Vernon," Nicole said as her left hand grabbed Trish's neck and her right fist connected with the makeup on Trish Hargrove's face. Trish's body propelled upwards and back into the crowd, landing with her legs spread eagle. Nicole shook off the distaste of her actions, turned and walked out the door. She stopped at the cashier's table as people rushed to see what was happening inside the room. She gave the woman the check for bachelor number eleven, just as Alicia came out of the ballroom with Trish's screams for someone to call the police vibrating through the room.

"Nikki, we have to get the hell up out of here."

"No, I'll wait." Nicole said as she took a seat next to the table.

"Nikki, they are calling the police," Alicia exclaimed

Nicole looked at Alicia. "What sense does it make for me to run? It's not like they don't know who I am. Did you reach Vernon?" Nicole asked as she crossed her legs.

"Vernon will be here before we get to the station," Alicia said as she gathered her things.

"We?"

"Yes, you go down, I go down."

"Shirley Ann is not going to like this." The women laughed as an officer approached Nicole.

Chapter 2

Nicole had been booked by the time Vernon arrived at the police station. The arresting officer described the incident to the magistrate, during which time he indicated he would have hit the woman too. The magistrate decided to release Nicole on her own recognizance.

Vernon Eugene Brooks was the attorney; other attorneys, stars and athletes went to when they needed representation. He was known as the cleaner. If anyone could sweep a crime under the court's rafters, it was Vernon Brooks. When Vernon walked into a courtroom he was respected. Hell, all some prosecutors needed to see was his name on a document and they would look for ways to settle the case to keep from being embarrassed in front of the court.

Alicia had no such affliction. Nothing about Vernon intimidated or frightened her. He entered the station, looked around, then walked directly to her. "Why am I not surprised to see you?"

He towered over the sitting Alicia, with his six-three sleek frame, dressed from head to toe in Armani, looking like he just walked off someone's corporate jet. "Do you always wear Armani? You should try Hugo. It would look good on you."

Vernon smirked. "Anything would look good on me. I've noticed whenever Nikki is in trouble, you are somewhere around."

Crossing her legs, Alicia smoothly replied, "Contrary to what you may think, I did not cause or encourage this one. However..." She smiled. "I don't blame Nikki for hitting the heifer."

He stopped and looked down at Alicia. She was always a sassy little vixen. Pretty as hell and a body most men would enjoy. The dress she was wearing would definitely capture a man's attention. He shook his head, it baffled him why she went to the other side. Nevertheless, that was not his concern.

"What happened?" he asked.

"Nikki placed a bid on this man Trish wanted."

Vernon raised his eyebrow. "Nicole put a bid on a man, for money?"

"Yes, we were at a charity event and Trish...."

"Trish Hargrove?"

"Yes, will you stop interrupting me and listen?" Alicia asked, somewhat exasperated. "Anyway, Nikki outbid her. Trish jumped in her face, proclaiming to the crowd that Nikki was spending her daddy's money to buy the man only because she wanted him. Then she said Nikki was a lesbian and didn't like men. Nikki turned to walk away and Trish added what she has always said. Nikki was a dummy. I think Nikki had taken enough and she swung. I mean she knocked the daylights out of Trish." Alicia laughed. "She fell into the crowd with her legs wide open, showing her kitty-cat and everything. It was a sight to see."

"I'm sure you enjoyed it," he replied sarcastically.

The sarcastic remark sobered Alicia quickly. "Vernon, you know where you can go. I've told you several times over the years. Just make sure Nikki is okay. I'm out of here." She turned and left the precinct.

Vernon approached the desk and advised the guard he was Nicole Brooks' attorney. The doors buzzed open allowing him entrance. There was his little sister sitting on a bench with her legs crossed holding a conversation with a woman of questionable character. He never understood why his siblings had this inbred need to associate with people beneath their status.

They were all multimillionaires. Each child to Avery and Gwendolyn Brooks received twenty-five percent of Brooks International when they turned twenty-one. Nicole inherited the CEO position with Brooks International, plus a ten million dollar trust fund when she turned twenty-one. James, the second oldest child went into State Government work, which paid little to nothing and now was working in President Harrison's administration. In Vernon's opinion, James should be President. Then there was Nicolas, Nicole's twin brother. He decided to become a sports agent. A potential gold mine, if he chose to open up to some of the advantages offered under the table to him for his client's services. Nick wasn't the type. He preferred to keep his clients free and clear from what he considered the sharks of the game.

Nicole, Vernon was sure, was talking to the woman offering her a bank account or a job with a ridiculous wage attached just to get her off the streets. When would she realize not everyone can be saved? Vernon, who was one of the top criminal defense attorneys in Virginia, would never assist anyone unless it was family, or there was something in it for him. It couldn't be money, because he had plenty of that. No, his clients had to bring prestige or publicity to the table for him to consider taking them on.

He cleared his throat. "Nicole," he said in an irritable tone.

She stood. "Hello Vernon. Glad to see you."

"Why on God's green earth did you call me out of my bed from McLean? James is fifteen minutes away. Why didn't you call him?"

Nicole tiptoed up and kissed Vernon's cheek. "James comes with TV reporters."

As hard as he tried, Vernon found it difficult to refuse Nicole anything. He was the black sheep of the family, but Nicole always showed him unconditional love. He smiled inwardly, of course, at her kiss, but continued his assault. "Why didn't you call Nick? You two always cover for each other."

Nicole was signing her release papers as she responded. "Nick is in Florida recruiting some baseball player. Besides, he's still a little pissed at me about his girlfriend."

"I happen to think you were right about her," Vernon huffed, not revealing that Nick and the lady were no more.

"Right or not, I should not have interfered. He has a right to love whom he chooses."

They continued to talk as the doors buzzed open. "They seem to be happy."

He shook his head. "I'm the last one to comment on anyone's relationship. I have my own to deal with."

Nicole stopped and scowled at him. "Constance is not going anywhere. What are you worried about?"

"I don't know, Nikki," he began as they walked through the outer doors into the cool night breeze. "We are having our differences concerning Taylor."

He walked towards the curb where a black sedan with a driver waited. The driver came around to open the door.

"You can handle her, Vernon. I know you can."

"I'm not sure I want to."

Nicole stopped, then turned back to look at her brother. Before she could respond, fluttering started in her stomach.

"Nicole Brooks?"

She knew to whom the smooth, silky voice belonged before she turned around.

Vernon stepped in front of Nicole. "Who are you?" he asked, shielding Nicole behind him.

Stepping back in front of Vernon, Nicole's eyes shimmered at the sight of the man up close and personal. He was simply delicious. Her stomach was doing somersaults. She turned to Vernon. "Would you wait for me in the car?"

Vernon looked at her and then back to the man who stood about six-two. "He has plaits in his hair, Nikki."

"They are braids, not plaits. Now, wait for me in the car," she said again politely. Vernon glared at the man. "I'll leave the door open," he said as a warning.

Xavier Davenport gazed at the beautiful brown skinned woman smiling back at him. No one in this life had captured his attention as this woman had the first time he laid eyes on her in the ballroom. His nerves were getting the best of him while sitting in the room with the other men, waiting to be paraded in front of women like cattle. If it had not been for the fact that it was his company that was designing and building the recreation center, he would not have been in this farce of a charity. Nevertheless, when he saw her walk into the ballroom, he said a silent prayer. If he had to endure a weekend with a woman, let it be her.

Standing in front of her now, he found himself at a loss for words. She was even more captivating up close. His only saving grace was that she seemed to be as entranced with him as he was with her.

A police officer standing outside observed the two for a few moments. He decided somebody had to make a move. The officer walked over to Xavier, then shoved his shoulder. "She ain't gonna bite man. Say something." Then he walked off.

Xavier smiled and extended his hand. "Xavier Davenport. Are you all right?"

Nicole placed her hand in his. She now understood the meaning of still waters. Everything within her said a simultaneous ahh. Calmness settled over her and the fluttering in her stomach stopped. "Nicole Brooks," she replied while staring into the dark brown eyes with gold flecks shining through. "Yes."

Still gazing at her he heard her response, but was lost. "Yes, what?" he asked, not ready to let her hand go.

Nicole blushed. "Yes, I'm all right." She smiled. "It was nice of you to come here to check on me. I think Trish was trying to convince the officer not to grant bail. She believes I am a menace to society."

"Are you? I mean do you go around striking people at will?"

"Believe it or not, that was my first time in about ten years."

"Was it worth it?" Xavier grinned.

That crooked grin was her undoing. It was the most alluring vision she had ever seen. Nicole reluctantly pulled her hand from his and immediately regretted the move. "Yes, and I would pay fifty-thousand dollars to do it again."

"Speaking of that, I tried to retrieve your check, but I'm afraid the sorority would not hear of it."

"I don't want it back; it's for a good cause." Nicole smiled.

"In that case, it seems I owe you a dinner and a weekend getaway."

Nicole was so caught up in his smile that she did not hear Vernon call out to her. "Nicole!"

"So, will you join me for dinner?"

She smiled. On top of his good looks, kissable lips and a body to die for, he was also a gentleman. "You don't owe me anything. I've embarrassed you enough tonight for a lifetime. I'll say we are even."

He stepped closer, he wasn't ready to part ways with her yet. Just about a breath away from her, he whispered. "You paid for a weekend getaway and I plan on delivering. I missed dinner. I'm certain you did as well. We both have to eat. Why not do it together?"

She was tempted to reach up and touch his braids that were a perfect frame to his face. She wondered if they were as smooth as they looked. Instead, she placed her hands inside her blazer pockets. "It's late. I'm sure they will not allow me back into the reception at the hotel."

"I happen to know a place that's open and is in walking distance. Will you join me? I mean you have to eat, right?" He smiled.

She was mesmerized by his smile. "All right, I'll be happy to join you."

"Nicole!" Vernon called out.

She walked over to the sedan and whispered to Vernon. "I'll see you later."

"I don't think so. You don't know that man," Vernon replied as he stepped out of the vehicle.

Xavier pulled out his wallet and gave Vernon his driver's license. "You may hold on to that until I return her safely."

Vernon glared. "You give me a driver's license in exchange for my little sister."

Nicole laughed. "Seems like an even exchange." She kissed Vernon's cheek. "I'll see you later."

"Nicole, where are you staying?" Vernon asked.

"With James," she replied as she stepped away from the vehicle.

Vernon put the driver's license in his pocket. "I'll be at James'. I expect you home soon," he replied looking at Xavier.

"Okay, daddy," Nicole laughed. Vernon scowled at her as he climbed into the car.

As the sedan pulled away, Nicole turned to Xavier. "Where to Mr. Davenport?"

Xavier placed his hand on the small of her back. "This way, Ms. Brooks."

***

The breeze was warm for an October night as the two walked down Jackson Street. "I'm told you are visiting Richmond tonight. Where do you live?" he asked as they turned to stroll down Leigh Street.

"I currently live in New York. My parents' home is in Mclean, VA."

"James is?"

"James is my middle brother."

"James Brooks, advisor to the President?"

"Yes, you know him?"

"I do." Xavier nodded.

"Well, I have three. Vernon, whom you just met, is the oldest, and my twin Nicolas, lives in Georgetown."

"You are the baby and only girl?"

"Yes." She smiled. "What about you? Do you have any brothers or sisters?"

"One brother, Zackary," he replied as he guided her across the street.

She stopped and looked at her surroundings. They had come to a black wrought iron fence that was about eight feet tall with a double gated entrance that appeared to be locked. Xavier punched a code into the keypad and the gates began to slide open. There was a building with two archways, allowing the traffic to flow under it in both directions. The sign in the middle of the median strip read, "Davenport Circle." They strode along the walkway to the right. A doorman appeared at the entrance to the building. Nicole looked around. "What a wonderful retreat, right in the heart of the city."

"Good evening Mr. Davenport, Miss," the doorman greeted.

"Hello, Joe. How are you this evening?"

"Fine, thank you, sir," he replied as he opened the door. "A package arrived for you today, sir, it's at the concierge's desk."

"Thank you, Joe." Xavier replied as they entered the lobby area of the building. In the center was an oval shaped fountain encased in marble, with cushioned bench seats surrounding the outside. To the right was Marco's Restaurant, which catered to elegant dining, and a number of patrons were waiting to be seated. Next to it was Karen's, a coffee shop and restaurant, Karen's, catered to casual dining and also had people waiting. On the left was a hair salon, a spa and a gym. On the far wall were two elevator doors and an exit to the courtyard. Xavier stopped at the desk to pick up his package. He joined her at the fountain. "Would you mind if I take this upstairs, before we have dinner?"

"You live here?" Nicole asked.

"Yes."

"In the middle of downtown Richmond?" she asked, surprised.

"Not exactly the middle, but yes." He smiled. He guided her toward the elevator. He placed his palm on the glass next to the key pad. The wall behind the elevator opened. Nicole hesitated and looked up at him. He stepped back, placed his hand on the small of her back to guide her inside. "It's a private elevator that goes directly into my home," he explained.

Nicole stepped inside and was surprised to see the glass interior. The elevator doors closed and began traveling upwards. The grounds on the other side of the building came into view. To Nicole's surprise, there was a small park with homes built in a semi-circle. "What a beautiful community in the middle of the city," she exclaimed. "It seems so exclusive. The homes here must cost a small fortune."

"To the contrary, they are very affordable. That's the concept of the community. Beautiful, safe and affordable homes for the average working family."

The elevator stopped and opened to the foyer of Xavier's penthouse. "Lights," he ordered. Lights illuminated the room. Xavier placed the package on the breakfast bar and turned back to Nicole. "Shall we go downstairs for dinner?"

Nicole's interest in real estate got the best of her. "May I see your place?"

Showing pride in his work, he was pleased with her request. He smiled. "Allow me to give you a private tour." He extended his hand to her. She placed her hand in his. A surge of energy flowed through him. He stared down at the small, well-manicured hand that lay within his. Rubbing his thumb across it he smiled up at her. "Do you feel that?"

Nicole knew what he was talking about but was afraid to acknowledge it. She'd set eyes on this man for the first time less than four hours ago, but there was an undeniable force flowing between them. "Yes, I'm just not sure what it is."

The moment was charged with so much energy that it seemed to clog his throat. He swallowed hard and decided to ease the moment. "I know what it is." He smiled as he placed her hand in the crook of his arm and guided her out of the foyer.

"You do? Please share your thoughts with me."

"I will." He smiled. "Sinergy."

Nicole stopped and looked up at him with questioning eyes. "Synergy?"

"Yes, sinergy. Sinful energy."

"I've attended many business seminars and that was not the definition given for synergy."

"You're speaking of synergy." He spelled the word. "I'm talking about sinergy. It describes the sinful energy that takes place when we look at each other. If we aren't careful, it will erupt at any moment."

"Sinful energy." She tilted her head to the side and smiled up at him, "I think I like that."

Her smile was so radiant, he wanted to kiss her, but instead he turned away. "This is my kitchen, where I tend to spend a little time."

"You like to cook," she stated as she followed him through the room.

"It was a matter of survival." He smiled. "This is my dining room, where I hope to someday have large family meals in front of the fireplace. After which we could then move into the living room and enjoy the same fire and lively conversation."

Nicole loved the double sided fireplace. However, she was amazed by the view from the living room more. She pulled away and walked over to the window. Below was the community and the courtyard. "It's magnificent." She turned to him and their eyes held. Passion blazed so strong she could feel the heat from where she stood. She looked away breaking the spell.

"Not to mention a football game or two," she stated at the sight of the sixty-two inch television mounted on the wall opposite the fireplace.

"Of course, or a quiet moment in front of the fire with a special lady."

His eyes were captivating and Nicole was finding it difficult not to stand there and stare into them. She smiled and exhaled. "I'm sure there have been many."

"Only you." He turned, took her hands and pulled her behind him. They walked down a hallway passing a bedroom and an office. At the very end of the hallway was a set of double doors. On the other side was a walkway with a walk in closet on the right and a bathroom suite on the left. An archway led into the sleeping area of a bedroom that covered the entire front side of the building. Walking under the arch, downtown Richmond appeared before her through the wall length window. In the far distance, she could see the James River, with its deep history shimmering beneath the water surface.

"This, as you can see, is my sanctuary. Everything I could possibly want is in this room."

Nicole walked over to the windows and looked out at the city skyline. "You have a taste of suburbia at one end and the bustle of the city on the other." She turned to him. "It seems you have the best of both worlds."

Xavier could not resist the urge any longer. Standing in his bedroom in front of the windows, the outside light radiated a mesmerizing glow upon her. She had to be the most beautiful woman he had ever seen. She was barely five feet, six inches tall in three-inch heels. If she weighed one ten it would surprise him, however, everything about her was just right. From the short curly hairstyle to the luscious subtle fragrance of the cologne she was wearing.

Walking toward her it seemed she was in control, but her eyes told another story. There he could see the same confusion he was feeling. There had been women in his life, but never one to capture him so thoroughly. He stopped in front of her and could see the anticipation in her eyes. He put his finger under her chin and gently brought her lips within inches of his. He wondered for a moment what happened to his declaration on monogamous relationships. There was something about this one staring up at him that made him forget the declaration.

"I'm going to kiss you, Nicole Brooks. If you have an issue with that, now is the time to speak."

Speak, hell it was hard to breathe with him that close to her. Nicole breathlessly whispered, "No issue."

A smile began at the corner of Xavier's lips. He may not know much about this woman, but he knew that she had no problem expressing what she wanted. Their lips tenderly met in a sweet, sensuous kiss that touched the very soul of each of them. No other part of their bodies touched, but both, with a gentleness that neither could explain, felt the caress.

Xavier slowly pulled away knowing he had just had his last first kiss. He said a silent prayer that she realized it too.

"I believe I need to feed you." He smiled as he swiped a curl from her face. "If we stay in this room, we may not eat for days."

With her head tilted, she noted that the gold flecks in his eyes had lightened, making them look more sensuous. "I had a big breakfast."

He laughed, took her by the hand and began walking out of the bedroom. "For future reference, if you bait me like that again, I will rise to the occasion."

**

The sound of a text message coming through on his phone caused Isaac to look up from the report he was reading. The message read. *Brooks-Urgent: Email forthcoming.* Touching the screen on his computer, Isaac opened his email. There was an arrest report on Nicole Brooks that was less than four hours old. He opened the file and read the report. He sent a message back. *I expect a full report on Trish Hargrove by nine a.m.*

Isaac sat back contemplating how he could use this incident to expedite his plans.

Chapter 3

Sunday
Richmond, Virginia

Sunrise was shining brightly through the window as the automatic drapes opened. Xavier did not move even though the view of the city appearing before him would normally stimulate him, but not today. The vivid image of Nicole standing by that window played across his mind. He lay there with his hands behind his head contemplating how the events of the day before had changed his life.

Twenty-four hours earlier he was cursing his sister-in-law, Diamond, for involving him in the event. Since he was the lone bachelor in their company, he was the logical choice to participate. Diamond had used their company's status within the community and the connection with their project as the reasons why someone from Davenport Industries had to participate. *'It's good public relations to have a representative in the event.'* She'd said. Now, he had to kiss her. If it had not been for her persistence, he would have never met Nicole, the woman who mesmerized him.

His mind wandered to one or two concerns. What woman in her right mind would shell out fifty-thousand dollars on a whim? Even for a good cause like the recreation center. The next question he pondered while taking his shower. If she could drop fifty-thousand, how rich were her parents? As he sipped his second cup of coffee, the most difficult problem came to mind. Was Trish being vicious, as he knew she could be, or was what she said true? Did Nicole prefer women to men? It was her business if she did, however, it did cause a problem for him. He had a serious sexual attraction to her. Just thinking about her was getting a rise out of him. His gut told him no woman could kiss a man the way she'd kissed him if she preferred women. His cell phone buzzed. He had turned the ringer off during the auction and had forgotten to turn it back on. The caller ID indicated it was Grant calling.

"Early on a Sunday morning, this should be good."

"X-man," Grant laughed into the phone. "You my friend have the world talking."

"About?" He sat back in his chair as he listened to his friend's laughter.

"You, Trish, the auction, some woman."

"Ha ha." Xavier grinned. "Only you could find humor in something so barbaric."

"Two women fighting over you? That's not barbaric, it's a man's dream. So tell me, is she the one?"

"She who?"

"The woman whose fist met with Trish's jaw."

Xavier stood, sat the empty plate in the dishwasher and thought for a moment.

"Yes."

Grant was speechless for a moment. "And you know that, how?"

A seductive grin appeared on Xavier's face as he thought about the word they created the night before. "Sinergy." He laughed as he disconnected the call.

Xavier glanced at the clock above his fireplace, it was almost seven. Whenever they could, he and his brother Zackary would meet at the downstairs gym to work out in the mornings. Dressed in sweats, t-shirt and sneakers he was picking the keys up from the table next to his bedroom entrance when he heard the elevator open. He stepped into the foyer to see Zack walking through the door with two cups of coffee and the newspaper under his arm.

"I was on my way to meet you at the gym." Xavier smiled.

Zack, who was taller and thicker than he, walked into the kitchen He placed a cup of coffee on the breakfast bar, then took a seat. "I think the gym is going to wait today, Xavier."

Xavier knew his brother well. If he came in calm, there was definitely something wrong. That was a concern for he never wanted to disappoint his brother, who had sacrificed so much for him. There was nothing Xavier would not do for his brother, because there was nothing Zachary had not done for him.

When their father passed away, Zack left college to raise him. Never once complaining about giving up his life to ensure his little brother was cared for. Zack began working for a construction company and when the time came, he sent Xavier away to college. Xavier received a degree in Engineering with a minor in Architecture and began designing homes, small communities and shopping malls. Together, they formed Davenport Industries. Xavier designed the communities and Zackary built them. They were recently featured in Black Enterprise magazine as one of the fastest growing African-American firms in the country. They were not rich, according to some standards, but they both knew how to work hard to acquire a good life.

Zackary and his wife Diamond lived in a beautiful home in Davenport Estates, the first development they'd built together. Xavier once lived in the penthouse of the condominium there, but now lived in the penthouse of their latest community, Davenport Circle, which was less than ten minutes walking and five driving from his brother's home. His number one rule was to never design anything he would not live or work in.

If something was up, Diamond would have given him a heads up call. He hadn't spoken to her, therefore, he had no idea what was on Zack's mind. However, he knew something was up because his brother had called him Xavier, not X-man.

"Something wrong, Zack?" Xavier asked as he took a seat across from him at the breakfast bar.

Zack opened the paper. "There's an article in the paper this morning about a fifty-thousand dollar man." He looked over the top of the paper at Xavier. "Any idea who he may be?" The cup Xavier held in his hand froze midway to his lips. Zack looked back down at the paper. "Nice picture, too."

Xavier snatched the paper from his brother's hand and began reading the article. He stood as he continued to read. "Oh, man, she is probably freaking out."

Zack watched his brother pace back and forth between the foyer, the kitchen and the living room reading the article. His brother hated publicity of any kind. He preferred staying in the background. Once he was scheduled to receive an award for his design of the Ward Community, he sent Diamond to pick it up because the event was being covered by local television. He wondered why X-man, as he called him, was not upset about his picture, but was upset about

Nicole Brooks' picture in the paper. Xavier walked back into the kitchen and sat at the bar.

Zack, who had fought hard as hell on his drive over, not to laugh at his little brother's predicament, was finding it increasingly difficult to hold it in. When X-man looked up at him, he had to let it go. His laughter roared throughout the penthouse.

"Okay, man, let me get this straight. You received a bid of fifty-thousand dollars at the charity auction. What in the hell did you do to get that kind of bid?" He continued to laugh. "Wait, wait, it gets better," Zack pulled the paper from Xavier and searched for the statement. "Immediately after being granted the winning bid, Ms. Brooks was approached by Trish Hargrove and an altercation ensued. The two millionaires involved, both from McLean, Virginia, were visiting Richmond for the charity event." He put the paper down and looked at Xavier. "You had two women fighting over you. X-man, I have to tell you, if I had thought growing my hair long would have garnered that much attention, I would have stopped going to the barber years ago."

"Ha ha, I'm happy I could amuse you and Grant early this morning. There's one correction. It's her parents who have money, not Nicole." Xavier replied, throwing the paper at his brother who seemed to be getting a kick out of an embarrassing moment in his life.

"That's true for Trish, but not for Nicole Brooks, my brother, she has money." He gave him the bio on Nicole Brooks he had pulled from the internet after initially reading the article. "Yes, her parents are filthy rich, but at the age of twenty-one each of the children received control of their trust funds." Zack noticed the crease in Xavier's forehead. "She also heads up the real estate division of Brooks International, in New

York. In fact, we applied for a grant from them to fund the recreation center."

Xavier thought for a minute. "No, I'm sure Trish said she was spending her daddy's money."

"Trish maybe spending her daddy's money, but Nicole Brooks has her own." Zack stopped laughing when he saw the expression on Xavier's face. "What is it, X-man?"

"Nothing man. I just..." He hesitated. "I liked this woman. We connected. You know." He exhaled. "We are supposed to go out next weekend."

"What's stopping you?" Zack asked.

Xavier stood and exhaled then said a little agitated. "I planned to take her to Shenandoah to spend the weekend at the Martha Washington Bed and Breakfast."

"Sounds like a nice weekend. What's the problem?"

He sneered. "Can you imagine a multimillionaire spending a weekend in Shenandoah?"

"Man, if you are with the right person, it doesn't matter where you are or what you are doing. Besides, I have never known you to renege on a deal. The woman paid fifty-thousand dollars for a weekend with you. The least you can do is show up." Sensing Xavier needed some time alone. Zack hugged his brother. "Seems like Nicole Brooks made an impression on you. The woman can't help that she has money. You need to find out if the woman behind the money is worth having." He walked over to the elevator. "Look at it this way," he said as the doors opened, "If it doesn't work out, you always have Trish." He stopped, then walked back over to Xavier. "Oh, one more thing, before I go. Would you mind logging into your computer?"

There was a smirk on Zack's face, which caused Xavier to frown. "Okay." He logged in then stepped aside.

Zack pulled up the Internet, then keyed in a few words. He turned the computer to Xavier. "You've gone international." Zack hit Xavier on the shoulder, laughing as he walked back to the elevator. He was still laughing when the doors closed.

Xavier looked at the monitor. He could not help but laugh at the picture of Trish's legs up in the air. "There should be a ban on cell phones with cameras." He began reading the blog.

Rumor Has It

Can you say catfight? Well, I would normally begin with rumor has it, but, darlings, this is fact. Billionaires Nicole Brooks of Brooks International, you know the Real Estate mogul, and the daughter of millionaire Teddy Hargrove, Trish, literally let their claws out at a charity event of all things. It seems society darling Trish had issues with the elusive Nicole stepping in to take the winning bid on a man in the auction. The two came to blows when Trish insinuated Nicole did not indulge in men. Gasp!

Picking up his cell, Xavier dialed the number Nicole put in his address book a few hours earlier. She answered groggily. "Hello."

"Good morning."

"Xavier," she purred as she sat up in bed. "Good Morning...again."

"Well, I'm not sure if it is a good morning for either of us. Have you taken a look at this morning's paper or the internet?"

Nicole threw the comforter to the side and stepped out of bed. "No, I've learned not to read the papers or the internet after they published my report card freshman year of high school."

"I take it you are used to your face being on the breakfast table of strangers?"

Not sure where his feelings were on the matter, Nicole held her tongue. She liked this man and wanted an opportunity to get to know him. However, not everyone could deal with the publicity that comes along with being a Brooks.

"Is it that bad?"

"Let's say the camera and Trish were up close and personal, with her legs spread eagle."

Nicole shook her head. "I'm going to have to write a big check for this one."

"You handle things by writing a big check? Have you ever tried a simple apology?"

"I'm not in the habit of buying people, if that's what you are asking. For normal people an apology would do. I am a Brooks. People don't accept apologies from us unless a check is attached." She hesitated and then added. "That's a way of life for me, Xavier." Nicole held her breath for his response. The last thing she wanted to do was frighten him away. Nevertheless, he needed to understand what baggage came along with her. "Xavier, like it or not, people target us for money. Not everyone, but enough for us to understand how the game is played. What you've experienced this morning is probably lightweight. The more time you spend with me, the heavier the coverage will get."

Xavier liked her frankness. The press comes along with her. Could he handle that? "Someone with a voice so sensual it causes my pulse to race is worth having to put up with the press. Try the apology without the check and we will talk later."

Nicole fell across the bed kicking her legs in the air and giggling. "Really?"

He smiled at her giggled response. "I just found you. I'm not ready to give up, yet."

"It seems we are on the same page, Mr. Davenport. Just so you know, it's the crooked grin of yours that got me." Nicole smiled as she disconnected the call. She breathed a sigh of relief and thought about the events from earlier that morning.

It was about four am when Xavier brought her to James' house. She had to drive his vehicle because Vernon had his license. That, in itself was an experience to remember. He drove a Lincoln Navigator, which appeared to be the size of a small house to her. For the last few years, she had been chauffeured around New York. A car would take her to work and home when she was ready or she would simply walk home. Driving a Navigator was a stretch. Xavier had to pick her up to set her inside. Her skirt moved up exposing a good portion of her thighs. He kissed both thighs, sending shivers up her spine and then tugged the skirt down. His lips were tantalizing, his smile enticing and his eyes dangerous.

A knock on the door interrupted her thoughts on the charming, braid wearing brother that had her captivated. "Come in," she responded.

Vernon walked through the door. "Good, you are awake. Your father has summoned you home."

"Okay, I'll be home this evening." She jumped up and hugged him.

"Save those kisses. Your father wants to see you within the hour. The jet is waiting. James, Ashley and the children are joining us."

She stepped back. "What's going on? Why are we taking the jet and not driving?"

"I don't know, James took the call," Vernon replied as he leaned against the door jam. "It could be that your escapade from last night has reached our father and he is eager to speak with you on the matter. I hope this Xavier Davenport is worth it."

She gave her brother the side eye. "You had him investigated, didn't you?"

Vernon grinned, "See you downstairs," and walked out the door.

Chapter 4

Sunday Noon,
McLean, VA

Nicole walked into her childhood home and was greeted by her mother and father. The foyer of the Brooks' home was large enough to hold two hundred people comfortably. Therefore, when the roar of Avery Brooks' voice sounded, it seemed as if a surround sound system was connected to it and continuously repeated itself. "Nicole Cheyenne Brooks, what in the hell have you gotten yourself into? And what is the meaning of this statement?" He looked down at the morning paper. "'You do not like men, you like women.' Explain yourself young lady, and at the moment I am using that term lightly."

Gwendolyn Brooks, with her short sassy haircut, size ten figure and wearing an angry look, left her husband's side and went to her daughter who was standing in the middle of the room, dazed by the tone of her father's voice. Nicole had heard her father angry many times, but there was something different in his voice today. He was hurt.

"Avery, you will not attack my child with that tone. Gather yourself." Gwendolyn matched his anger. The two had argued for the past two hours about the article that had reached the paper in Mclean. She was determined to keep Avery from alienating his daughter. She had made that mistake with their son James, and it had taken them years to reconcile. She was not going to have that kind of friction in her family again.

"Hello, sweetheart." She kissed her daughter's cheek. "I heard you had an interesting evening. Come into the family room and talk to us about it." She looked back over her shoulder at her husband warning him to watch himself.

Nicole looked from her mother to her father and now understood why James and Ashley had come along. "Hello, Poppa," Nicole smiled. She didn't care how angry he was or why, he was still her father and she loved him without question. She kissed his cheek and stared into his eyes, he was mad. "I'm not sure what I have done to cause you to be angry with me, but I'm sure we can work it out."

Seeing the two, his wife and his baby girl standing together looking like Siamese twins, he couldn't help but let his anger melt away a little. But damn it, this was still his baby girl smeared in the paper and it was his responsibility to protect her against any and all perpetrators. Even against herself. "Is it true?" he asked roughly as his heart melted a little more from his baby's kiss.

"Hello, Pop," James smiled as he walked through the door holding the hand of his daughter Jayda, who had been through a traumatic experience and was still very clingy.

Avery smiled at his son. He was so proud of all he had accomplished in his life, but nothing made him prouder than his children. "Well hello, Jaybird." He bent down and kissed his granddaughter on the forehead, worry etched in his brow over the change in the once rambunctious child, making him forget about Nicole's situation for a moment.

"Any progress with the doctor?"

"Some." James nodded his head. "We're still working on it, right Jaybird?" He smiled as his wife, Ashley, walked through the door.

Gwen waited with open arms as Jayden, her grandson ran to her. "Grandma, Grandma, we going to save Aunt Nikki?"

Jayda pulled away from her father to join her brother. "Me too, Grandma. We not going to let Poppa get her."

Nicole walked over and took both of the twins' hands, then walked into the family room.

"They are under the impression that you plan to spank Aunt Nikki." Ashley stated as James winked at her. "I have no idea where the notion came from."

Vernon walked over to Nicole and whispered. "The twins have given you a moment to get your response together before Pop remembers why we are all here. I suggest you use the time wisely."

Ashley, who had become a friend as well as her sister-in-law, came to her side. "You realize this distraction is only going to last a few more minutes."

"Yes, I know," she sighed. "Now if I could just figure out what Pop is so mad about."

Ashley smirked. "You can assume it's one of three things - the possibility that you are gay, you just dropped fifty-thousand dollars on a man or you got arrested. I would go with the gay part if I were you."

Nicole looked at the family gathered in the foyer and exhaled. "I hope you are wrong ,Ashley, because if that's the issue, we are going to have a problem."

"Well, whichever one it is, James and I have your back."

"Ashley," James called out, "let's take the children upstairs while Pop gets started with Nicole."

Nicole kissed her niece and nephew goodbye then sat back and closed her eyes. The family room under different circumstances was a happy place. Many family discussions filled with laughter and her brothers getting into trouble had taken place there. Very seldom was she the focus of her parents' displeasure. It was important to her not to cause them any trouble, for she had disappointed them so with her learning disability. Her brothers, all attorneys, were brilliant in their respective fields. Nicole struggled. She had to work harder than any of them to succeed. The fact that her father was upset with her about something so personal did not please her, not one bit. However, angry or not, she was raised to respect her parents. She would allow her father to have his say about the situation. At the moment, she was a little afraid of which position he would take. As an attorney, she was sure he would understand why she had not dispelled the rumors regarding her sexual preference. As a father, she was sure he would want to know if the rumor was true. After all, she was his baby, and he wanted to protect her against any harm, real or imagined, no matter what.

When she was in high school and the talk began about her being dumb, her father had been working on a highly publicized civil rights case in Georgia. She came home crying to her mother about the kids in school calling her a dummy. Of course, the group of girls teasing her were all friends of Trish. Gwen immediately called Trish's mother and had more than a few choice words with her regarding her daughter's cruelty. She then advised Mrs. Hargrove, that if she did not find a way to curtail her daughter she would make a personal trip to their home and teach both of them what the back of her hand felt like. In turn, Mrs. Hargrove told her husband who then gave the information regarding the threat to the tabloids. There was no mention of the reason for the threat.

Avery asked for a continuation on his case and came home the same day the paper hit the newsstand. He talked through the night with his daughter until he understood exactly what her learning challenges were. After gathering information from teachers and other students who'd witnessed or taken part in taunting her, he confronted the school administration about allowing this type of bullying to take place. He then took steps to have her tested to determine the exact nature of her learning disability. The next step he took surprised Nicole. He made an appointment with Mr. Hargrove. Went to their home and followed through on the threat her mother had made. Instead of the back side of his hand, Avery used his fist. Mr. Hargrove stated he would call the police and show the pictures of the attack to the tabloids if her Pop did not pay him one hundred thousand dollars. Thus began the monetary relationship between the Brooks' and the Hargroves.

"When did violence become the way we handle things in this family?" Avery asked as he joined his daughter on the sofa. "Haven't your mother and I taught you to handle things through open communications?"

"She used open communication, Pop," Vernon snickered. "It was her fist that was closed, see," he said pointing to the picture in the paper. Avery gave his oldest son a look to let him know he was not in the mood for jokes. His baby girl's reputation was at stake and it was not a laughing matter to him. "Pop, you have to find the humor in this, I did."

Avery turned to his son, who was now standing at the bar fixing a drink. "I haven't forgotten your part in this, Vernon. We will discuss why I did not receive a call from you last night."

"Pop, don't blame Vernon," Nicole exclaimed. "He did what any brother would have done. I am responsible for this. I lost my temper. I allowed Trish to get under my skin, again—and I am sorry. Tomorrow I will go to her home in Richmond and apologize in person. Of course the offer of restitution for any doctor bills will be made."

"You know that will not satisfy the Moneygroves," Gwen sneered as she sat on the opposite sofa, crossing her legs.

Nicole smiled. "Mother."

"Don't mother me, you know I am right. I'm surprised they have not called making their demands before going to the tabloids."

"Isn't a wing of their house called the Brooks wing, since we literally paid for it?" James smiled as he came into the room and mussed the top of Nicole's head, ruffling through her curls.

"If it's not it should be." Avery snickered. "Nevertheless, we have a situation here. It is only a matter of time before the New York media picks up this article, if it has not already happened. We need to have a response in place. How do you plan to nullify the statements in the paper regarding your sexual preference?"

Nicole looked around at her family. For the first time in her life, she was not sure they would continue to love her if she handled things the way she wanted to. This stupid incident could cause irreparable damage to her reputation if she finally took a stand.

"I don't."

The two simple words she'd just spoken, captured the attention of everyone in the room.

"Explain yourself, young lady," Avery demanded.

"Poppa, it's simple. It is no one's business what my sexual preference is. What goes on behind my doors is my business. It doesn't change who I am in the board room. I don't ask Hayward Ellington what he does behind closed doors. I have no plans to address that issue at all. I will apologize, for my actions, but that is as far as it will go." Nicole stood and took the glass of wine Vernon extended to her. She looked at him for a sign to see where he stood on her decision, but was not able to read him. The expression on James' face encouraged her to stand her ground. However, the look on her father's face cautioned her to step lightly.

"Nicole, I will love you until the day I die and will stand behind you no matter what. If you tell me you are..." Avery hesitated.

"Gay, Pop? Or you could use the politically correct word lesbian. But either way, she should not have to answer that question, not even for you."

Everyone turned to see the six-one, slim, serious face of Nicolas Brooks who stood in the doorway dressed in jeans, and a sweater with his arms folded over his broad chest.

"Nick, what are you doing here?" James asked as he stood and shook his youngest brother's hand.

"I called your place. Claire indicated you would all be here."

"Nicolas, welcome home. It is so wonderful to see you," Gwen smiled as she hugged her son.

The relief that washed over Nicole was unmistakable. Her other half was there. Based on his statement, she knew he understood and supported her decision. There was never a time when her older, by five minutes, twin brother was not there for her. The last few months had been miserable without him around. She'd made a mistake and came between him and his girlfriend. She now knew that was wrong. In her mind she was only trying to protect him, but in the end she realized she was being judgmental. That, she thought, had cost her, her brother's love, but it seemed she was wrong. Placing the glass on the table, she went over to Nicolas, put her arms around his waist and hugged him. The hold was so tight, Nick stumbled to keep his balance.

"Hello, baby sis." He returned the hug filled with eternal love and forgiveness. He looked at her. "Did you think I was going to let you have all the fun on this one?"

Nicole smiled up at him. "I think it's time to merge Brooks and Brooks, protectors of the Fourth Amendment."

"Nicolas, I'm going to tell you the same thing I told Vernon, stay out of this," Avery warned.

"No way, Pop. Nicole has a right to her privacy," Nick stated as he accepted the drink Vernon offered. Nick took a seat between Nicole and his father. "Butchie," he called out the family's nickname for his brother James. "Where are the children?"

"They are upstairs with Ashley," James replied.

"James Jr. too?" Nick asked, ready to challenge the boy to a game of basketball.

"No, he's visiting Georgetown's campus with friends this weekend."

Gwen loved having her family in the house. The huge home had been feeling empty, but today just about everyone was home. "I'm going to have Helena prepare something for dinner."

"I have a taste for an Uncle Butchie burger on the grill," a young voice stated from the doorway.

"Taylor," Vernon called out with surprise as he walked over to the doorway. He picked his twenty-year-old daughter up and swung her around, then hugged her fiercely. James looked at Nick and they both had the same question on their minds. *What's up with Vernon?* This was a man who shows no emotion and he was displaying signs of joy at the sight of his daughter.

"Where's your mother?"

"I'm not sure." Taylor said as she slipped from her father's arms and walked over to Nicole. She hugged her. "My stylist told me about the article on the internet. I took the jet home. I'm not sure what I can do to help, but I'm here for you." She took the seat on the other side of Nicole.

"This sofa is getting mighty crowded." Avery growled.

Nicole smiled and hugged her niece. To think she'd come from Atlanta and left a busy touring schedule just to support her, meant a lot to Nicole. Taylor, known to most of the world as Lil Tay, was a multi-platinum recording artist who was supposed to be on a concert tour.

"In the kind words of Bartle and Jayme, thanks for your support."

"Who's Bartle and James?" Taylor asked.

"Never mind," the group echoed in unison with a chuckle.

"This is between Nicole and I. Everybody out," Avery commanded.

"I love you, Pop, but I respectfully disagree," James stated. "This is about family."

"What Nikki's sexual preference may or may not be is her business," Taylor added.

"I agree." Vernon added. "The question on the table should be, what we are going to do to stop the continuous extortion of money from this family by the Hargroves?"

"We could all whip the woman's ass, give her a check and call it a day," Ashley suggested as she strutted into the room and took a seat next to her husband.

"You are becoming more like a Brooks every day," Nicole smiled at Ashley.

"Thank you."

"Nicole in my office—now." Avery pointed to the door across the foyer.

Nicole jumped to her feet. "I'm coming with her, as her attorney," Nick insisted.

"I'm her attorney," Vernon argued.

"Actually, I am also an attorney," Nicole said to stop all of them. "I will state my own case to Poppa." She turned to her father. "I'm ready," she said, then marched across the foyer with her head held high.

Avery looked at his family as they watched Nicole walk across the foyer into his office. They all looked as if they were ready to pounce on him.

"I'm not going to kill her, you know," he said to defend his actions.

Taylor walked over to her grandfather. "Poppa," she said with sad eyes as she took his hand. "I know you are not going to kill Aunt Nikki, but can I please just sit in the room and hold her hand while you fuss? It always made me feel better when you held my hand while Daddy fussed at me."

Avery swore he saw crocodile tears about to fall from Taylor's eyes. This was his first grandchild and he did not have the power to deny her anything. He kissed her forehead, took her hand and began walking toward the office.

Taylor looked over her shoulder and winked at the family.

Vernon smiled. "That's my girl."

James and Nick turned to Vernon with raised eyebrows.

***

Avery walked into the office, crossed the length of the room with four long strides and took a seat behind his desk. The office was decorated with deep, rich mahogany furniture, with plaques and accolades of all kinds for his different court battles or actions concerning civil rights. There were pictures of him with political powerhouses, leaders of the world, and others. The big chair he sat in was made to intimidate those opposing him. However, he could feel this battle with his only daughter was going to be his toughest yet. Of course he understood her stance, hell he fought for people to be able to take the stance. Here, there was another element in play. This was his baby—his daughter, the apple of his eye and he would move heaven and earth to keep her safe—protected from all. He would not stand for her reputation being slandered in the media. For as her father, that was his job. His family was low on girls. His daughter and granddaughters were his pride and joy. Now he sat there looking at two of them across from him and knew, he was in trouble.

Nicole sat and waited. She knew her father was not going to speak until he felt he had intimidated his opponent into submission. She always admired his tenacity when it came to waiting out his opponent. She just never thought she would ever be on the receiving side. His problem, however, lay in the fact that she had inherited that trait from him and so had Taylor. She knew they were his one weakness, with the exception of her mother. However, she feared her love for him may overrule her right to privacy and she would give in to him. At the moment, Taylor squeezed her hand. She glanced at her niece and read what was in her eyes.

You can do it, Aunt Nikki.

"The London deal goes to the board next Thursday. Ellington and Warner will have the final vote on the acquisition going through. What do you think their stance will be once this story reaches them?"

That was totally unfair. She wanted to yell objection, but they were not in a court of law. They were in the courtroom of Avery Brooks. He played to win—she had forgotten that.

"That's what I thought your reply would be." Avery leaned forward with his hands folded on top of the desk. "You see, Nicole, as unfair as it may seem, in this instance when you and Brooks International have so much on the table, you have allowed your personal life to interfere with your professional. If it were not for this incident, you could very well have continued as you have, keeping your personal and professional lives separate. Your actions have forced your own hand. To keep the London deal alive, you will now have to publicly declare your sexual preference."

Nicole stood and began to pace the floor in front of her father's desk as she had as a child when she was trying to work something out in her mind.

"That was smart, Poppa," she said as she folded her hands behind her back and continued to pace. "Approaching this from a business standpoint was an intelligent move. However, you know and I do too, Ellington would never vote with me on this acquisition. He may sway Warner. Our only recourse was to develop a plan that would impress the London team to a point where they would provide the funding needed to complete the project."

"Therein lies your problem."

She stopped pacing and faced her father. "Jacob Allen."

Avery nodded his head. "Jacob Allen."

Nicole's shoulders slouched as she sighed.

"Who is Jacob Allen?" Taylor asked, unable to wait on the two legal minds.

"Jacob Allen is the developer working on the plans for the London project." Nicole began to explain. "He, his family and everyone that works at their firm are right-wing Christians who condemn homosexuality."

"What does any of that have to do with business?" Taylor exclaimed. "You're not asking to have sex with any of them. You just want them to design your building or shopping center or whatever it is you do. You shouldn't have to declare your sexuality publicly with anyone at any time. That's a private issue and it should remain that way."

Nicole and Avery could see Taylor was becoming emotional, but neither could understand why.

"Anything sexual should be between two consenting adults, it should not be forced, coerced or openly discussed by others. It's a private matter and if Aunt Nicole does not wish to announce to the world which sex she prefers she shouldn't have to Poppa."

Nicole stared at her niece, something wasn't right, she thought as the distress showed on Taylor's face. Nicole glanced at her father. Avery returned the look, then turned back to Taylor, concerned.

"Taylor," Avery gently spoke, "come here, darling."

Taylor wiped the tears that had unconsciously dropped while she was talking. "No, Poppa, I don't want to."

"Come over here Taylor, now." He spoke quietly, but firmly.

Taylor hesitated, then walked over to her grandfather. "I'm too old for the lap, Poppa."

Avery pulled her onto his lap. "You are never too old for this lap." He tucked her head in the crook of his neck. Her legs were longer than he remembered and she clearly was not a little girl any longer, Avery thought as he pulled her snuggly onto his lap. He motioned to Nicole to leave the room.

She mouthed Vernon, wondering if she should have her brother come into the room. Her father shook his head, no. Nicole opened the door to leave the office, then stopped. "Poppa." She hesitated at the door. "I'm not gay."

"I know."

"How do you know?"

"You paid fifty-thousand dollars for a man," Taylor cried while sinking in the safety of her grandfather's arms.

***

"What happened?" Nick jumped up as Nikki walked back into the family room.

Sighing as she slumped into the seat next to Ashley, she said, "We do have a problem." She sat up. "Vernon how can we get rid of the charge and the story?"

"The story is out. Pulling it back will not prevent other media outlets from picking it up. The charge, that's easy. The Hargroves are about money. Dangle enough in their faces and they will go away."

"Only to be resurrected again," Gwen said from the doorway. "I am tired of making their lives easier. They are leeches. It's time to teach them a lesson. Vernon, set up an appointment to meet with the Hargroves. James, contact the media to set up a press conference, it's time to put a stop to this madness."

Nicole looked from Nick to James then back to their normally reserved mother. They had all witnessed Gwendolyn when someone attacked one of her cubs.

"Mother, thank you for the support. However, we have to proceed with caution. Brooks International is in a very delicate phase of negotiations with London on a multibillion dollar deal. I'm afraid my actions haven't given us any other option than to pad the Hargroves' bank account again."

"Then what is going to stop them from coming back again, and again, and again," Ashley asked hesitantly. "I mean, according to what I'm hearing, extorting money from the Brooks' is the Hargrove family business. It also gives me the feeling that we are buying people off instead of dealing with the situation." James touched Ashley's hand. "Please hear me out. I don't mean to be disrespectful in any way." Ashley turned to Gwendolyn. "I am a Brooks now therefore, I have a stake in this as much as the rest of you. I don't know the Hargroves or their history. However, I can tell you the way to deal with a bully is to get in their face. If you keep doing the same thing you always have, the results will be the same. I say squash their little behinds and call it a day."

The room was silent for a moment as they all considered Ashley's words.

"She may have a point there," Vernon nodded.

"What would you do, Ashley?" Nicole asked.

"That would depend on what's at stake. You mentioned a deal. How does this incident impact the deal?"

"The owners of one of the companies we are depending on to pull the London deal through are devout Christians. The accusations about my sexual preference have been an issue for them in the past, however, they have never questioned me on it before, because it was basically in-house."

"Now that Trish has made it public, they will expect you to take a position one way or another, and you believe it's a private matter." Nick summarized.

"Precisely." Nikki nodded.

"What if you spoke with them privately, one CEO to another," Ashley asked.

"The CEO represents the company," James stated. "His first priority will be to keep his company's public image intact. He will want Nikki to make a public statement, or his company will withdraw from the project."

"You can't be certain of that until you try."

"I'm afraid we can, Ashley," James stated. "Allen and Allen are politically connected and support only candidates that have the same beliefs."

"They are the same in business," Nikki added. "When we first approached them, they were very interested in working with us. Then one of my partners, Hayward Ellington, conveniently dropped a hint about my administrative assistant's sexual preference. I couldn't lie and say she wasn't gay."

"Is that why Alicia came out," Nick asked.

"Yes. Fortunately, Jacob Allen was impressed with the idea of designing a community in London, so he stayed with the project."

"It's one thing for an employee to go against what he believes in, quite another for that employee to be the CEO. This situation may push him to withdraw," Vernon summarized.

Nicole sat back and sighed. "That is my fear from a professional standpoint, just not my biggest concern."

"What is your other concern?" Nick asked.

"What does Xavier think of all of this? Does he believe Trish? Will he still be interested in me with all the baggage? I mean he was supportive when I spoke with him this morning, but in the grand scheme of things how long will that last?" Her head dropped to the back of the sofa in exasperation. "Good Lord that man can kiss."

The room again was silent. None of them had ever heard Nicole express concern over a man's feelings towards her. Oh, she had had boyfriends here and there, but her attitude was always, had fun—time to go.

"Well, that answers the question on if she is gay." Ashley smiled at her husband.

"Who in the hell is Xavier?" Nick asked.

"The man she paid fifty-thousand dollars for," Constance replied from the doorway. "Where is my daughter?" She frowned at Vernon.

Vernon straightened from the fireplace where he was leaning. "You're her mother. You should know."

Constance put her purse on the table next to the door. "I'm not in the mood for you today, Vernon. Where is she?"

"Our daughter is with her grandfather," he replied through clenched teeth.

"Why," an angry Constance demanded. " What lies has she told him?"

"Is there something wrong with Taylor?" a concerned Gwen asked looking from Constance to Vernon. Neither replied. "I don't give a damn what's going on between you two. I asked a question and I expect an answer," she demanded.

"Constance." Vernon glared towards his wife. "Is there a problem with Taylor?"

"Yes," Nicole replied. "However, Poppa is handling whatever is wrong."

"What do you mean?" Constance snapped.

Nicole sat up, looked around then looked back at Constance. "You have mistaken me for your child. Try again."

Constance pushed her now auburn hair from her shoulders and remembered her situation with this family. As Vernon's wife she was to be seen, not heard. "I did not mean to snap, Nicole. I'm just concerned about Taylor. She took the jet and left without telling me where she was going. After speaking with her people I guessed she was here."

"That's what family does when one of us is in trouble," Nick responded as he took in a head to toe view of Constance. "You look different."

"Yes, you do," Ashley added. "Hello, Connie."

"Constance," she replied to Ashley with a defiant look."

"Not that Ashley cannot speak for herself," James stood as he walked over to the bar. "In her defense she calls you Connie because I do." He refreshed his drink then walked over to Constance. "And I would thank you not to take that tone with my wife." He held her eyes until they softened. "Welcome home, Connie. How are you?"

James always treated her with respect, as if she was a true member of the family. Their true bonding point was formed when he caught his wife in bed with his brother, her husband. James was able to leave, go on with his life away from the house and the family. She had to stay and deal with the humiliation. "Hello James." She spoke for the first time in a civil tone. "Thank you and I'm fine. I just want to make sure Taylor is okay."

"Why are you concerned with her being here, Connie?" Vernon continued to glare at her. "This is her home, after all."

The venom returned to Constance's stare, as she looked around James. "Because she is my child. I am always concerned about where she is and what she is doing. Always have been, can you say the same?"

"Excuse me Mrs. Brooks." They all turned to Helena, the cook. "Dinner is ready."

"Thank you, Helena." Gwen replied. "We'll be right in." She turned back to Constance. "I asked you a question. What's going on with Taylor?"

"She's a teenager, Gwen," Constance smirked, "there is always something going on."

"Taylor is twenty, not a teenager." Vernon walked over to his wife. "Look at me Connie."

Venom would have been sweeter than the look she gave him. "The days of me jumping at your command are over," she snarled.

"Really?" Vernon raised an eyebrow. "As long as you carry the name Brooks you damn well better jump." He walked by her toward the stairs leading to their wing of the estate. "Connie," he commanded.

Connie looked around at the family members. James was the only one who looked remotely embarrassed by the scene. He nodded to her to go with Vernon.

The thought that haunted her years ago when she caught Vernon in bed with James' wife the first time, was whether she had married the wrong brother. She glanced at Ashley and wondered if Vernon had had his way with her as well. She lowered her eyes and followed Vernon out of the room.

Nick stood, pulling Nicole up with him. "Saved by the ever forbidding Connie." He hugged her. "I'm hungry, what about you?"

"I'm starving." Nicole returned the affection she had been missing from her brother. "I missed dinner last night and breakfast this morning."

"For fifty-thousand dollars the man should have at least bought you dinner," Nick smirked.

"At least a hot dog," James added as they all walked toward the dining room.

Ashley, looked up at James as he took her hand. "I have a feeling she got something hot last night that was better than food."

"Ashley I don't give it up on the first date," Nicole frowned, then smirked. "He can certainly hit it tomorrow though."

"Hey." Ashley gave Nicole a high five as they walked through the dining room door. "Clearly, she is not gay," Ashley said as she took a seat next to her husband. "Since that's the case, couldn't Nicole sue for defamation of character or something?" Ashley took the platter from Nick, without noticing that the room had grown quiet.

Nicole stared at Ashley, and then slowly drifted her eyes to Nick. James took the platter from Ashley after she had taken what she wanted, and just stared at her, then looked up at Nick and Nicole.

"Out of the mouth of the non-lawyer in the family," Nick said as he began to nod his head. "Why not?"

"Why not what?" Ashley asked.

"There are four elements to defamation." James began. "Prove the statement was made."

"The statement had to be made publicly," Nick added.

"Hell, you can't get any more public than an auction filled with people and press," Gwen huffed.

"The statement had to be negligent and we must prove damages." Nicole nodded, thinking the process through.

"Think this through, Nikki," James cautioned. "Your sexual behavior will come into play if you take this course of action. You will have to prove, in a court of law that the statement is false. A few moments ago, you didn't want to acknowledge your sexuality to your own father. Are you willing to swear in court that you are not gay?"

"That's right Nikki," Nick added. "You will have to prove not only financial damage, but personal damage to your reputation. What do you think Alicia's reaction will be if you use the approach that being gay or accused of being gay was damaging?"

"Before you make a decision," Gwen reached across the table to grasp her daughter's hand, "speak to your father. No one knows discrimination law like your father."

The discussion continued as Nicole contemplated her next move. It now seemed she had options.

***

"You have two minutes to tell me what's going on with my daughter." Vernon entered the sitting area in the wing of the Brooks Estate that he called home. His footsteps, though angry, were cushioned by the thick Persian carpet as he walked towards the bar. Seconds later, Constance entered the room just as Vernon put the glass of brandy to his lips. He paused, watched as she placed her purse on the table next to the bedroom. There was no mistake; Constance was still a beautiful woman. Nothing could change his thoughts on that front. It was her heart that caused him to push her into the hell hole of the abyss.

The demure walk towards him, with her hands folded in front of her was a farce. He took the shot of brandy in one gulp, then placed the snifter on the bar. "You're down to one minute." In that minute, he decided to pray for control.

"Taylor is a typical twenty-year-old." Constance sat in the Queen Anne chair near the fireplace on the other side of the room and crossed her legs. "She feels she knows what is best for her."

"Which is?"

"Vernon, I have been managing Taylor's career for five years now," she hissed. "I know the music industry inside out. I know the players from the fake, to the legit."

"I don't recall asking you what you know. Game recognizes game. And you, Connie, are a master." He stepped from behind the bar, then towered over her. "Don't make me ask again."

"She wants out of her contract." Her voice level raised. "If she does that, it's going to appear she is difficult to work with. It will tarnish her career. I'm not going to allow that to happen."

His cell phone buzzed, as he gave her a speculative look. "Brooks," he answered the call without taking his eyes from her. He listened for a moment. "Mr. Hargrove. I've been expecting your call. Before you go any further, please know, there will not be a settlement out of court this time. We'll be in touch." He hung up the telephone, bent over and placed his hands on the arms of the chair, boxing Constance in. "For the record, I didn't fall for that crap you extracted. You can go back to Atlanta, Taylor stays."

"Taylor is in the middle of recording a CD, she has contractual responsibilities."

"Present the contract. I'll find a way to break it." He stood to walk away.

"You can't do that."

"Yes, I can and I will."

"I won't allow it." Constance jumped up.

Vernon was back in front of her so fast Constance fell backwards into the chair. "Allow? You-" He stared down at her. "I've allowed you to take my daughter from her home to assist with her wishes to perform. I...allowed you to manage her career." He hit his chest with the palm of his hand. "I allowed you to have your freedom." His voice dropped low. "You didn't allow anything." He stood up attempting to get his temper under control. "Make no mistake, Connie, if any harm comes to Taylor I will kill anyone I think is responsible. Do we understand each other?"

***

Hayward Ellington sat in his luxurious sunroom in his Hampton estate reading the entertainment section of the Sunday paper. The usual nonsense was being reported, this one carrying that one's bastard child. This one is sneaking around with someone other than his wife. One would think there were better topics to put in a newspaper. Turning the page, a caption caught his attention just as he was about to toss the paper aside. *Real Estate Mogul Called Out of the Closet.* Beneath the article was a picture of Nicole Brooks standing over a woman with her legs up in the air. His face frowned in disgust. How could she be so stupid?

"Mr. Ellington," his butler called out. "You have a call." He gave the telephone to Hayward.

"Ellington here."

"Mr. Ellington, I believe you have a vote this week regarding a real estate deal with Nicole Brooks."

"Who is this?"

"Unimportant. Your question should be how can I assist you in eliminating Brooks International from the deal?"

There was hesitation. "I'm listening.

Chapter 5

Monday
Richmond, Virginia

Early Monday morning Trish Hargrove sat in the reception area of Davenport Industries dressed in an indigo designer dress, a thick black belt around her tiny waist, matching red heels and a pair of large designer sunshades. Her legs crossed and swinging. *This is going to be a good day*, she thought as she patiently waited for Xavier to arrive. The events of the weekend put her in a perfect position to be set for life. Things could not have turned out better if she had planned it herself. Before the week was out, she would be financially set, without selling her soul to the devil. With any luck, by the end of the day, she would have Xavier back in her bed. She flipped her shoulder length hair from her neck and tilted her head slightly to the side.

The pictures of the communities designed and built by Davenport Industries hung proudly along the wall in the lobby. This building itself, was designed by a man with vision and passion. That's what drew her to Xavier, his passion. Yes, his bank account was what caught her attention, but it was his passion that reached in and took a little piece of her heart. She wanted to feel that passion again. She wanted Xavier Davenport.

The last time they were together, she did not understand that good things came to those who wait. She tried to rush things with Xavier. Now, she had the patience it would take to get what she wanted. The man and financial security were within her grasp thanks to Nicole Brooks. Sitting up straight, her smile brightened. Who would have thought it? Nicole not only pushed the man into her arms, but would be the person filling her bank account with a digit and lots of zeroes behind it, once her attorney filed the law suit. Her parents played games in the past whenever the mighty Brooks stepped out of line. With her, it was be a very different story. Hell, she had pictures to back her claim.

"Trish?"

The voice radiated warmth so deep, the moisture could be felt between her legs. The vision stirred it more. "Xavier."

"What are you doing here?"

Her body slowly rose, revealing her long legs and curvy figure. The move was a practiced one that was meant to grab a man's attention. "I had to stop by in person to apologize." She placed her clutch under her arm. "Do you have a few minutes to talk?"

"Sure." Xavier put his hand on the small of her back, guiding her toward the elevator. "Good morning Lafonde," he spoke to the receptionist who handled the administrative offices. "Do you have any messages for me?"

"Yes, sir." Lafonde gave a stack of messages to Xavier, while giving the woman a side eye. "You have a ten-fifteen with the board, your mother's physical therapist would like for you to call, and your lunch appointment will be about fifteen minutes late. Would you like for me to hold your calls?"

Xavier glanced at his watch to determine how much time he had to speak with Trish. Something compelled him to have this conversation now, rather than later. "Yes, thank you."

"You're welcome."

Walking into the plush office it was clear this was an executive's space. The cherry wood desk, sat in front of a wall of windows with a view of downtown. A conference table, with the model of the current project in development spread across it, was at one end of the room. At the other end sat a drafting table, with a sketchpad, pencils, straight edge aid and a computer with a large monitor, with designs flashing on the screen.

"Have a seat Trish." Xavier pointed to the chairs that sat directly in front of his desk as he placed his portfolio on the drafting table. "How are you?" he asked looking over his shoulder.

"A few bruises here and there, but nothing major. No broken bones or anything," she joked as she sat and crossed her legs. The hem of the dress rising to show, smooth solid thighs. "I really want to apologize for the ugliness that took place on Saturday. It was so unfortunate to have that type of element at such a worthy event."

As he walked to his desk, he raised an eyebrow. "What type of element would that be, Trish?"

"Oh, you know, Xavier. Violence is not the way to settle anything. Anyone who cannot control their temper should not be allowed around civilized people."

"You questioned her femininity. Did you think your comment would go unchallenged?"

"Why would she challenge what is true? Her history has been with women, not men."

"How do you know that?"

"I've known Nicole Brooks all my life. We went to middle and high school together. There has never been a boyfriend or a man in her life. She went away to college and the only person she has ever brought home was that Alicia Robinson," she huffed.

"Have you ever been intimate with her?"

Trish pulled her shades from her eyes and glared at Xavier. "I am one hundred percent female. I love the feel of a man between my thighs. There is nothing, let me express that again, nothing, a woman can do with this." She motioned her hands around her body.

"Then my question is how do you know Nicole does not feel the same way?"

It took her a moment before the realization that Xavier's responses were not what she'd expected. "Because I know," she replied. "Look at my face Xavier. I can't believe you're sitting here attempting to justify her doing this to me." She looked as if she would cry.

"Trish, you and I have played this game for a while. I know you and I thought you knew me. Unfortunately, I'm beginning to see that you don't." He sat up in his seat. "If you did, you would know I don't deal with drama. For the brief time we were together, you brought drama into my life. Like then, I turn my back on that. You know this about me, or at least I thought you did." He shrugged his shoulders. "I don't know the history between you and Nicole. However, from what I saw on Saturday, I strongly suggest you pick another target. For it does not seem to me that Nicole Brooks is someone you want to go up against."

"Are you taking her side, after what she did to me?"

"No." Xavier shook his head. "I'm not taking anyone's side. I'm saying, look at your face, then take a look at hers. That observation should clearly tell you to watch what you say to her, for she strikes back—hard."

Trish stood with her hands on her hips. "Are you laughing at me, Xavier Davenport?"

"Yes, Trish. You knew before you made the statement that it was going to evoke a reaction from her. That's why you looked back at me and grinned before you said it." He stood and walked around the front of the desk to stand before her and leaned against it. "I never understood why you thought the way to get attention was to belittle or humiliate others." He tweaked her chin. "You are much too fine to have to resort to things like that. If a man is going to be with you, let him be there for the beautiful person Trish is, not for the fault you can show him in others." She smiled.

He removed her hands, and stood. "I think you are physically a very beautiful woman, it's the person inside that's a little scary."

"I can change for you, Xavier. You know I will."

"You shouldn't have to. There is a man out there that will accept you as you are. I'm not him, but he does exist."

"Xavier..."

"No." He kissed her forehead. "It's not going to happen. We've had this discussion before and nothing has changed." He took her shades from her hands and placed them back on her face. "Go home and take care of that eye and for goodness sake, stay away from Nicole."

Trish picked up her purse. "I believe you still care, Xavier."

"I do." He placed his hand behind her back and guided her to the door. "Just not the way you want me to." He opened the door. "Now go."

She stepped out the door, then came back with a frown. "Why do you keep referring to her as Nicole? You don't know her."

"I met her Saturday," he replied.

"When?" Trish asked. "When did you meet her?"

It was too late by the time he realized his mistake. "I went to the police station to bail her out of jail, but her brother was there and she didn't need me." He shrugged his shoulders.

"Really? You went to bail her out while I was laying on the floor bleeding and humiliated."

"Trish, your screams had garnered all the attention in the room. You didn't need me."

"So you took it upon yourself to go to Nicole Brooks' rescue."

"I did."

"Really."

"Yes, Trish, really. She did donate a huge sum of money to the recreation center. It was the least I could do."

"Is that all it was about—her donation?"

Focusing now on the notes for his meeting, Xavier replied without thinking. "I would be lying if I said she was not an intriguing woman."

"How can you be interested in her?" she yelled as she stomped back into the room. "She doesn't like men. Do you not understand?"

The anger in her voice caused him to look up from his notes. The glare he gave her was cold. "I'm a grown man, Trish. I don't deal with children."

Trish closed her eyes to rein in her temper. "Xavier," she spoke in a controlled manner. "Nicole Brooks is not the woman for you," she cried out. "Can't you see, I'm standing right here in front of you?"

"We tried that, Trish, it didn't work." He picked up his notes. It wasn't that he wasn't sensitive to her feelings. He knew if he attempted to console her in anyway, she would take it as a sign of affection he just did not have for her. "I have a board meeting I have to attend. I believe you know your way out."

"X-man, do you have the new specs on the Cedar Street strip mall?" Zack stopped as he noticed Trish standing near the desk. "I'm sorry, I did not know you had a visitor. Hello, Trish."

"Hello, Zackary." Trish turned to walk out. "Please stop calling him X-man, it's so childish." Trish stood there, not believing what he just said. "All right, Xavier." She pushed her purse under her arm. "Remember you set these wheels in motion," she said then walked out.

Xavier shrugged his shoulders wondering if he should have handled that differently.

"Women problems?" Zack grinned.

"Not really." Xavier picked up his notes then his tablet with the diagram for the strip mall.

"Trish looked a little upset."

"Trish is always upset about one thing or another."

"True," Zack replied as he tried to get a read on his little brother. X-man always kept his feelings close to the vest. He rarely expressed anger or frustration. The only time Zack could remember X-man having a cross word with anyone was when he had treated his wife badly. His wife, Diamond, had been X-man's best friend all through college. Anger was Zack's way of keeping Diamond from capturing his heart and X-man did not like it one bit. In addition to that, X-man did not like the fact that he kept the truth about their mother from him. Since that time Zack did all he could to keep the lines of communication honest with X-man. Besides, as his big brother it was his responsibility to protect X-man in all things. "A woman scorned is hell on wheels, X-man. Learn from my mistakes. Don't underestimate how far Trish will go to get your attention."

"Trish isn't a woman scorned Zack. I was very clear with her. A relationship between us is not in the future, especially now." Xavier said as he walked toward the door.

"Because of Nicole Brooks?"

"Yes." Xavier stopped and looked at his brother.

"Did you tell Trish that?"

"No, not really. She asked about Nicole and I didn't lie. I am very interested in Nicole."

"And you told Trish that?"

Xavier stepped through the door. "Why do you keep asking me that?" He looked back over his shoulder at Zack. "I told her the truth."

Zack chuckled as they walked down the hallway to the conference room. "When it comes to women, there's the truth and then there's their truth."

Xavier frowned at Zack. "There is only one truth, Zack. I'm not interested in a relationship with Trish."

"Because of Nicole Brooks."

"No," Xavier said as he opened the door to the conference room. "Because of Trish."

Zack pushed the wood door closed. "I'm willing to bet, what Trish heard you say was you are not interested in a relationship with her because you are now interested in Nicole Brooks."

"That's not what I said, Zack. I lost interest in Trish months ago. She knows that."

"All I'm saying is she may have heard it differently." He opened the door and pushed X-man inside.

Xavier stepped into the room as the occupants stood to applaud. In the front of the room, Diamond stood next to a banner that read, *Davenport Industries, Home of the $50,000.00 Man.*

The members of the board, Reese Kendrick, head of security, Jake Turner, the Human Resources Director, Julia English, the Corporate Attorney and the newest member, Neil Jeffries, Director of Finance, laughed as Xavier's head fell to his chest in embarrassment.

"Ladies and gentlemen, the fifty-thousand dollar man, Xavier Davenport single handedly secured the initial funds for the Recreation Center." The members of the board threw long stem roses at Xavier's feet.

"Ha, Ha, very funny," he laughed at Diamond, then turned to Zack. "You were in on this?"

"Of course not." Zack grinned. "You know I'm all about business."

"Yeah, right." Xavier grinned.

"Did you really think we were going to let this opportunity to pull your chain slide?" Zack affectionately hit Xavier on the shoulder, and then took his seat at the head of the conference table. "Be happy I took all the red lace panties they planned to throw."

Xavier laughed, as he took his seat. "Thank you for the little things."

"If everyone will settle down. Before we begin with our scheduled board meeting, we have a special announcement." Diamond clicked the remote control, and the monitor dropped slowly down from the ceiling. She clicked another button and Nicole Brooks appeared on the screen.

"Good morning, Diamond, and members of Davenport Industries' Board of Directors. Thank you for the opportunity to speak with you. My name is Nicole Brooks. It was my honor to be the donor of $50,000.00 toward the construction of the Recreation

Center. Diamond was kind enough to send me the specs for the center and plans for services to be offered. I was impressed, very impressed with the project. More so with Davenport Industries' pledge to cover fifty percent of the cost. As the CEO of Brooks International, we are always searching for projects that concentrate on improving communities. I have a decent understanding of the cost to build the wonderful facility you have planned. The funds collected from the charity event represent approximately twenty percent of the total budget. We believe happy families build strong communities. After a careful review of this project, we believe the services this facility will provide will have a significant contribution to building family unity. For that reason, we have decided to guarantee the remaining balance needed to construct the recreation center." The room erupted in applause. Nicole smiled. "Brooks International extends our congratulations on your efforts to improve communities across the country."

"Good morning Ms. Brooks. Zackary Davenport here. On behalf of Davenport Industries and the Highland Park community, we accept the offer and thank you for your generosity."

"You are welcome. Our financial department will be in touch. Congratulations again to Davenport Industries."

"Thank you, Nicole," Diamond said as she clicked off the connection, then turned and took her seat at the table. "Now, that's the way you get corporate donations."

Neil Jeffries shook his head as he spoke. "The purpose of my report today was to advise the board that funding of this project may create a cash flow problem for the company." He picked up the report. "I can now shred this."

The murmur of conversations raced around the table with excitement. Zack's attention fell on his brother. While X-man smiled with the others, Zack could see that he did not welcome the announcement. Zack knew that the board anticipated having to take the brunt of the cost for constructing the center, for they understood the chances of raising the additional funds needed were slim. Nicole Brooks had just lifted that burden from them.

Reese looked down the table at Xavier and laughed. "It seems you made quite an impression on the lady, X-man."

Xavier did not respond. The joy of seeing Nicole changed with her announcement. He had spoken to her last night before going to sleep and she did not mention this. Of course their conversation was more on the personal level. However, he had a concern with crossing the personal and professional lines. Hearing the excitement around the table, he looked up, smiled then caught his brother's eyes. He quickly masked his anger.

"While we are excited about this announcement, we have other business at hand." Zack turned to Diamond first, knowing X-man needed a moment. Smiling at his wife, he asked, "What plans do we have for the grand opening of Davenport Circle?"

Xavier listened as the meeting progressed around him. His mind, however, was on his mixed emotions about Nicole.

***

After the meeting, Xavier returned to his office. The first item on his agenda was to finalize the draft for the strip mall. However, now that the funding was in place for the recreation center, that would take priority. Placing his tablet on his desk, he walked over to his drafting table, turned on his computer, then stared at it. The creativity was not there yet. He turned towards the windows that covered the back wall of his office and stared at the outline of the city with the James River in the distance. The scene always sent inspiration his way. This morning, it wasn't working. He turned to the sound of a soft knock at his office door.

"Am I interrupting?" Diamond asked from the doorway.

"No, come in."

"Is it safe?" She smiled, showing those deep dimples he loved so much.

"I haven't decided yet," he replied as she sat on the windowsill.

"Oh, come on. I never would have thought so much drama would have occurred at the auction. You can't still be mad at me."

"I can." He raised an eyebrow. "But, I'm not."

She jumped up and kissed him on the cheek, then sat back down. "I'm happy to hear that. So, tell me about your plans for Nicole Brooks."

"I haven't finalized them yet." He sighed.

"You're not going to do the Shenandoah? I love that area."

"I'm not sure Nicole Brooks will go for the outdoor events I had planned."

"Why not?" Diamond asked a little surprised.

"She's a billionaire, Diamond." He stood and walked over to his desk. "I'm not sure how to plan a weekend for her."

"Xavier." She walked over to the desk and gave him a gentle push. He fell into the chair behind the desk, faking injury. "Nicole is a female first. Anything romantic will impress her." She put her hands on her hips. "Millionaire, billionaire, what's a few thousand dollars amongst friends. Don't allow what you hear or her money to dissuade you from fulfilling your obligations. Besides, I think she likes you."

"Why, did she say something to you?"

"No, we never mentioned you. We only discussed the project this morning. From what Alicia told me, you are the first man she has shown any interest in for a few years."

"Is that so?" He picked up the tablet on his desk as if he was not interested in the subject. "Who is Alicia?"

"She's my soror and she is Nicole's personal assistant."

"Nicole isn't a soror?"

"No. She was at the event with Alicia."

"With Alicia?"

The way he asked the question made her smile. "Don't believe the rumors, especially from Trish. I don't know much about Nicole's personal life. According to Alicia, she's a loner. She is all about Brooks International. If she takes this weekend off with you, it will be a first." She took the tablet from his hand and placed it on the desk. "Look, you need a break. You've been working non-stop since Davenport Estates. Take the weekend, enjoy the company of a woman. Who knows, you may find something special in Nicole Brooks."

"You don't believe the rumors?"

"No, and you shouldn't either. Find out for yourself."

He sighed. "I'm concerned about the move she made this morning."

"The announcement about the recreation center?"

"Yes."

"Why are you concerned about that?"

"I don't like the idea or the appearance of having been bought."

"Sorry to tell you this, but that ship has sailed. The price and all was published in the newspaper and on the blog *Rumor Has It*."

"Another blog?"

"Oh, man, are you out of it." She laughed as she pulled the blog up on his computer. "There's a few blogs connected to just about every family of substantial wealth. It seems the Brooks' have captured the attention of this particular blogger. You, my friend, have been identified. You don't need to read it. It's just a weekend obligation for charity." She turned to walk out. "I have to go. Be sure to have Lafonde set up those plans for you."

He watched as she walked away. "Hey, you're filling out those pants, girl."

Diamond stopped in the doorway. "You're not supposed to be looking at my butt."

"Dimples, I've been looking at that butt for ten years," he replied laughing.

"I'm your brother's wife."

"Don't make the butt no less phat."

She gave him a mischievous grin. "I'm going to tell your brother," she said then walked out of the office.

Xavier smiled as she walked out. He was very happy his best friend married his brother. The two complimented each other well. Looking at the computer, he began reading.

Rumor Has It

This blogger has identified the $50,000.00 man. Remember the cat fight I mentioned on yesterday, well, rumor has it Nicole Brooks paid

$50,000.00 to have a romantic weekend get-a-way with an Architect from Virginia. His name is Xavier Davenport. Can you say FINE! Check out the pic below. Trish Hargrove may be in trouble. It seems Xavier and Nicole have something in common. The brother is one half of Davenport Industries, a commercial development firm. I wonder what designs he has for Nicole for the weekend.

Xavier stood and walked over to the window as his thoughts went to Nicole. He now wondered if she was the one. The woman who could make his heart smile at the sight of her. It certainly was not smiling this morning when she made that announcement. Call it machismo or whatever; he had a problem with the world thinking he could be bought. The thought of her investing in the recreation project because of him was an issue that needed to be cleared up. Before he allowed this woman to creep into his heart any more than she already had, he would have to get the answers to a few questions. He walked back over to his desk and pushed the intercom for Lafonde. "Will you get me the address to Brooks International's corporate office and find out if Nicole Brooks is in the office today."

Chapter 6

Monday
Manhattan, New York

Brooks International's offices were in a buzz. The telephones were ringing off the hook, several employees were gathered in pockets at their desks and Alicia was in a bad mood. Nicole did not have the luxury of any office interactions this morning. She was in cleanup mode. The calls were coming in fast and while she had no intention of discussing her sexual preference with any of the callers, a few demanded at least a conversation about the articles from the weekend. To add to the lovely morning she was already having, Steven Warner was sitting in the chair across from her desk waiting for her to deal with the third interruption since he arrived, fifteen minutes ago.

"I understand your concern, however, Brooks International has no interest in interfering with the policy of your agency regardless of what's written in a blog." She listened, then nodded. "I totally agree and if we have any reason to withdraw the notice will come from this office. Thank you for the call."

Nicole closed her eyes and exhaled. When she opened them Steven was staring at her. "Don't you dare laugh."

"I would not dream of it." Steven wiped an imaginary piece of lint from the trousers of his five thousand dollar navy suit. The dark tie against the crisp white shirt was his trademark. And he wore it well for a sixty-something year old mogul who resembled the movie star Clark Gable. "It seems the articles have ignited a little nervousness among your clientele. You do realize this is only the beginning?" He raised an eyebrow.

Nicole sighed. "I do. My sexual preference has seemed to generate unrest in the world. Who would have thought it?"

Steven smiled. "My dear, anything about a young African-American billionaire will generate talk. The thought of you having a questionable sexual appetite is like ice cream on top of a thick brownie with nuts."

"Oh, that sounds delicious."

"Yes, it does. However, my dear you will have to address this issue one way or another soon. You should know I received a call from Ellington, your troubles are only beginning." He uncrossed his legs and stood. "He's coming after your share of the London deal full throttle. I suggest you contact Jacob Allen before he does."

Nicole stood to see him to the door. "Bend down here so I can kiss your cheek." The six-foot man did as requested with a smile. She kissed him. "Thank you for the heads up. I expect Jacob will attempt to pull out of the deal."

"Not attempt, my dear. He will pull out of the deal. However, Allen and Allen are not the only commercial architects in the world. There are others."

"Just the best and I have to say I love their ideas for the London project." She looked up at him. "Are you still with me?"

"You keep solid funding and Warner Industries is with you. However, Ellington is coming after you. He does not want Brooks International on this project."

"What you mean is he doesn't want a little girl with brown skin on this project."

"That is true."

"It was our idea. We did the leg work with the London officials. He needs us as much as we need him. He doesn't have the funding to go it alone."

"Don't underestimate Ellington's' goal. He wants the project to proceed. If there is another source of funding out there, he will find it. He does not want Brooks International to spearhead such a groundbreaking project. At this moment, I'm certain he is speaking with Jacob Allen trying to convince him to pull his design, forcing you to pull out of the project." He kissed her forehead. "Tread lightly, my dear. I'm in your corner."

"Brooks International owns the property."

"A small technicality, my dear."

As soon as Steven left the office, Alicia walked in. "How did it go?"

"He's still supporting the project, for now. If Ellington is successful in pulling Jacob to his side, we may have a problem."

"Problem is on line one." Alicia frowned.

Nicole sighed. "No interruptions, Alicia, okay."

Alicia turned to walk out. "Oh, and tell Stacy if one more call comes in on my line from the media, I'm going to assume she is unable to handle her job and find a replacement. One more thing, Steven mentioned articles. I know about the one, see if there are more. Then see if we can block them. I don't need this on Page Six."

"Be happy to." Alicia replied and closed the door behind her.

Nicole took a deep breath, then picked up the telephone. "Good morning, Jacob."

"Is it, Nicole?" Jacob's voice echoed in the phone.

"Any morning I wake up is a good one for me. How is your day so far?"

"My day began at seven when I received a conference call from Hayward Ellington and Steven Warner. You seem to have some dissension on the London project."

"Brooks International is fully committed to the London project. I just spoke with Steven Warner. He has assured me Warner Industries is committed as well. I cannot, however, speak for The Ellington group."

"Nicole, it goes without saying Brooks International is well respected as a leader in real estate development. However, recent events have created a buzz about its reputation."

"Brooks International's reputation has not been tarnished in anyway. We have an AAA rating internationally in addition to several awards for commercial excellence. We stand on our reputation."

"Nicole, you are the face of Brooks International. As unfair as it may seem, the news reports over the last few days have tarnished that reputation in the eyes of my agency. However, a public announcement on your sexual preference could eliminate this situation."

"No one should have to publicly announce anything about their sexual preference. Are you willing to do that Jacob?"

"I don't have to, Nicole. I'm not about to lose a multibillion dollar project."

She knew Jacob was right, but she was not willing to give in. "You know me, and you know how I handle business."

"I represent an agency, Nicole, and so do you. We do not have the luxury of our own convictions. I have to protect the investors. This call is a courtesy to advise you of a board meeting that will take place this afternoon to discuss our continued presence on the London project. You will have my vote. However, I'm only one in seven and Ellington is gathering his votes. I suggest you do the same."

"I understand your position, Jacob. Will you at the very least promise me this? Do not give the design you shared with me to Ellington, regardless of the outcome of the board's vote."

He hesitated. "I'll give you thirty days. After that, I can't promise anything."

"Thank you, Jacob."

"Nicole, I want to work with you on this project. Reconsider your position."

"I'll think about it, Jacob," a dejected Nicole replied. "I'll think about it."

Nicole stood to look out the window hoping the view of Central Park would calm her rising anger. The morning had started out so promising. The offer to help build the recreation center in Richmond felt good. The proposal from Davenport Industries was impressive. She wondered if Xavier had any part in that. She knew he was one of their architects, but that was about all she knew. How much input he had on their projects, she did not know. She reached up and touched her lips, remembering the kiss they'd shared. A warmth spread through her as she replayed the conversation from the night before. The man's voice was like a smooth caress. It was funny how the few times they had spoken it seemed as if they had so much to talk about. They had just met, yet he seemed so familiar. She wanted to see him again, but there was no way she could go back to Virginia right now.

So much was happening at the office that even the weekend getaway was questionable. Glancing at her watch, she saw it was a little after one. She wondered if Xavier was free to talk, just for a minute. She pulled her cell phone from her purse then dialed his number. The call went directly to voice mail. She sighed, threw the cell back into her purse. It was just as well, there were a few calls she had to make.

She was about to push the intercom on her desk, when it buzzed. "Alicia, good, I was about to buzz you. Have you had lunch?"

"Um, no. With everyone so busy I ordered in. I ordered you a sandwich and a salad. Why don't I send that in?"

"Bring your thinking cap. We have to work on a game plan for Jacob."

Alicia hesitated. "Before we do that, you have a visitor."

"Is it Ellington? I can't take discussing my sexuality with another man right now."

"Oh, I don't think you'll have a problem with this one. I'll send him in."

Alicia disconnected the call before Nicole could respond.

"Oh hell," she murmured as she sat behind her desk. A second later she jumped up. "Oh, hello."

The man was finery at its absolute best. Xavier stood there in a pinstriped Armani suit, with a crisp pink shirt, a solid black tie and his hair bound in a band. His six-two, slim frame was mouthwatering and there was no way she could hold her smile back.

"Hello, Nicole." Xavier stood there leaning against the door, still wondering why the very sight of the woman affected him. "I was instructed to deliver your salad. I'm to tell you it looks delicious."

He said something that she was sure of. For the life of her she had no idea what. The first and last time she saw him he was leisurely dressed. Today he wore business attire and damn if he didn't look good from head to toe. Then he smiled. The crotch of her panties filled with moisture. The man made her come just by looking at him. "I am in so much trouble."

"If I'm allowed to enter I may be able to help." He raised an eyebrow. "May I?"

He was still standing at the door with a knapsack over his shoulder and her lunch in his hand. "Oh, please do come in." She quickly walked toward him taking the lunch container from him, placing it on the desktop. As she turned back to him the urge to throw herself into his arms was so strong she took a step forward, then stopped.

He reached out, wrapping his arm around her waist and gently pulled her to him. They stood there, staring into each other's eyes. "May I kiss you before you kick me out?"

Without responding, she tiptoed up to gently kiss his lips, but the feeling was so glorious, and the morning had been so crappy, she just couldn't stop. When his fingers cupped her head, holding her lips securely to his, her need to taste him increased.

Xavier's intent was to talk with her face to face about his concerns. Then based on her response, make the plans for the weekend. Seeing her brought an entirely different response. The combination of the sunlight pouring through the window behind her, the look of surprise in her eyes, the radiant smile she gave him, all knocked the wind out of him. Urges, like he had never experienced before, flowed through him. All he knew for sure was if he did not kiss her right at that moment, he was going to die. What in the hell was happening to him?

The knapsack dropped to the floor, as her arms circled his neck. The mystical surges of desire rose quickly as the warmth of her mouth pulled at him. It was as if his tongue was seeking to take every inch of her and more if he could get it. His arms tightened around her, lifting her from her feet, bringing her more securely nestled to his body. A sound or something triggered him to stop. His mind thought, not just yet, just one more taste.

Slowly, he lowered her back to the floor, ended the kiss, then smiled at her kiss swollen lips. He ran a thumb over them and smiled. "Thank you."

There was no way she could let go. She held on to the strong arms that circled her and laughed. "You are welcome, but I swear it was my pleasure."

A glorious smile appeared on his face. It was her words that put it there. "Tell me what spell you cast over me and please tell me there is an antidote."

"I wish I could, and if there is an antidote I'll take it first." They stood there for another moment before he released her. "What are you doing here?" Nicole asked still holding his hand.

"Hmm, the magic is about to end."

She stepped back. "That doesn't sound too good." She walked around her desk. "Please, have a seat," she said as she sat down. "Welcome to New York."

Xavier looked around the plush office, as she picked up the knapsack and placed it in a chair, then sat in the other facing her. "I thought we needed to talk in person. I promise you I did not come here to eat you alive."

Nicole laughed. A deep rich laugh that came from within. "I hope you enjoyed that meal, it was delightful and you can't know just how much I needed it."

"Rough morning?"

"Very," she replied. "Whatever brought you, I'm happy you are here."

"I hope it stays that way."

She sobered. "Doesn't sound good. What is it?"

"We need to discuss your offer this morning."

"What offer?"

"The recreation center."

"Oh, yes. What about it," she asked, a bit bewildered.

"Why did you make the offer?"

"Why?" She frowned. "It's a wonderful project and a well written proposal. It's just the sort of project we fund."

"Why did you choose to finance it now?" The moment she realized the direction of his questions the brilliance in her eyes disappeared and he wished he had not voiced the thought.

His words answered her prayer to stop the flood from flowing between her legs. God works in mysterious ways. Nothing like a splash of cold water to stop a damn wet dream. No he did not just insinuate she was trying to buy his affections.

"Xavier Davenport." Her voice was smooth and deadly. "Make no mistake about it. I am immensely attracted to you. My panties are soaked just sitting here looking at you. However, there will never be a time when I have to buy the affections of you or any other man. I sincerely hope that was not what you were alluding to, for the other thought which has crossed my mind is that you feel I need to have a man appear in my life to refute the recent news articles." Her arms crossed over her breasts. "Frankly, either way, your visit, as joyous as the first five minutes were, is now over. You found your way in, I'm certain you can find your way out." Nicole turned to her laptop to turn it on.

"Nicole, please listen."

"I think not." She stood, ran her hand down her thighs to smooth her skirt down. "I have had it with men today. A freaking pastor on whether or not I was going to try to change his policy on gay rights in the church has questioned me. I've read a blog that has openly discussed my sexual preference. Then a business partner who has threatened to withdraw from a multi-billion dollar project if I don't go public with my sexuality. And now, you. The man who makes my inner lips moist on sight, has the audacity to ask if I'm trying to buy your affections by contributing to a project we picked up on months ago, before I even met your fine ass. It is just a little too much for one day." She picked up his knapsack, threw it in his lap and pointed. "The door is that way." She walked back around her desk, picked up a file and began reading.

Xavier stood. "Nicole, I had to ask."

"Xavier, please, just go." She began working on a file on her desk.

He stood there staring down at her. "We need to discuss the weekend."

"We really don't." She looked up shaking her head. "I release you from any obligations for the weekend." She looked back down at the papers.

He pulled the file from her desk. She jerked her head up. "We will have this weekend, Nicole. I flew here to ask you a question, not to accuse you of anything." He placed the file back on her desk and turned towards the door. "Just so you know," he said before walking out, "I have no questions about your sexuality. However, I was wondering..."

She glared at him.

"How wet are your panties?" He closed the door behind him as he walked out.

The elevator door on the thirty-fifth floor was about to close when a hand blocked it.

"Hold on," Alicia said as she stepped in.

Xavier stood with his hands in his pockets as if he did not have a care in the world.

"Well," she began as the door closed, "that started with such promise, but did not end the way I envisioned."

"You always listen to what happens in your boss' office?"

"No, however things got a little loud at the end and I couldn't help over hearing."

"Un huh." He looked suspiciously.

"What time is your flight out?"

"Why?"

"I thought it would be a shame for you to have come all this way and not see New York. Is this your first time here?"

"It is."

The elevator door opened and a tall red-head walked in. Her eyes raked over Xavier from head to toe. "Hello, Alicia."

"Candace," she responded.

"Candace Mercer, and you are?" Candace asked, never taking her eyes from Xavier.

"A visitor," Alicia replied.

"Oh, I know he doesn't work here. I know all the men in this building."

"And she means that literally," Alicia remarked as the elevator doors opened to the spacious lobby.

Xavier stepped out and walked towards the exit.

"Xavier," Alicia pulled his arm. "You did not come all this way just to confront her about the offer. I know that and you do to."

He stopped and looked down at her. "I'm not going anywhere..." He hesitated.

"Alicia," she supplied her name.

"You're Diamond's friend."

"No, I'm Diamond's soror."

"Okay." He smiled, "I stand corrected, her soror. She mentioned you. Look, I didn't come here just to ask Nicole about the donation. You're right about that. I needed to make sure I'm not a part of this game between her and Trish Hargrove."

"Nicole doesn't play games, especially with Trish Hargrove." She smiled, "So you're not leaving?"

"No."

She grinned. "So what are you going to do about Nicole? She's pretty pissed at you right now."

"I'm going to check out a little of New York. Come back here around five and wait for her."

Alicia laughed and walked towards the door. "There's a flaw in your plan. Come take a walk with me." They walked out of the building then turned right to join the busy pedestrians.

"So, tell me. Why is my being here so important to you?"

"Who said it's important?" Alicia asked.

"Your actions."

Alicia looked to the side, smiled up at Xavier then looked away as they walked down the street. "Nikki is in this mess because of me."

"How so?"

"Well, for one, people think she is gay because she is my friend. She's my friend because she was the one person that looked confused when I announced to all my so called friends in college that I was gay. She had no idea she was supposed shun me." She shook her head. "Silly rabbit."

He shrugged his shoulders as she stopped in front of a glass front building. "She wasn't. That's no reason to shun a person."

Alicia chuckled and shook her head. "You are as bad as she is." She turned to the man in the tailor made uniform. "Hello, Henry. This is Mr. Davenport. He's a friend of Nicole's. Would you get him settled in her place?" She turned back to Xavier. "This is Nicole's Palace. We both live here. You can hang here until I send her home. I'll try to get her out before your flight."

"My flight leaves at eight fifty."

"I know." She grinned as she began walking away. She turned back, "Do me a favor?"

"What's that?"

"Whatever happens, don't give up on her. She is a good person who needs a good man in her life. I think that man is you."

"You're a good friend, Alicia."

"I know." She waved and walked back to the office.

Xavier turned to the man in the uniform. "Mr. Henry?" he asked.

Mr. Henry smiled and opened the door. "Yes sir. May I have your name?"

"Xavier Davenport."

"Is this your first visit to New York?" he asked as they entered the huge marble floored lobby.

"Yes, it is."

"Allow me to give you a tour of Nicole's Palace."

"That won't be necessary. I'll just wait here for her."

Henry laughed. "The building's name is Nicole's Palace. Her father had it renovated a few years ago, when Ms. Nicole took over the reins at the Real Estate firm."

Xavier took a moment to look around. He noticed the concierge's desk with the italic N inscribed in a black emblem on the front. The two elevator doors had the same design. The marble tile also had the emblem every fifth tile. He could see his reflection in the various light tan shades of color in the tile. His eyes took in the crown molding, the floor to ceiling ancient columns, the gold and black trim, the chandelier lighting and the overall airy feel of the lobby.

"Joseph, have someone take over the door while I take Mr. Davenport up to the penthouse." He motioned for Xavier to follow him. "Her father wanted to ensure her safety here in the big city. He wanted a place fit for the princess she is," Henry stated as they stepped into the elevator.

Xavier did not miss the message in the statement. "She is a special woman." He nodded his head with the acknowledgment.

"That she is. I heard Ms. Alicia say your flight leaves tonight." He inserted a key into the elevator panel, then pushed a button, which had no floor number on it. The elevator began ascending.

"Yes, it does."

"You have a few hours to spare before Ms. Nicole arrives. It would be an honor to have our concierge arrange for what we call a nickel tour while you wait."

"That sounds nice, thank you, Mr. Henry."

The doors to the elevator opened to a foyer much like the lobby downstairs. The difference being the warmth he felt the moment he stepped into the room. There was a bank of windows on the far side of the foyer, which opened into a great room. Most people would first notice the fine furniture in the room, not Xavier. His eyes went to the structure of the room, the way the windows were placed to capture the outline of the city as if it were a painting in the room.

The placement of the furniture would impress Diamond. To the right was the entrance to the kitchen, a dining room table was placed in the center of the window to the right. A sofa and chair were center wall on the left, columns lined the entrance leading to the black baby grand piano in the center of the window directly in front of him.

"Wow, this place is a palace." Xavier turned to see Mr. Henry still standing at the elevator. He reached into his pocket and pulled out his wallet.

Henry shook his head. "We don't accept gratuities here. We are well compensated. This is a private elevator. If you decide to go out, the guest code is located here." Mr. Henry turned, then pointed to a panel on the wall next to the elevator. "Will you be needing anything else, sir?"

"No, thank you." He looked around. "I think I'll wait for Nicole."

"As you wish, sir. Enjoy your stay."

The elevator swooshed closed. Xavier looked around, placed his knapsack on the breakfast bar between the kitchen and the dining room. He pulled out his sketchbook, took a seat on the piano bench and began drawing.

* * *

It had been a hellish day and all Nicole wanted to do was take a shower, crawl under her blanket and cry like a baby. Not only did the meeting at Allen and Allen go against her, that rag of a blog posted another article. This time about her niece Taylor walking off of a video shoot. Now Vernon was up in arms. A nice glass of merlot would ease the pain of the disappointing day.

Nicole threw her keys on the breakfast bar, reached in the cabinet, then the wine cooler under the cabinet, poured a glass and was about to take a swallow when she noticed the knapsack on the bar. She placed the glass down and looked at the knapsack.

It was the one Xavier had with him at the office. She walked out of the kitchen and looked around. Nothing seemed out of place.

She called out, "Xavier." There was no reply. "No he is not." She stomped down the hallway, checked her bedroom. He wasn't there. She checked the spare room, the office and the theater room. Nothing. She walked back into the great room looked around again. The knapsack was still there, but there was no sign of Xavier. She felt a breeze and looked over at the patio door. It was cracked open. She walked over, pulled the door open and there sat Xavier.

The sun was setting casting a shadow over him. His back was to her, feet up on the railing, shoes next to his chair, his suit jacket hanging on the back and earplugs in his ears. He was drawing on a pad. From the looks of the drawings on the table he had been at it for a while. She noticed he used old-fashioned pad and paper, not a computer to design. His touch was smooth as he moved across the page. For a moment she considered getting him a glass of wine, he looked so at home. The thought made her smile until she remembered she was mad at him.

Something must have alerted him to her presence. He turned and smiled. Damn if her legs weren't trembling. Stop it, she demanded.

He pulled the earplugs out and stood. "Good evening."

"What are you doing here?"

"Alicia showed me where you live and Mr. Henry let me up."

"Just like that, he just let you into my apartment?"

Xavier nodded. "I think he likes me."

"I don't like you very much right now. Why are you still in New York?"

He frowned. "I thought I told you why I was here. We have things to talk about."

"We talked."

"No. I asked a question, you yelled and asked me to leave. In my book that was not a conversation." He looked at his watch. "My plane leaves at eight fifty. We can talk here or at the airport, Nicole, but we are going to talk."

She turned to walk back into the penthouse. "This has not been a good day and probably is not the best time for us to talk. My emotions are high at the moment and you are not helping."

"I'm here, Nicole." He put his pad on the table and followed her into the kitchen as she picked up her glass of wine. "Give me five minutes and I'll leave."

She stared at him over the rim of her glass. He really—really looked good standing in her kitchen, with his shirt sleeves rolled up and his tie loose. Hmm, if she could have her way he would stand there all night and she would stand right where she was staring at him.

She exhaled. "You have five minutes."

"Your announcement this morning surprised me. We had talked last night and you did not mention anything about the donation."

"I don't..."

He cut her off. "I only have five minutes. I need that time. My attraction to you is an issue for me. I tend to think long and hard before I become involved with someone. My mother played games with my father. The last woman I was involved with is a master at games. For my sake, I had to ask the question. You are a very wealthy woman, Nicole. That's a concern for me. I don't know the rules for your games. Buying your way may be the norm for you. I don't want you to think for one moment that I can be bought. When we are together, and make no mistake about it, we will come together, it's going to be because of this insane mutual attraction we have going on." He stepped closer to her then gazed into her eyes. "We have a date. On Friday, I'll pick you up at the airport at six. We are going to spend some time outdoors, so bring comfortable clothes. I'll return you to the airport on Sunday at six. Is that agreeable with you?"

"I don't mix business and personal."

He took the glass from her hand. "I'm happy to hear that." He took her hand and pulled her to him. He could feel her heart rate increasing against his chest.

"I don't play games, either," she whispered close to his lips.

"Good." His lips captured hers. The heat in the room intensified as his tongue traced her lips, his hands roamed her body and settled on her firm behind. He pulled the v of her thighs to his swelling member and plunged his tongue into the warmth of her mouth.

She moaned at the steel feel of him. Not the material of his pants, nor, that of her skirt were protection against the heat generated when their bodies touched. It was as if nothing was there. He lifted her onto the breakfast bar, pulling her to the edge. She wrapped her legs around his waist then moaned at the hardness of him between her thighs.

He broke away from her lips, pushed the blazer off her shoulders and open mouthed her nipple through her blouse. The blood rushed to her head as she leaned back, urging him to take more of her breast into his hot mouth. She squeezed her legs, grinding against him, relishing the feel of him. He pulled her blouse from her skirt, kissed her navel, then the area where her panties were wet. He inhaled. Her scent was calling him, beckoning him to taste her. He pushed the material aside and slowly licked, long and hard. "Sweet," he moaned, as he slid her wet panties down her legs, knocking her shoes to the floor. He pulled her body back down to his now pulsating shaft, kissed between her breasts, her neck then back to her lips.

The heat was overwhelming, she wanted to feel him, his natural meat between her legs. She pulled at his belt, released the hook and unzipped his pants. Her hand wrapped around him. The heat from his skin was scorching, his penis thick, long and hard. She wanted to feel that. The alarm on his cell phone sounded. They both froze, breathing hard, unable to speak. They stared into each other's eyes. Their passion filled the air. "I did not bring protection with me."

She heard him, but did not have the strength to pull away. She placed him between her thighs, tightened her legs around him and began to grind slowly against his thick, long meat.

He held her head against his shoulder, slowly moving his body in rhythm with hers. How he wished he was inside of her. Her juices coating him as she glided over him, was hot. He felt her body begin to tighten.

"Xavier," she moaned.

"Come for me, Nicole, come for me," he moaned into her curls.

"I'm coming," she breathed. "I'm..." Her body exploded.

He laid her back, dipped down and allowed his tongue to dive into the free flowing juices. He licked and sucked until her body jerked again, and again and again. He spread her thighs, holding her to his lips, until every drop of her had been consumed.

The alarm sounded again. Neither could speak nor move. Xavier was the first to recover. He stood, looked down at her passion filled face. "Sinergy," he said as he pulled his pants up.

They exploded in laughter. He held his hand out to pull her up, then he lifted her from the breakfast bar. "It's already out of control." He adjusted her blouse, then straightened her skirt, rubbing her curves as he moved down her thighs. He picked her panties up off the floor, sniffed them, then placed them in his pocket. He ran his fingers through her now unruly curls. "I'll wash up and catch a taxi to the airport."

"No, I'll go with you."

"I'll miss my plane if I sit in the back of a car with you." He walked around the corner to the half bath.

"I'll have a car brought around," she called out to him. She placed the call, then put the phone back on the receiver. On wobbly legs, she walked over to the balcony to get his jacket and pad. On the table she saw several sketches. She picked them up glancing through the discarded sheets. They were drawings of the buildings around her apartment. The building in the center wasn't one she recognized. He came out of the bathroom as she walked back into the great room. "The car will be downstairs when you get there." She looked up at him with the drawings in her hand. "These are good. Did you draw these?"

He retrieved his sketchpad and suit jacket, and then took a quick glance at the drawings. "Yes, those can be thrown away, they're not good," he said as he put his jacket on and placed the pad in his knapsack. Putting the knapsack on his shoulder, he turned back and pulled her into his arms. "I'm sorry if I offended you earlier. I don't know where this journey is going to lead, but I know I don't want any questions between us along the way." He gently kissed her on the lips. "I'll call you as soon as I land." He hurried to the elevator and pushed the button. She walked over towards him.

"Xavier."

"Don't," he said without looking back. "If you touch me right now I won't make that plane."

"Would that be so bad?" she asked.

"Yes," he said as the elevator doors opened. He stepped in, then turned to her. "I may never leave. Sinergy."

Nicole laughed as the doors closed, and just like that, he was gone. Her home suddenly felt empty. In the hour that they had been together, he had filled her home with joy and excitement. "Sinergy, sensuous energy," she thought, then shook her head. "Sinful sensuous energy." She laughed as she wrapped her arms around her body and walked down the hallway to her bedroom.

Chapter 7

Tuesday
Manhattan, New York

"Good morning Nikki." Vernon's voice came through the phone. There was no question she loved her brother. However, him calling her this time of morning could only mean he was about to ruin the tranquility of her morning.

"Hello, Vernon. How is everyone?"

"The family is fine. I'm keeping Taylor here with me for a while."

"How does Connie, oh I'm sorry, Constance feel about that?"

"She's here as well, for now."

"What happened on the video shoot?"

"Connie claims it was nothing. Taylor is withdrawn, not saying much to anyone."

"Jayda withdrew when she went through that ordeal in Washington. See if Ashley can get Taylor to talk to her."

"I'll get to the bottom of it before Taylor goes back on the road." He cleared his throat. "I received a call from an attorney representing Trish Hargrove. They want a meeting to discuss a settlement."

Nicole sighed, turned her chair to face the window. "Vernon, I did hit her."

"A good solid hit, from what I'm told."

"She deserved it." Nicole stood as she spoke. "Vernon, before it was Pop and Mom who were affected. They had a say in settling. I'm not sure I want to give Trish a dime."

"All right. We have options. If we don't settle out of court, you are going to be tried for assault and battery. You will probably be found guilty."

"Probably? You think you could win this?"

"Of course I can. The question is, do you want this to go to trial. If she wants a few thousand, I say pay her and be done with it."

"Vernon." She shook her head.

"Hear me out. Trish is about money. That's all she has ever been about. You have a business and a reputation to uphold. She damaged your reputation causing financial damage to your business. If you are up for it, I say go with Ashley's suggestion. Sue Trish for defamation of character. Ask for punitive damages equaling what you would have earned if the project succeeded."

"You're talking billions of dollars, Vernon."

"And? Didn't you just lose an integral partner in this deal due to comments Trish Hargrove made in public?"

"Yes."

"Then she is subject to compensating you because of that loss."

"I don't want money from Trish. I just want all of this to stop. At some point, it has to stop."

"Nikki, it's time for Trish to pay. She has been getting away with this crap for too long."

Nicole nodded her head. "Let's meet with them. See what they have to say." Nicole hung up the phone, then pushed the intercom for Alicia.

Alicia knocked on the door and walked in. "Yes, Ms. Brooks."

"Don't yes Ms. Brooks me. I'm still not speaking to you."

"Okay, see if I ever put a man in your apartment again to get you mind blowing sex."

Nicole grinned. "We did not have," she hesitated, "intercourse. We did some really heavy grinding and whew, I don't know what you call what he did with his tongue."

"Girl, please. That is just too much info."

Nicole laughed then fell back into her chair. "I can only imagine what a full blown love making session with Xavier would be like." She closed her eyes and drifted back to yesterday for a moment. Opening her eyes, she sat up. "Okay, I'll have to fly to Richmond this afternoon. We are meeting with Trish Hargrove and her attorney."

"They are going to try to settle out of court again?"

"Probably, but I'm not sure I'm going to settle."

"You shouldn't. However," Alicia exhaled. "If you go to court, the reason for the recent conflict between you two is going to come out. You will also eventually have to declare your sexual preference publicly. Are you ready to do that?"

"What I do behind closed doors is my business. I don't have anything to be ashamed of and neither do you."

"You know that and I know that. But, I have to say the world is a different place since I came out."

Nicole looked at her concerned. "Has something happened?"

"No, and I wouldn't tell you if it did."

"I can't understand for the life of me why anyone would care about two people loving each other. There is enough hatred going on in this world. We should celebrate when a person finds true love."

"Have you met my mother, Shirley Ann? Mmm hmm, you should tell her that."

Rumor Has It

The feud between billionaires Nicole Brooks and Trish Hargrove, is heating up. Rumor has it, the oh so fine architect from Virginia, Xavier Davenport, flew to New York to spend the day. As you can see in the pic below, he is standing outside Nicole's Palace. You got it, the home of Nicole Brooks. It seems the building isn't the only thing Nicole's name is on.

Trish wanted to throw the computer out the window. Her plans were slowly slipping away. She grabbed the glass of wine she had poured, then walked over to the window of her condo. "I can't believe he went to New York to see her." She was steaming. What was it about men when it came to her? Stepping away from the window, she looked in one of the many mirrors she had throughout her house. Reflected back, was a tall, slim woman, with curves in all the right places. "I'm taller than she is." She turned to the side. "I got the bam, bam going on with the booty, the perky breasts." She tilted her head. "The body is happening." She sat the glass on the table under the mirror, fanned her hair out with her hands, then stepped back with her hands on her hips and smiled. "I am fine." Her telephone buzzed.

She took a deep breath when she saw the number. "Hello, Mother."

"Trish, did you see this post on the internet?"

"I saw it."

"What are you going to do about it?"

"I'm working on it Mother." She rolled her eyes as she sat back down on her chaise lounge. "Mr. Michaels and I have a meeting with Nicole Brooks this afternoon."

"That's my girl. Do you have any pictures of you and Xavier together?"

"Yes, why?"

"Fight fire with fire, Trish. Girl, haven't I taught you anything? Post those pictures. Better yet, get pictures of Nicole with that girl of hers, whatever her name is. Whoever is behind the *Rumor Has It* blog will post them." She huffed. "I don't know what you did to lose Xavier, but you better get him back or find a replacement or do the unthinkable, get a job. Your father is serious. Come January you are on your own. That little trust fund will hold you for a while, if you live within your means. What fun is that?"

"He doesn't like the way I do things." She sighed. "Mother, I don't know what to do here. Xavier is slipping away."

"He's doing more than slipping. Men like Xavier do not up and visit a woman in New York for the fun of it. He is definitely interested in her. You're going to have to find a way to keep them from getting closer."

"What do you suggest?"

"Well, what's your end game? Do you want Xavier to be your husband or do you want a healthy bank account?"

"Both," Trish replied to the ridiculous question.

"Okay, there's not much you can do with Nicole, other than line your purse. The Brooks' are always a good financial resource. As for Xavier, you were with the man for months, what is his trigger? What is the one thing he cannot tolerate in a woman? Work it from that angle. Whatever you do, don't delay. Nip this now or you can kiss Xavier goodbye."

Trish finished the conversation with her mother then walked into her bedroom. From the closet, she pulled down boxes filled with photos from high school and college. There had to be pictures of Nicole and Alicia in there somewhere. Her cell phone rang again. Thinking it was her mother, she answered without looking.

"Yes, Mother."

"This isn't your mother, Ms. Hargrove. I'm the person who holds the key to your bank vault."

"Excuse you," she screeched.

"I see you've made a habit of lining your pockets with dribbles of coins from your confrontations with Nicole Brooks."

"How dare you?"

"I dare that and much more, however I don't have time for childish games. You have a meeting with your attorney this afternoon. Vernon Brooks will shut him down. If you are interested in beating the Brooks' and lining your pockets, call this number after your meeting."

The call ended. Trish looked at the number, then disregarded it. She didn't have time to play phone games, she had to win Xavier back. First she had to find just the right picture, then she had to find the identity of that blogger. By the time she was finished, Xavier was going to wish he had never heard of Nicole Brooks.

* * *

The offices of Tillman and Michaels were located in a plush building, located in the far West End of Richmond. Vernon and Nicole walked through the glass and chrome doors, stopping once they reached the receptionist's desk. The words spelling out the firm's name, Tillman and Michaels', were lodged in large chrome lettering on a wood panel wall behind her desk. Pictures of the two partners were like book ends next to the name.

The receptionist, a non-descriptive blonde, greeted them. "Tillman and Michaels. How may I help you?"

"We have an appointment with Aaron Michaels."

"Your name?" the receptionist asked.

"Vernon Brooks."

"Have a seat, Mr. Brooks. I will let Mr. Michaels know you are here."

Vernon and Nicole took seats in the burgundy chairs aligned in a semicircle to the right of the receptionist's desk. Vernon reached for a magazine, crossed his legs and sat back. Nicole noticed he was as nonchalant as ever. In a way that was comforting, because it appeared this was just a social call and he didn't have a care in the world. She on the other hand was nervous. It wasn't a judgment on Vernon's ability to handle the situation. No, this was about her indecision on how to handle this situation. The statement Alicia made was still reverberating in her mind. If we don't settle, a court case will ensue. That could drag her family, friends and possibly Xavier into a courtroom battle. That she wasn't sure she was ready for.

"Here, with me, you can look nervous," Vernon, said as he continued to flip pages in the magazine. "However, once we are in their presence, do not show any sign of doubt or indecision."

The statement surprised her because she did not think Vernon was paying any attention to her. She should have known better. This brother missed nothing. "What makes you think I'm nervous?"

"You're fidgeting and biting your lower lip. Again, with me, that's okay. With them we show no fear." He looked up to see Aaron Michaels walking towards them. "It's game time."

"Vernon." Aaron Michaels extended his hand. The man certainly looked the part of a successful attorney, dressed in the power color navy blue, single breasted, Italian made suit, crisp white shirt, navy and white striped tie. His light blonde hair was cut short and piercing blue eyes, glaring as if he could read everything about you with one look.

"Aaron." Vernon shook his hand. "My sister, Nicole Brooks."

Aaron shook her hand. "Ms. Brooks. It's unfortunate we have to meet under these circumstances."

"Mr. Michaels." Nicole shook his hand.

He cupped her hand and held it. "Let's see if we can put this incident behind us in a way that is beneficial to all."

"Time will tell." Vernon did not give Nicole a chance to reply. He pulled her hand from Aaron's sending a clear message; this is not a friendly visit. Knowing his sister, she would probably reply, 'I'm certain we can settle this.' The simple response would give the opponent insight to their willingness to settle. The last thing Vernon wanted Michaels to think was that they were going to settle anything.

They followed him to the conference room to find Trish Hargrove already seated along with the other partner, Chase Tillman, at the table.

"Well, two for the price of one. How very fortunate for you Trish." Vernon nodded his head as he took a seat. Michaels pulled out the chair for Nicole.

"You're paying for them," Trish smirked. "Why not have the best your money can buy?"

"Presumptuous of you, isn't it?" Vernon replied as he crossed his legs.

Nicole did as Vernon asked and remained expressionless as the conversation continued.

"Mr. Brooks, for the time being we will ask you to refrain from speaking with our client. If you would, please address your comments to us."

"I'm always game for intelligent conversation, Mr. Tillman. You requested our presence. How may we assist you?"

"I believe it's more of what we can do for you Ms. Brooks." Aaron smiled towards Nicole.

"I'm going to ask you to refrain from speaking to my client and direct all comments and/or questions to me."

"Vernon," Aaron cautioned, "let's keep this cordial. I understand Trish and Nicole have been friends since high school. We would like for them to leave here with that friendship intact."

"Cut the crap, Aaron. They are not friends, never have been and never will be. Do not refer to my client by her first name. Her name is Ms. Brooks to you and anyone associated with your firm. What do you have?"

"Very well, Mr. Brooks." Tillman smirked as he pushed a button on the remote control sitting in the center of the conference table. A video appeared on the large screen monitor mounted on the wall at the far end of the room. "This was retrieved from the cell phone of one of the witnesses to Ms. Brooks assaulting our client. In fact, it's one of many videos and still shots recovered that night." He pushed play and the video clip played. Afterwards, he pushed the stop button and turned to Vernon.

Vernon was smiling as he turned to Nicole. "I am so proud of you. You got that right jab from Mother, didn't you?"

Nicole was doing all she could not to laugh at her brother, but he just would not stop. "Do you remember when she did that exact thing to Mrs. Hargrove? It's like a part two. Knock the shit out of a Hargrove - the sequel." He made a motion in the air similar to the title of a movie running across the screen.

There was no holding it back. Nicole had to laugh.

"Did it feel good? It felt good to me just watching it."

Nicole nodded her head at him. "Yes, it did."

He smiled at his sister, she was playing right into his hands. "Then it was worth it." A frown appeared as he turned back to Tillman, whom he did not like one bit. "We stipulate to the assault on Ms. Hargrove. What do you have?"

"We have twelve months in jail, and a fine."

"It's a misdemeanor, and her first offense. They let her out on her own recognizance. That's how seriously the police took the situation." He uncrossed his legs and sat up. "Here's what I propose. While I'm doing this case pro bono-"

"You are," Nicole interrupted. "Thank you."

"Of course I am. You're my little sister. I would do anything for you."

"Mr. Brooks," Tillman called out annoyed.

"My apology." Vernon looked toward Trish. "Where was I? Oh, I know. I propose you stop wasting my time and come to the point of this meeting. Trish is going to have a problem paying your fees as it is."

"I don't think I will." Trish smirked at Nicole.

Nicole smiled in return.

"Very well." Tillman sat forward and pushed a folder towards Vernon. "Five million, a public apology, and your client is not to have any contact with an Xavier Davenport. A million per occurrence fee will be added if your client so much as has a conversation with the man."

Vernon opened the folder, reviewed the document inside. He pulled a pen from his breast pocket as he turned to Nicole. "Sounds reasonable. What do you think?"

Nicole watched as Trish smiled at Tillman. He gave her a cautious look. "Do you think for one moment Xavier will have anything to do with you when he hears about this?"

"There's a gag order included. Neither party may discuss the details of the settlement."

Nicole looked up at her brother. "Is there something in there to ensure there will be no jail time and what about future occurrences? If I hit her again, will we end up in court anyway?"

Vernon made an effort of looking through the documents. "You can't hit her again, Nikki, ever."

"I can't hit her and I can't see Xavier?"

Vernon nodded. "Right."

Nicole sat back dejected.

Vernon turned to Tillman. "It's a fair offer." He pushed the folder back down the table. "We have no intention of settling. We welcome the opportunity to have this play out in court." He turned his cold hard eyes on Trish. "By the time I finish with you, the jury will line up to knock you on your ass." He sat back. "Here's what I am going to do. You have five minutes to have the charges dropped or we are going to sue you for defamation of character to the tune of five hundred and fifty-million dollars."

"Five hundred and fifty-million dollars?" Trish spat out. "What in the hell for?"

"Ms. Hargrove please let us handle this," Tillman stuttered. "Brooks, we have your client on tape. We will play this tape on every news channel across the country. Your client's reputation will be put on trial."

"So will yours." Vernon stood, taking Nicole's elbow to help her up. "Let's see who has more to hide." They turned to walk out of the conference room, when Vernon stopped and walked back over to the table. He reached inside his ten thousand dollar suit jacket and pulled out a folded blue summons and placed it on the table. "You've been served." He took Nicole by the elbow, opened the door and walked out of the room.

Trish ran out the door after them. "Nicole." She jumped in front of them. "What in the hell are you doing?" she spat out. "This is not how the game is played."

Nicole stepped into Trish's face and smiled. "Taking the game to a new level, Trish. I hope you are ready to play with the big boys." She turned and walked out the building with Vernon, as they heard Trish demand that they come back.

Vernon stood in front of the building looking up toward the sky. "That was better than sex." He turned to Nicole. "How was it for you?"

Nicole laughed at her brother, as she shook her head. "You need to get a new sex partner. That didn't touch what I've been experiencing lately, and we're just at first base."

"Damn," Vernon laughed as his driver pulled in front of the building. He opened the door. "Davenport," he asked.

Nicole smiled brightly as she slid across the back seat of the sedan.

"I guess Trish's amendment is out the window." Vernon slid in beside her.

Chapter 8

Richmond, Virginia

Trauma, at times can take years to overcome, if the person was weak-minded. Ann Davenport was a lot of things, a terrible mother, an ex-drug addict, even homeless at one time. Weak...never. The woman was a survivor. Over the past year, she had proven that to her sons. Today was her sixtieth birthday and if it had not been for her daughter-in-law, Diamond, she would not be here. Just about a year ago she'd suffered third degree burns when one of the homes on Davenport Estates exploded. Diamond literally pulled her from the blaze, saving her life.

It was a long painful road back to recovery, but she survived and was grateful. Having her boys with her to celebrate in their home was more than she deserved. She had been a terrible mother. Oh, she loved her sons and her husband for that matter. But the drugs ruled her. She'd turned her back on her family and left her boys to be raised by their father, King Arthur Davenport. He was a damn good man and did not deserve what she had done to him. How she wished she could have told him that before he died. Her actions caused Zack, who was in college at the time, to leave school to take care of Xavier,-her X-man, as she called him. For years Zackary would have nothing to do with her. Oh he made sure she had a place to sleep and food to eat. But, until Diamond came along, he kept her from his and Xavier's lives even after she had cleaned up her act. Ann understood his reasons, but desperately wanted to be a part of X-man's life even if Zack wasn't willing to let her into his. Zack stood firm and threatened Ann's life if she ever went near Xavier.

Right before the explosion, Xavier and Ann had met. He did not know who she was for a while, which gave them a chance to get to know each other. She liked the man he had become. Once he found out that she was his mother, he walked away. They never had a chance to explore where the mother-son relationship could go before the fire happened. Since that time, both her sons had visited her regularly in the hospital and then moved her into the house she'd left so many years ago.

Over the year, she noticed the emotional damage she had caused both her boys. Because of her past actions and the pain inflicted by Zack's ex-girlfriend, he shut down when it came to women. To say he'd hated them, might be harsh, but he sure as hell didn't trust them. Until Diamond came along and taught him how real love could heal. Now, he was so damn happily married it was sickening.

Then there was Xavier. Where Zack wore his feelings on his sleeve and everyone knew what he felt, X-man kept it all inside. No one ever knew what he was feeling unless he chose to tell you. For a year now, he had visited her regularly. Every visit revealed a little more of him. When he felt she was getting too close to what he was really feeling, he simply pulled away and she wouldn't see him for a few days. Then he'd come back around with those bright eyes ready to let her pull him right up in her arms. Trust issues arise in people in different ways. As quiet as it had been, X-man's trust issues were much deeper than Zackary's. Ann was trying to gain his trust, because the boy needed someone to talk to. He kept things bottled up so tight that one day she knew he was going to explode.

Xavier reached down to hug his short mother, standing 5'5' and maybe 110 pounds. He was careful not to hug too tightly. The burns had healed, but from time to time she was still in pain.

"Happy birthday, Ann." He gave her a bouquet of flowers, then kissed her cheek. "Are you ready for dinner?"

"Thank you X-man," she turned to pull out a vase from under the kitchen sink as he sat at the kitchen table. "Let me put these in some water and I'll be ready to go. Where's your brother?"

"He and Diamond are going to meet us at the restaurant."

"These are beautiful," she said while arranging the flowers. "I called you last night, didn't get an answer. Were you out on a date?"

Xavier sat back and thought about his night. The truth was he had thought about little else since leaving Nicole's apartment. The taste and scent of her were still fresh in his mind.

Ann turned to put the vase with the fresh cut flowers on the table. She stopped at the sight of her son. It was uncanny how much he looked like his father with his trimly cut beard, and mustache. The look of total bliss was on his face.

"Wow, who is she?"

Xavier focused to see his mother standing at the table staring down at him. "What did you say?"

"I asked who in the hell has you smiling like you're the cat who ate the canary?" Smiling, he shook his head and stood. "No one. Are you ready?"

"Hell no, sit down, we have time."

"Ann."

"Sit down, I said." She laughed at the boyish look on his face as he sat back down.

Ann took two glasses from the cabinet and pulled out a bottle of wine from the refrigerator. "I'll pour, you talk."

"Not much to talk about, yet."

"Ah-ha, so there's potential."

Xavier smiled as he took the glass from her. "A little." He blushed.

"Sounds and looks like a lot." She grinned. "I know that look."

"What look?"

"The 'I got me a little piece of heaven last night' look."

Xavier burst out laughing. "You are too much Ann. You really are." He took a drink.

"Yeah, I know. So tell me about her."

Sitting the glass on the table, he picked up her sweater from the chair. Ann rarely went out without a sweater to cover the scars from the fire. "Why don't I tell you about her on our way to the restaurant?"

"Aw, lil-man, you can give me something."

"Okay, I'll tell you this." Ann looked over her shoulder at him expectantly. "She's short, just like you."

Ann hit him in the chest. "Boy, you can give me more than that."

Xavier laughed as he opened the door and helped her into his truck. "She has short curly hair and the most adorable smile I've ever seen."

"Well, now. That's something." She got into the car thinking, her son is falling for someone. What touched Ann more was he told her about her. When he closed the car door after getting in, she looked over at him. "It's not that Trish girl, is it?"

"No," Xavier almost laughed. "They are as different as day and night."

Once Ann settled into the seat she looked over and asked, "Is she worthy, son?"

"What do you mean?"

She reached over and touched his hand to keep him from starting the vehicle. She waited until he turned to her. "I loved your dad. I really did. But I wasn't worthy of him. As much as I loved him and he loved me, I wasn't worthy of the love he gave me. That Trish woman is not worthy of you, Xavier. Now, I don't know about this new woman, but that last one, was trouble with a capital T. I should know. Game recognizes game." She pulled her hand away. "Don't make the same mistake your father made."

Xavier didn't say anything for a long minute. "I'm not so sure that's true. What other woman could have given him sons as good looking as me and Zack?"

***

Jamming the key in the door, Trish pushed the door open then stomped inside. After slamming the door, she pulled off her four-inch pumps and threw them into the great room. Dropping her purse on the sofa, she walked to the kitchen, poured a glass of wine and consumed it before pouring another.

"Those damn Brooks'. I hate every one of them," she screamed, taking the frustration of the afternoon out on the empty apartment. She slouched onto the sofa, causing the wine to spill a little. Swiping at the red liquid, she screamed again, then exhaled. To say she was a little upset would be inaccurate. She was livid as she recapped the meeting in her mind. That damn Vernon and his slick ways, he had her attorneys shaking in their boots. She had Nicole on film for goodness sakes. There was no way she could be found not guilty. "No way." She emptied the glass, and threw it against the wall, where it broke, dropping pieces near the picture she kept on the table of her and Xavier.

It was a short six weeks, but the best of her life. Trish picked up the framed picture and held it to her chest as she sat back on the sofa. "What went wrong, Xavier?" Each day she awakened with the same thought. If only she hadn't said anything about his mother. The only reason she said something was to protect him. Hell, his mother was a drug addict. She had turned tricks to get her fix. There was no telling what the woman was capable of. The words came back to her so clearly.

'Xavier, I don't understand your concern for her. She was gone for damn near twenty years. You definitely don't need her now. You've got me.'

There was no immediate reaction from him. To this day, she still wasn't sure that was what separated them. All she knew was that he's stopped calling, or coming by. When she asked him about it, he simply said, 'I don't see us working out.' What in the hell did that mean? They were perfect together. Xavier had a very successful business, even though he had to share it with his brother. But she had plans for him to go out on his own. He was so damn fine. She held the picture up. "We look good together." She placed the picture back on her chest, laid back and placed her arm over her forehead. She thought about the blog post from this morning. "Why were you in New York, Xavier?" She sat up, put the picture back on the table, then stood. "If you think I'm going to let you have Xavier, Nicole Brooks, you are mistaken. Damn lawyers." She picked up her laptop, and began a search for a new lawyer, then stopped. Trish jumped up and grabbed her purse. She went into her phone log and found the number she was looking for, then pushed the redial button.

"Ms. Hargrove, I expected your call earlier."

"Well, you got me now. What can you do for me?"

* * *

Xavier's telephone chimed while he sat at the table laughing at Ann and Zack go at each other over her smoking. He shrugged his shoulders at Diamond. "I guess old habits are hard to break." He pulled his cell out. Seeing it was Nicole, he excused himself.

"Hi, I was in Richmond and wondered if you were free for dinner?"

He looked at his family. "I'm with my family celebrating my mother's birthday. You're welcome to join us."

"No, I don't want to intrude. I'll call when I get home."

"It's not an intrusion. Please, join us." He gave her the address, then returned to the table with a smile a mile long. "Nicole is in town. I hope you don't mind, I invited her to join us."

"Nicole?" Ann questioned.

"The woman who paid fifty-thousand dollars to spend a weekend with X-man." Zack teased.

"Well, she got a bargain if you ask me." Ann smiled at Xavier.

"You're his mother, you have to say that." Diamond laughed. "I went to school with him, I know better."

"Doesn't make it any less true. Besides, anything is better than that Trish woman."

"Ann," Xavier warned.

"I call it like I see it, X-man. I was afraid for your life. Cause if you had brought that home talking about marrying her, I would have killed you."

Zack laughed. "She is a little out there. Told me I couldn't call you X-man."

"It was juvenile." Xavier laughed.

"Really?" Diamond exhaled. "Are you really over her?"

"Hey, it was my first try at a monogamous relationship."

"Good riddance." Ann chuckled. "Is this one snooty like the last one?"

"No," Diamond responded.

"As different as night and day," Zack added.

"Nicole is warm. That's the first thing you see when she smiles. You feel it, in your bones, you know what I mean?" Xavier nodded as he spoke. "It's that feeling you get when you spread butter on a hot roll. You know you're in for a treat. Like home, you know?" He sat up. "You know what else, she makes you wanna laugh every time you see her. Even when she's upset with you, the feeling doesn't change, you still want to be in her presence. Yeah, Nicole's aura is unique." He didn't say anything more as his family stared at him.

"Like home," Zack repeated with a twinkle of laughter in his eyes.

Xavier snapped his fingers, then pointed at Zack. "Exactly." He sat back as if satisfied with his description.

Ann started first. That laughter that begins in the pit of your stomach then works its way up and out. Then Zack jumped in with his rich deep chuckle that resonated around the room. Next were the smooth sweet sounds of Diamond's laughter added to the mix. They all turned when Nicole walked up. The three of them nearly fell out of their seats with laughter.

Xavier had to laugh. "Ignore them." He kissed her cheek. "My family is a little touched."

"Somebody is touched, that's for sure." Ann laughed as she extended her hand. "Honey don't judge us. I'm Ann Davenport, the mother."

Nicole shook her hand. "It's nice to meet you, Mrs. Davenport."

"Just Ann. Mrs. Davenport belongs to Diamond. Have a seat. Since the butter is here I'll see if the waitress can bring us some hot bread."

Zack and Diamond burst into laughter again.

Diamond looked up at Nicole, trying to compose herself. "Nicole." She chuckled. "Please excuse us. Xavier, who is standing there acting innocent, put us in this state." She cleared her throat. "One day, please ask me to tell you about this dinner."

Nicole smiled. "I certainly will."

"She will not." Xavier pulled out a chair for her.

Nicole pulled out a box and gave it to Ann. "This is for you. Happy birthday, Ann."

Ann looked up at the woman, surprised. "You brought me a present?"

"Yes, Xavier indicated it was your birthday. It's not much. But I believe every birthday should be celebrated in some way."

Ann was touched. She took the small blue box, removed the top and set it aside. There was an opal pendant necklace with matching earrings. Ann looked up in shock.

"Opal is the birthstone for the month of October. I'm told it's unique. I hope you like it."

Ann's look from Nicole to Xavier, then back to Nicole. "It's beautiful," she said as a tear escaped. "You got this for me? Why?"

Nicole looked nervously at Xavier. "You're Xavier's mother and it's your birthday. Is it too much?"

He took her hand under the table. "No, it's perfect."

"Thank you." Ann wiped the single tear away, as the waitress arrived with the hot rolls. "You can keep the butter, we'll just spread Nicole on them."

Chapter 9

Thursday
Manhattan, New York

It was official; the London deal had been placed on hold for thirty days. The board would not go forward until Allen and Allen made a final decision. Nicole was disappointed. She had worked on the London project for over a year and for it to end because of personal issues was unbelievable.

"This may be a blessing, Nicole," Steven said as they walked from the conference room into the hallway.

"A blessing," Nicole questioned with a frown. "How could losing a year's worth of negotiations, planning, and securing the property be a blessing?"

"Nicole, if this project was to go through..."

"When," Nicole said, not ready to concede defeat.

"Okay, when this project goes through, you would have to report every step of the way to Ellington. Everything you do would be open to scrutiny by a man you despise. You don't need that. You can do this project on your own." Nicole started to walk away, but Steven stopped her. "Listen to me Nicole. Allen and Allen are not the only architects in town."

"No, Steven, they aren't the only, but they are the best."

"Are they?" Steven gave Nicole a folder. "I'm ashamed to say, I was online reading this blog called Rumor Has It. You'll never guess what it stated." He waited as she looked up impatiently at him. "Aren't you going to ask?"

"No, Steven. What does a blog have to do with this project?"

"Everything my dear. Hear me out. While reading this blog I learned that a certain real estate mogul was involved with this bright young architect. So I took the liberty of doing a little research on the young man." He pointed to the folder. "Take a look at some of his designs. I think you may be surprised." He waved as he walked off. "Keep in touch."

Hayward Ellington and his assistant walked out just as Steven walked away. "Interesting meeting, wouldn't you say, Ms. Brooks?"

Her parents taught her to respect her elders, however, this man with his lopsided toupee was bordering on a cursing out. Taking a second or two, Nicole turned. "Very, Mr. Ellington. I would think the outcome disappointed you. The Allens did not pull out of the project."

"On the contrary. While they are contemplating your role in this project, I've offered them a feasible option."

"We were in the same meeting. I did not hear a counter offer."

"It was private session, dear. The best deals take place in private."

"You care to enlighten me?"

"I'll do you one better and give you the same advice I gave my daughter," he smirked. "Take the next thirty days, find a husband, if that's your preference, move back to Virginia and have a few babies. Make your life count for something." He turned and walked away.

Nicole walked back to her office, infuriated. She wasn't sure if she was angrier about the advice he gave or the idea of him making a deal with the Allens behind her back. Hell, she knew this was business, more deals are made on the golf course than in the boardroom. However, when Jacob gave his word, she expected him to keep it, not make a contingency plan with Ellington.

Walking through the corridor, she noticed several employees looking her way, then turning away quickly. Today was not the day to mess with her.

Walking by the cubicles, she approached her office, where a few employees were leaning over Stacy's desk with their backs to Nicole as she walked in.

"What's so fascinating, ladies?"

Several of the women jumped at the sound of her voice.

"Nothing," they said as the group quickly dispersed.

Nicole noticed Stacy push a button on her computer, clearing the screen. She walked over, reached across Stacy's shoulder and pushed the space bar. Nicole looked at the computer, which had a picture of Xavier and Trish. The blog read:

Rumor Has It
People say a picture is worth a thousand words. Rumor Has It, Xavier Davenport, the architect from Virginia who Nicole Brooks paid $50K for spent the night with Trish Hargrove. Seems Trish is getting it for free. Hmm, I wonder if he has anything left for

*Nicole? For 50K he better be giving up
something. IJS.*

"Since you're not giving it up to a man, he got it
somewhere else," Stacy smirked.

This was not the day. Nicole looked around the
office. There were several employees at their desks
watching the commotion. She turned to Jake Gordon,
an administrative assistant who had been with the
agency when she took over.

Turning back, she glared at Stacy. "Jake," she
called.

"Yes, Ms. Brooks." He walked over to the area and
stood in the doorway.

"How much do you make a year?"

"Um, fifty-two thousand a year. But I'm not
complaining."

"How much do you make a year Stacy?"

"I'm paid for the job I do."

"That is not what I asked you." She glared at the
woman. Alicia stepped out of her office when she
heard Nicole's raised voice.

"One hundred and twenty-thousand a year and I'm
worth every dime of it."

Nicole smiled. "Maybe to someone else."

"I've worked for this agency for the last twenty
years. Before you were placed in your position. I have
clout. You can't do a thing."

"I would think a certain amount of loyalty would
come with that type of salary. And the clout you speak
of just ended."

"I'm loyal...to the agency."

"I am the agency," Nicole barked, then took a deep
breath. She knew Stacy had worked for her father
when he was running the agency, but her superior ass
behavior had run its course. "Jake, you have a new

position, your new salary will be one hundred fifty a year. Your first task, have this woman removed from my agency." She turned from Stacy to look at Jake. "Can you handle that?"

"Mr. Brooks will reinstate me before you can change the locks on the door." Stacy smirked as she reached for the telephone.

"Don't touch my telephone," Nicole barked at the leggy, blue-eyed blonde. "Get your purse and get out. Be here in the next two minutes and I will have you arrested for trespassing."

Stacy looked around at the people in the office. "She can't fire all of us if we walk out together," she said. "None of you like working for a woman who has no business being here." She continued to look at the people in the office. "Don't be afraid of her. You all know Mr. Brooks is not going to uphold this action. We will all be back. She will be the one removed."

One girl snickered. "I like my job, you are on your own."

"Ms. Crane, you were asked to leave the premises," Jake said. "If you believe you have a grievance, file the proper paperwork with Human Resources Management. They will review your grievance and be in touch. For now, I need you to leave."

"You, of course, she would have your support. You're a freak just like her."

"Well, this freak is putting your ass out. You can walk out on your own, or I can assist," Jake said as he moved his head from side to side. "Freak that."

Stacy grabbed her purse from the bottom drawer and reached for a binder as she looked back at Nicole. "You are going to pay for this," she spat.

Alicia grabbed the binder from her. "This is the property of Brooks International."

A stunned Stacy turned to the woman behind her and reached for the binder. "That is personal property."

"We'll ship it to you, once it's been reviewed."

Stacy looked around the office, then stormed out the door.

Nicole scanned the room at each employee, expecting others to walk out behind Stacy. Instead, one person began to applaud, then another and another.

"It's about time you stood up to her," Alicia said from behind her.

Nicole turned to her friend. "I need to get away."

"Going back to Richmond?" Alicia grinned.

"I need to regroup. Think the project through. Can you hold down the fort?"

"We lost the vote?"

"Not completely, but it's heading that way. Ellington made them an offer."

"Are you going to sell the property to Ellington?"

"Hell no," Nicole replied as Jake walked back in.

"Ms. Brooks, I stopped by IT and requested all Ms. Crane's access be terminated. I'll go back to my desk now."

Nicole stared at him. "This is your desk now, Jake." She turned to walk away.

Jake frowned at her. "You're serious?"

Nicole turned back to him. "Do you want the job?"

"Yes, he wants the job." Alicia grabbed Jake's arm and pushed him into what used to be Stacy's chair. "The first thing I want you to do is see what's in this binder."

Nicole laughed as she walked into her office. Losing a deal was not familiar to her. She picked her projects carefully. Expanding Brooks International into London was an idea she came up with when visiting there. She loved the feel of the city, the flats, the bakeries with fresh pastries daily, the nightlife. Yes, it was selfish of her to purchase the property when she was there, knowing she had no plans for it. The thought of renovating the area with the palatial style homes where everyone would feel like royalty appealed to her. She wanted to keep them that way, by modernizing the shops below, maybe adding a garden in the center. When she told Jacob about her ideas, he drew up the plans. They weren't everything she wanted, but he had certainly captured the essence of her vision.

She dropped the folder Steven had given her on her desk and grabbed her purse. "Jake," she called out as she walked out of her office. "Call my pilot. Tell him I'm flying home in an hour." She waved as she walked out. "The place is yours until my return Alicia."

"Have fun this weekend," Alicia yelled after her, then turned to Jake. "Call her pilot first, then arrange a pickup from her apartment and one to pick her up from Richmond International. Afterwards, place a call to the Washington office advising them Nicole will be in the area."

Jake flipped through the phone listing on the computer as he spoke to Alicia. "You do know Stacy is not going away quietly. It's not in her nature. Expect repercussions."

"It's now your job to ensure those repercussions have no impact on Nicole or Brooks International."

* * *

"She just fired me." An angry Stacy yelled into the phone. "The bitch just up and fired me for showing the damn blog."

"It was inevitable."

"Well, what do I do now? I can't get you information now that I'm out. How am I supposed to live?"

Singleton sat back in his chair, pleased by the turn of events. "I'm certain there is another way to earn your keep. I'll be in touch."

Richmond, Virginia

"Mr. Davenport," Lafonde called from the doorway of Xavier's office. "Mrs. Hargrove is here to see you. I've explained to her that you are not available, however, she is insisting."

"Get out of my way." Estelle Hargrove pushed her way past Lafonde. "Xavier, I want to speak with you...now."

Xavier stood, as did, Zack, Diamond and Reese, who were in his office. "Mrs. Hargrove, I'm afraid this is not a good time."

"Make it a good time."

Zack looked from the woman in the doorway to Xavier. There was something in the way the woman was speaking to X-man that bothered him.

"Excuse me. We are in the middle of a meeting."

"Xavier, now." She completely ignored Zack and the others as she walked over and set her purse on his desk.

"We'll give you a minute, Xavier."

"No, Diamond." He stared at Mrs. Hargrove. "Zack." He stopped his brother who was about to bear down on the woman. "I'll handle this."

"Did you have anything to do with that piece of trash written about my daughter?"

"Mrs. Hargrove, this is my place of business. If you would like to meet with me," he pointed to Lafonde, "you schedule it with her. You will not disrespect my place of business." He turned, "Lafonde, show Mrs. Hargrove to your desk, make an appointment for her at my earliest convenience, then show her the door."

"How dare you. I have never been treated so rudely."

"It's an honor to be your first." Xavier nodded to Lafonde. "The door."

Reese snickered, as Zack cleared his throat.

"Mrs. Hargrove." Diamond stepped forward. "Allow me to help you."

"I don't need help from the likes of you," Mrs. Hargrove sneered at Diamond. "As for you." She looked at Xavier. "I have no idea what my daughter sees in you, you are so beneath her." She pointed a finger at him. "I will tell you this, I will sue you and your little firm for every dime if my daughter's reputation is ruined in this mess with Nicole Brooks." She turned and stormed out of the room. Lafonde followed her out.

The occupants of the room turned to stare at Xavier. "What was that all about?" Zack asked as he took a seat.

"I have no idea," Xavier replied as he sat down.

"She seems very angry at you," Diamond shook her head, "and at everyone else." She took her seat, as did Reese.

"I apologize for the way she spoke to you, Diamond." He looked up at her. "That was disrespectful."

"Is that Trish's mother?" Zack asked.

"Yes." Xavier looked down at his paper work. "Let's get back to the meeting."

"Don't you want to talk about this X-man?"

He looked up at Zack. "No, I want to get back to the meeting."

Zack started to say something, when Diamond touched him on his arm, then shook her head.

The group settled back into the meeting, only to be disturbed again fifteen minutes later.

"Xavier," Trish called out as she stomped into his office. Xavier stood as Trish ran into his arms. "I can't believe you did this." She waved a piece of paper around. "Why would you do something like this?"

"Trish." Xavier held her at arm's length. "What are you talking about?"

"This picture of us...you know being intimate," a distraught Trish exclaimed.

"Trish." Xavier gently shook her. "I have no idea what you or your mother are talking about and frankly I don't give a damn. This is my place of business. You do not bring drama here."

"I'm so sorry," she cried into his chest. "How do you think it feels to have my personal pictures in some blog? And why would you do this? I don't understand, Xavier." Zack and Reese looked at each other and tried to hide a grin. Diamond hit Zack to get him to behave, then pulled up the internet on her tablet.

"Trish, look at me," Xavier spoke calmly to the hysterical woman.

She looked up at him with tears in her eyes. "Yes." She sounded so pitiful.

"Trish, you need to calm down."

"You know I would never allow my mother to hurt you. I will protect you at all costs, but Xavier, she's upset about this and so am I."

"Thank you Trish. But, as you can see, I'm in the middle of a meeting. We'll talk later."

Trish looked around the room as if for the first time noticing the other people in the room. "Oh." She wiped the tears from her eyes. "I'm so sorry," she apologized to everyone. "I'm so sorry. I'll get out of your way." She stopped at the doorway. "But we have to talk about this tonight. You promise to come by?"

"Yes." Xavier replied as he watched her walk out the door. He closed his eyes, dropped his head and exhaled, thinking, he really did not want to turn around.

"Well," Diamond said trying hard not to laugh. "It seems you have a few actors visiting you today, along with new popularity." She turned the tablet around. "You're a hit with 126,000 views and counting."

They all took a closer look at the picture. "Wow," Reese said. "You took nude pictures with Trish. She's more of a freak than I thought."

"I don't recall taking that picture."

"You probably didn't." Zack nodded. "She had the picture doctored then posted it."

"Hmmm, sounds familiar." Reese sat back down.

Xavier always controlled certain elements of his life, until he met Trish Hargrove. There was no controlling her. Now, he knew where Trish received that characteristic. He sat back in his chair, crossed his leg at the ankle and waited.

Seconds passed, not a sound was made. Reese was the first to speak. "Do you have a box of tissues? I think I feel a tear or two coming on." He coughed out a laugh.

Xavier smirked and shook his head. "What do you have to say?" he asked Zack without looking up.

"Not a word. So far we've had a tornado and a hurricane. I'm just wondering if we will finish this meeting before a tsunami comes through."

The people in the room began laughing. "Okay." Xavier looked at his watch. "We can still salvage this meeting."

"I don't know." Diamond smiled. "Do you have any other women, who are angry with you?"

"Or any other pictures you want to share?" Reese laughed

"Not that I am aware of." Xavier picked up his pen just as Lafonde walked in.

"Mr. Davenport."

Xavier dropped his head in frustration. "Is it too much to expect you to handle the front desk?" Xavier turned to see Nicole standing behind Lafonde.

"When you learn to handle your women, I'll be able to handle the front desk." Lafonde retorted. "You stated if Ms. Brooks came by to show her in. Well, she's here." Lafonde stormed off leaving Nicole and Xavier staring at each other.

"Your office seems to be as off center as mine." Nicole smiled. "I can come back if this is a bad time."

"No, no." Xavier shook his head as he walked toward her. He took her hand to pull her into the office. "I need to see you." He smiled down at her.

"You, Mr. Davenport have no idea how happy I am to hear that."

Reese cleared his throat once,-no response. Zack, Reese and Diamond looked at each other grinning. Reese cleared his throat again.

Xavier looked over his shoulder. "Say hello to Zack and Diamond."

"Oh, I must be chopped liver." Reese acted as if he had been insulted.

"Nicole, this is our head of security, Reese Kendrick."

She turned to Reese. "Reese. Hello."

Reese shook her hand. "Ms. Brooks, this is a pleasant interruption."

"One I must apologize for." She looked at Xavier. "I'm a day early for the weekend. I'll be at my brother's house. Will you call me later? Something's come up and I think we should talk about it."

"Don't leave." He glanced over his shoulder at Zack. "We will wrap this up in a few minutes." He turned back to Nicole. "We can start the weekend early."

"I can wait in the lobby," she nodded.

Seeing the protest in Xavier's eyes, Diamond spoke. "I have a better idea." She walked over to Nicole. "I would love to tell you about the joke from last night." She smiled at Xavier. "We'll let the guys finish up the meeting. They don't need me anyway." Diamond took Nicole by the arm and led her out of the room.

Xavier stood watching from the doorway after the women were gone. He had to do something about that sexual energy that hit him whenever Nicole was in the room.

Zack and Reese looked at each other. "He's gone," Reese said.

"No doubt," Zack laughed. "One question. What are you going to do about Trish?"

Xavier turned. "I have no idea."

"You do realize you are being played, right?" Reese asked.

"Those tears were so fake she could put a crocodile's to shame," Zack added.

"When you go to her place to console her she is going to be so distraught over the picture or because her big bad Mommy came to beat you up," Reese continued. "Then when you get there, she will be dressed so provocatively with the tear stained cheeks, and puffy eyes that the only thing you can do is to hold her in your arms. That's when the real trouble will start. You're going to feel those pillow like breast against your chest. Her nice firm body rubbing up against you. A man can't help but respond. So you pull her a little closer, then she kisses you on your neck, you know right in that spot that gives you an instant hard on. Next thing you know, bam you're doing the do. And there ain't no turning back at that point."

Xavier and Zack stood there watching as Reese continued to rant. When he finished, Xavier smiled. "Sounds as if you have a little experience in that scenario Reese."

"A little." Zack laughed.

"I was being kind," Xavier teased.

"Man, that crap ain't nothing to play with. I almost lost my wife that way. I'm telling you what I know. A woman like Trish knows how to play that game. Man I will bet you my Lexus her mother taught her."

"Her mother," Xavier laughed. "Come on, Reese."

"X-man, you're laughing, but I'm telling you, they are at the lingerie shop right now picking out the perfect seduction outfit."

Zack was laughing but he knew Reese was serious. "How did you handle it?"

"Wrong. I lied to Terry. Told her I hadn't slept with my ex since meeting her. You know what my ex did? Texted Terry pictures of me in her bed asleep with the date and time stamp on it. I'm telling you man, I wasn't drunk, wasn't high. It was those crocodile tears and those pillow soft breasts that did me in."

"So you're telling me to watch out for women with big breasts and crocodile tears?"

"Damn right," Reese laughed. "Along with a big butt and a smile."

Zack laughed, then turned to Xavier. "It doesn't seem we will get much done here. Why don't you join your visitor?"

That was exactly what Xavier wanted to do. "You sure you don't mind?"

"We have plenty to go on. Reese and I will get out of here so you can start your weekend early." Zack nodded at Reese as he closed his folder.

Xavier walked over to his desk. "I'll work on a few diagrams over the weekend."

"No." Zack demanded. "Enjoy your weekend with Nicole. We'll pick up on this Monday." He waited until Reese left before closing the door. "Interesting morning," he said as he stood in front of Xavier's desk.

Xavier knew the tone. He stopped putting things away, then took a seat behind his desk. "You're concerned?"

Giving a small nod, Zack agreed. "It's clear you have a connection with Nicole. Trish is not going to step aside quietly. She isn't a lady in that sense. However, Nicole doesn't appear to be the kind of woman to take whatever Trish dishes out." He grinned. "You're in for an interesting ride, little brother." He turned to leave. "Know I'm here when you need me. I know a thing or two about dramatic women."

Xavier laughed remembering the drama Zack went through with his ex-girlfriend right before he and Diamond were married. "I don't think anyone is going to burn down buildings to get my attention."

Zack was at the door when he looked back. "I wouldn't laugh too hard X-man. I won my woman. You have yet to close the deal. Have a good weekend," he said as he walked out of the office.

Xavier's head dropped as he exhaled. The day had been trying. This was something he was not used to. He led a quiet life for a reason. During college, his roommate went through a situation that nearly ruined his life. An ex-girlfriend claimed she was pregnant. His friend, trying to do the right thing, left the woman he loved to plan a life with the ex-girlfriend and the baby. When the child was born, paternity test was performed. The child was not his. His roommate was fortunate. The woman he loved, loved him enough to stand by him. The two married six weeks later and are happily married with two children. The drama his friend endured prompted Xavier to handle women in his life differently. First, he did not get into long term relationships. Second, he let them know up front what he would and would not deal with. Third, and more important than the others, he never—never had sex without protection. He thought those three rules would keep the drama at a minimum. Then he met Trish Hargrove and thought maybe, just maybe, he could have what Zack and Diamond had. He dropped rule number one and soon regretted it. Now, there's Nicole. Rules had no meaning.

Chapter 10

Xavier stood at the window behind his desk, with his shirt sleeves rolled up, hands in his pockets and legs braced apart as he took in the surrounding area of downtown Richmond, VA. The sight of the James River with its history of slave trade, auction houses, and the selling of human goods as if they were commodities like coffee and sugar, inspired him to make something beautiful from the not so pleasant past. Today, the scene symbolized him. He had to end his not so pleasant past with Trish, to begin what he believed to be his beautiful future with Nicole.

"I heard you had an interesting morning," Nicole said from the doorway. She stepped inside as Xavier turned towards her. Closing the door, she leaned back against it and sighed. "My appearing unannounced added to that. I'm sorry."

The appearance of Trish and her mother annoyed him. Nicole's showing up pleased him. He wondered why as he stood there staring at her. There was something about her aura that created a calmness about him. No, drama, no mysteries. Today, there was something in her eyes. It was clear to him, even with the beautiful smile and calm demeanor, something had upset her.

He walked over to her and gently kissed her lips, then smiled. "Your appearance brightened my day.

Now, tell me. What can I do to remove the sadness from your eyes?"

The warmth of his gaze touched her through and through. It eased the unpleasant events of the morning. "Take me away from here. Make the world around us disappear for a little while."

"Let me have your cell phone." Nicole reached inside her purse and gave him her phone. "Now, your tablet." She hesitated and watched as he raised an eyebrow. After a long moment, she pulled the tablet out and gave it to him. Xavier smiled as he walked to his desk, placed her devices along with his there, picked up his keys and suit jacket, then walked back to her. He opened the door. "Your wish is my command."

Arlington, VA
Thursday Afternoon

Gwen sat in the downstairs family room with a book in her hand. However, the story she had been waiting for months to come out, did not hold her interest. It was a crisp October evening, yet her granddaughter was more content to be out in the cool air than in her luxury suite upstairs, or on her cell phone texting friends, or listening to music. That was the one that concerned her more than the others. Taylor always loved music. She would have the house filled with the sounds of music she would be dancing to, or creating on the piano. It had been a week and Taylor had yet to touch the piano, or even hum a tune.

"Hello, Mother." Vernon gave her a kiss on the cheek, then walked over to the bar. "What are you reading, another romance novel?"

"Romantic suspense." She smiled. "How was your day son?"

Taking a seat across from her, Vernon could see he did not have her attention. Turning in his seat, he saw Taylor sitting out on the deck. He put his glass down and stood. "How long has she been out there?"

"Constance went upstairs about an hour ago, Taylor came down." Gwen looked up at her son. "She's been out there since then. Now son, I don't interfere in my children's lives unless I sense trouble. You need to find out what is going on with your daughter, now, before it settles so deep you can't get it out."

"Gwendolyn Brooks, your middle name is interfering." He walked out of the room. "And I love you for it."

Gwen smiled as she watched her son step out onto the deck, taking a seat next to his daughter.

"Did I hear Vernon come in?" Avery asked from behind his wife.

"Yes, he's talking to Taylor," Gwen responded as she continued to watch the scene unfold. "Do you think she will tell her father what's bothering her?"

Avery rubbed his wife's shoulder. She covered his hand with hers. "I think if anyone can get Taylor to open up, it's Vernon. The concern is what he will do once he finds out." Avery sat next to his wife, pulled her feet into his lap and began to massage them.

"Our children are very passionate about those they love. Ooh, move to the center." Avery moved his hands to massage the arch of her foot. "Yes, right there," Gwen purred. "Vernon will handle whatever is happening. What concerns me is Taylor's music. I haven't heard her singing."

"I miss her voice, but I miss her laughter more." Avery replied as he watched his son put his arm around his daughter. "I think Vernon is softening in his older years."

"He works too hard." Gwen frowned. "I want him and Connie to find happiness. If it's not with each other, then they should divorce and move on. No one should be as miserable as Connie."

"She brought that on herself when she married for money and not love."

"Oh, I think she loved Vernon at one time. It happened to be at a time when he was still trying to prove himself. Hanging out at all hours, sleeping around." Gwen shook her head.

"Let's not forget what happened between him and Butchie."

"Please don't remind me of that." Gwen raised an eyebrow. They held each other's eyes, then turned to the two on the deck.

"Daddy, can I stay home for a while? I have some decisions to make about my future."

Vernon looked at his daughter who had wanted nothing more than to sing since she was five years old. It seemed things had changed. He had no idea why, but he was going to find out before he allowed her to give up on her dream.

"Taylor, this is your home. You don't ever have to leave if you don't want to." He took his daughter's hand then walked down the steps, through the yard and did not stop until they reached the gazebo. "Let's talk for a while," he said as they sat."

Taylor wasn't afraid of her father, it just seemed he was always so distant from her. Like he never knew what to say or how to be around her. When she decided she wanted to sing, her mother handled everything. At the time Taylor thought he didn't want to be bothered. As she grew older she realized it was her mother keeping her away from her father. Yes, her father spent a lot of time working, and wasn't always available to attend her concerts, but she understood he was working. Now, she needed him like never before. She needed him to help her understand what had happened. Only a man can understand how another man acts. No, she wasn't afraid of her father, but she was afraid of what he would do when he found out what had happened to her. Worse when he found out her mother's reaction to it. The incident could impact her contract and her future with the record company. At this moment, she did not trust the people in her camp, including her mother. How could she explain her feelings without causing a bigger strain on her parent's marriage?

It felt a little awkward sitting with him now, but she knew she had to trust someone.

"Okay." She took a seat across from him, then crossed her legs.

Vernon watched her and it suddenly felt as if a ton of bricks had landed on his head. His baby girl was no longer a baby. She was a beautiful young woman.

"Who is he?"

For the first time in over a month, she smiled from deep within. That was the first time her father had acted like a father, a real father.

"There is no man, Daddy. You will be happy to know your little girl is," she hesitated, then sighed, "untouched in that sense."

Vernon breathed a sigh of relief. "I can't tell you how that pleases me." He smiled. "If it's not a man, then tell me, what is going on with you and your mother?"

Taylor looked away, pulled her jacket a little tighter as she hugged herself. She looked over the plush green grass and shrubbery that covered the area and wondered just how much she should tell her father.

"Daddy, I need to make a change. I've thought about it a lot and I think I'm old enough to make certain decisions."

Vernon listened without interrupting.

"I would like to move to New York with Aunt Nikki and attend Columbia. I've checked out the admission requirements and I've been studying for the LSAT. I'll take the test December."

Of all the things he expected her to say, that was not on the radar. "You should look a person in the eyes when speaking. It lets them know, you are serious and cannot be swayed."

Taylor looked up at her father. "I want to let music go for a while and attend law school. As you know I have an undergrad degree in music. Now, I want to learn the legal side of the business. I don't want to be in a position where I have to depend on anyone to handle my career."

Vernon nodded his head. "Columbia. Okay, have you discussed this with your mother?"

Taylor hesitated, then lowered her head. "I'm not sure Mother has my best interests at heart right now."

"Head up, Taylor.

Taylor looked up at her father.

"Your mother loves you, Taylor. She has dedicated her life to your career. I think you should at the very least inform her of your decision. I will support anything you want to do, as long as it is not something that will harm you." He sat forward, resting his arms on his thighs and clasping his hands together. "Sweetheart, your mother has spearheaded your career. She persuaded me to let you follow your dream. I have to say, Connie has done a damn good job with you. You are Lil Tay." He smiled. "Hell, I'm finding myself trying to live up to you and your accomplishments in the industry."

"Daddy, please," Taylor laughed and waved his statement off. "I know how famous you are. Even in Atlanta we hear about your cases. So don't even try that one." Vernon smiled. "But thank you. Sounds like you're proud of me."

He switched seats to sit next to her. "I'm very proud of you." He kissed her temple. "I wish I could take credit for you, but I can't. Connie and your talent made you Lil Tay. That makes me wonder why the hostility between the two of you. Before you answer, understand your old man deals with criminals. I have a bullshit radar that can detect from miles away." He gave her a tight squeeze, then looked down at her.

Taylor bit her bottom lip, wondering how much she should or should not tell her father. She had to talk to someone, but if she told him all, her father would have one of his clients take people out or worse, he would do it himself.

"Daddy," she began slowly. "I need my management team loyal to me. Their first priority should be my well-being, my career, my future. It seems Mother's priority is more with her these days. Please don't ask me to explain further. Just know I love Mother. I just don't think my career should remain in her hands."

"Okay. Do you have a management team in mind?"

"I do," she acknowledged. "Before I make that decision I want Mother to be open to what I want and what I will not tolerate in this business. I still want her involved, but as my mother, not my manager."

Vernon nodded his head. "I think that's fair. Do you want me to speak with your mother about this?"

"No. I want you to let us work it out. However, you should know I've made up my mind. I will not re-sign with B7 and Mother will not be my manager after this contract expires. I will no longer be Lil Tay. I will be Taylor Brooks."

Vernon and Taylor talked a while longer then walked back into the room where Avery and Gwen sat.

"Grandma, I'm moving to New York."

"New York?" Gwen smiled. "Don't you want to go back to Atlanta? I thought that was where all the big time music producers were located now."

"I'm taking a break from music to attend Columbia."

"Columbia? You're thinking about law school?"

"Yes, ma'am."

"Oh my. Avery, get off that phone. Did you know this?" Gwen beamed.

Vernon smiled. "I only promised to speak with her mother. I'm pretty confident I can sway her to our way of thinking."

It was the first time in a week Gwen had seen a light in her granddaughter's eyes.

"Did I know what?" Avery asked as he put the phone on the table.

"Taylor wants to go to law school," Gwen replied with pride in her eyes.

"Of course she does," Avery beamed. "She's a Brooks. It's in her blood."

"I have to get accepted first, Poppa," Taylor cautioned everyone.

"That's a given." Avery nodded.

Vernon sat next to his daughter and pulled at her hair. "Columbia is no joke Dad. It's not a guarantee."

"Columbia?" Avery's chest puffed out. "You could get a condo in Nicole's Palace while you're in school."

"Dad and I are going to take a look this weekend."

Avery looked at Vernon. "You're going to New York?"

"Yes, we're leaving tomorrow."

"Good. You can see what's going on at Brooks International. That was Stacy on the phone. It seems Nicole fired her today."

"About time," Gwen smirked.

"Gwendolyn."

"Don't Gwendolyn me. That heifer was too high and mighty for me. I still think she was the one who shared your plans for the convention center with that...what was his name?"

"Ellington."

"Yes, that Ellington man. The one who thinks only the purebreds of America have the right to network in his circle. I don't like that man and I do not like Stacy and I certainly never trusted her."

"Tell us how you really feel Grandma. Don't hold anything back." Taylor grinned.

"Oh you hush." Gwen smiled, then turned back to Avery. "Don't you interfere in Nicole's decision. If Nicole fired her, I'm certain she had a good reason."

"I have to agree, Pop," Vernon chimed in. "Nicole has a long fuse. It takes a while and quite a bit to get her to the point of firing someone. Have you spoken with her?"

"No," Avery replied. "According to Alicia she is off the grid until Monday."

"Ahh, it's the weekend getaway with Xavier Davenport." Taylor smiled. "I hope he is the one for Aunt Nikki. She deserves a sexy man like him."

"You think Davenport is sexy?" Vernon looked over his glass at his daughter.

"Yes, Daddy, I do. He has this strong, silent aura about him."

"And how would you know?" Gwen asked.

"I checked him out when Aunt Nikki won her bid. You have to be careful around men. Even the ones that seem on the surface to be good and trustworthy, you have to dig deeper before agreeing to be in the same room with them, much less in a hotel room with them." The members of the room looked from one to the other.

"I'm certain Nicole took precautions, Taylor," Gwen said in a soothing voice. "I think she likes him, quite a bit."

"Hmmm, that's an understatement," Vernon continued to take the hard glare of his parents from his daughter. Whatever happened, he was going to let Taylor tell him when she was ready. That didn't mean he was going to wait for that. "When was the last time you've known Nicole to take time off from work for any man?"

"Never," Gwen replied. "That's why that silly rumor about her being gay took off like it did. Nicole hasn't had a man in her life in forever."

"Nicole is selective," Avery stated. "This Davenport kid must be something."

"I question his judgment," Vernon stated. "He was involved with Trish Hargrove."

"Well, that's a mark against him," Gwen huffed.

"He dumped her," Taylor added.

"How do you know that?" Vernon asked.

"It was in that blog, Rumor Has It."

"You read that mess?" Gwen asked.

"I have to stay in the know and, like it or not, the person behind that blog has an inside track on us."

"Did you read the post on you?" Vernon asked.

Avery sat up. "Someone posted something on my baby?"

"No worries,wPoppa. It was true. Well, the gist of it was true. I did walk out on a session."

"Why? You're under contract. You have to honor you commitments."

"Yes, Poppa I do, when lines aren't crossed. However, my contract with B7 Beats ends in a few months and I have no intention of re-signing with them."

"You ever consider setting up your own studio?"

Taylor sat up. "Really, Daddy?"

"Damn right."

"I still want to go to law school. But it would be great to control my own music. I can produce the kind of music I like and don't have to cave in to others."

"You can create a masterpiece and if it's not on someone's play list, no one will ever hear it," Constance said from the doorway. "As I told you before, there is an aspect of this business you do not understand. The labels have connections with the radio stations that you will never be able to penetrate on your own, Taylor. As smart as you are you do not know everything."

Gwen looked at her granddaughter, and just like that, the light in her eyes was gone.

Taylor stood. "Excuse me. The atmosphere in the room just became a little stale." She walked out of the room.

"Do you have to stomp on her dreams like that?" Gwen asked. "At least let her try it her way."

"It costs money to build a studio, to hire producers, to get beats," Constance replied.

"Taylor has made millions off her music," Avery stated. "If that's not enough, hell, I have billions sitting somewhere, build her a damn studio, if that's what she wants."

"Money is not the solution to everything," Constance replied.

"No?" Vernon laughed. "When did you come to that realization?"

Constance poured herself a drink. "Oh, I don't know, maybe the morning I caught you in bed with your brother's wife."

Vernon stood.

"Vernon," Avery cautioned.

"It's all good, Pop. Connie is right. I did sleep with my brother's wife." Vernon stopped when he reached Constance's side. He poured another drink as he stood at the bar staring into his wife's eyes. "Why don't you divorce me Connie? It's clear you're not happy and the only happiness I know, you just squashed from my daughter's eyes. So, tell me, if money isn't everything, why in the hell are you still married to me?" They held each other's eyes for a long minute before anything was said. "Pop." Vernon never took his eyes from Constance. "Have an accounting done on Taylor's earnings. Let's see if she has what's needed to build her own studio."

"He can't do that. I'm her manager," Constance replied with a calm smirk.

"For now," Vernon replied. "That contract is coming to an end."

"I'm her mother. That's a lifetime contract."

"You will always be her mother, Connie. That is not the case as her manager."

Constance smirked. "You don't have the time or fortitude to manage her, Vernon. You are brilliant; I'll give you that. Management in the music business takes someone who can compromise. That eliminates you."

"If Taylor needs a new management team," Gwen spoke, "I'm certain Nick can assist."

"Taylor is my child," Constance snapped. "I will decide what is best for her."

"Correction Connie," Vernon spoke in a voice too calm to ignore. "Taylor is our child. One who is old enough to make her own decisions. If she does not want to sign a contract with you or B7 Beats, as parents we will support that."

Constance put the glass, which was now empty on the bar. "We'll see, Vernon." She tilted her head towards Gwen and Avery then left the room.

"What on earth has gotten into her?" Gwyneth proclaimed.

"A man," Vernon replied. "The only thing that would make Connie act this way is a man."

"One with wealth and power." Avery nodded his agreement.

"No," Gwyneth exclaimed. "Connie may be unhappy but I don't believe she would step out on Vernon."

Vernon watched as his wife walked up the staircase. He was certain that was exactly what Connie was doing. Her doing so did not faze him. What did was the role his daughter was to play in Connie's plans. "Excuse me for a moment."

Vernon walked out to the veranda where he and Taylor were sitting earlier. Pulling out his cell phone he dialed Nick's number.

"What's up, Vernon?" Nick spoke as if he was distracted.

"I need you to look into something for me."

"You need me?" Nick teased. "It's going to cost you."

Vernon looked incredulous. "You're going to charge me."

"Aren't you the brother who's always saying time is money? You're damn right I'm going to charge you." Nick laughed.

Vernon smiled and as he thought about it, he was pleased Nick had the knack for smoothing out a situation with humor. "It's Taylor. I want you to find out who is trying to sign her. I also want to know who you would recommend to take over managing her career."

"The last part is easy. My partner Tyrone Pendleton is the best in the business. He will also be the person to answer your first question. He is wired into the music business like you wouldn't believe."

"Get what you can from him." Vernon hesitated. "I don't like the vibe I'm getting from Taylor."

"What's going on with her?"

Vernon stood feeling helpless. "I don't know, Nick." He shook his head. "I just don't know."

"Did you ask Constance?"

"She gave me some bull about Taylor being young and thinks she knows everything."

"She is only twenty, Vernon. I deal with kids in Taylor's situation every day. They are millionaires ten times over, with people trying to tell them what to do." Nick sat back in his seat. "I have this one kid, Jason Whitfield. He is barely twenty, struggling to adjust to his new circumstances. If it hadn't been for Persuasion, I would have lost the kid."

"Who is Persuasion?"

"My team of investigators." Nick laughed. "When any of my clients have situations that could cause them problems I have Persuasion investigate and fix it."

Vernon thought about this for a moment. "Look, I have investigators at my firm, but I don't want them in my personal business. You think your team can check things out discreetly?"

"I'm sending the contact information to your phone. Tell them I sent you. If something is happening, they will uncover it. Be sure to ask for Naverone. Whatever is happening, nip it now, before it causes issues for Taylor's career."

Constance paced the suite wondering if she should make the call. Vernon was smart and determined. It would be better if she let this deal with Taylor drop. Now she just had to convince Isaac. Stepping out onto the balcony, so she would not be over heard, Constance dialed the number.

"Let me speak to him."

"Mr. Singleton, Connie is on the line."

Isaac looked up from the contract on his desk, then motioned for the phone. "Connie, are you on your way home?"

"No, there's been a complication."

"Nothing we can't handle, I'm sure."

Constance hesitated. "Taylor has decided she doesn't want to come back right now."

Isaac held his temper, keeping the goal in mind. "I'm sure you can convince her otherwise."

"It may be best to let her stay. Her father is beginning to ask questions."

Isaac smiled. Vernon was the person at the center of his plans. "He's doing what he thinks is best for his daughter. I would do the same if Taylor was mine. However, you should remind him, Taylor has a contract with B7 to honor."

"This family isn't concerned with money, Isaac. They have money and power."

"Ah, I forgot we are talking about the mighty Brooks'," he snorted. "If Taylor does not honor her contract, B7 will have no choice but to execute the clause which states, she will be prohibited from signing with any other studio for the next five years. That could destroy her career."

"Isaac, this is my daughter," Constance pleaded.

"Yes, and this is business. If she doesn't complete this CD with Nail and all that it entails, including videos, it will cost the company millions, not to mention my reputation." He hesitated. "Now, Connie, you know how people in this business can get when their rep is in question."

"You wouldn't allow them to do anything to Taylor, Isaac, she's my blood."

"I'll hold them off as long as I can. Get Taylor back here to complete the CD. I'll see you when you return." He disconnected the call.

"You want me to contact Nail?" his assistant asked.

"No," Isaac stated. "He's doing what we paid him to do."

"How he's doing it is what concerns me, Mr. Singleton. My job is to protect your back. If what he did was criminal, I don't want that to backfire on you."

"Is it criminal?"

"That's just it, sir, we don't know."

Isaac nodded. "Where do we stand on the others?"

"We have an opening to Nicole on both levels, personal and professional. As for Vernon, well, you're sleeping with the man's wife and we have control of his daughter's career. The other two Brooks siblings are well protected."

"No one is clean. Keep digging. In the meantime, work on the daughter. "

Chapter 11

Richmond, VA

The sleek black BMW sedan pulled into the parking space next to the SUV Xavier was leaning against. His eyes followed her legs and moved upward as she stepped out of the automobile. The impact was like a punch to his gut. For a week, Xavier had been trying to determine what it was about Nicole, this woman, that made him think of giving up everything he ever thought of doing, just to have a few moments with her.

Nicole did not think, wonder, or care she simply walked right into his embrace. Her fingers pulled the band from his braids, then spread them across his shoulders.

"What is it about you that makes me want to strip bare and watch you make love to my body with your eyes?"

A curl from her hair tickled his nose as he lifted her into his arms. Her legs instinctively wrapped around his waist as he turned and braced her body against the SUV. Her skirt inched up, leaving her thighs exposed to his touch. His hands smoothly caressed her thighs as he settled his body between them. They were smooth to the touch. Almost as smooth as her lips, but not as tasty, he thought, right before he devoured them. The kiss was slow, deep and thorough as he touched every corner of her mouth. He braced her face between his hands, going deeper, demanding every morsel of her sweetness to satisfy him.

Her legs tightened around him, pulling him snug at her junction. The heat from his erection seared through her, causing her stomach to contract and juices to saturate her panties. Their bodies merged as if they were well-oiled machines working in tandem to accomplish one mission—satisfaction.

His braids shielded her face as he ended the kiss and gazed into her eyes. His thumb rubbed across her lips. "If we stand here one moment longer, I'm not going to care who pulls into this garage."

"I'm ahead of you, I don't care."

"I don't want to share our moment with the world." He kissed her, then set her back on her feet. He smoothed her skirt down.

"You're getting good at dressing me, Mr. Davenport. Are you as good at undressing?"

Xavier took her hand, picked up her purse, which had dropped to the ground, then began walking towards the elevators. "I am better." He displayed that one sided grin, she had come to expect as they walked behind the main elevator doors. On the other side he placed the palm of his hand on the display next to the elevator door. It opened. He backed her in, pinned her against the wall with her arms above her head with one hand. The elevator doors closed as his other hand moved stealthily up her chest, flicking the buttons from the white blouse open. As he reached the pink lace bra, he unclipped the front latch. He released her hands pushing both items to the floor. Before she could get a giggle out he had captured her right nipple between his lips.

She moaned from the softness of his lips, the wetness of his tongue, the power of his suckles.

"Xavier," she groaned as he left one breast to capture the other with the same torment. She didn't feel the release of her skirt until it hit the floor. His hands roamed the curve of her hips, as his tongue blazed a trail of heat between her breasts and down her stomach until he reached her navel. His tongue darted in and out of her tiny belly button, driving him to the brink of no return, for the scent of her awakened his primal need to have her.

"Nicole." Her name came out in a growl as he returned to her lips.

"Yes." The sweet word echoed out, filled with surrender, just as the elevator stopped and the doors opened into the hallway of his bedroom. Xavier picked her up and carried her to his bed. "Lights low," he moaned as her body sank into the plush comforter and his body covered hers. He pushed the curls from her face, then stared down into her shimmering brown eyes. "May I have the honor of making love to you?"

"Yes." Her eyes captured the promise of sweet ecstasy in his. They were hypnotic and she did not want an antidote.

Xavier stood gazing down. The sight of her lying on his bed enthralled him. She had to be the most exquisite creature God had ever created was his thought as he dropped his suit jacket and shirt to the floor.

Nicole drooled at the sight of his bare chest. He was magnificent. Strong shoulders, a broad chest, and chiseled abs. He was too tempting to lay there. She came to her knees, touching his bare chest with her index finger, running it down the middle until she reached his belt. She unbuckled it, then unzipped his pants. When they dropped to the floor, she sat back on her haunches and took in all the wonder of Xavier Davenport.

"God must truly love me."

Xavier reached out cupping her face in his hands, bringing her lips a breath away from his. "You, Nicole Brooks, are the personification of grace and beauty. In this moment I know God exists for only He would have the power to create something as alluring as you. I want to spend the next seventy-two hours getting to know every inch of you."

Her hands covered his as he gently kissed her lips, pushing her backwards onto the bed. He raised her hands above her head entwining his fingers with hers. He kissed the tips, taking each tantalizing digit into his mouth and sucking as if her fingers were different flavors of lollipops.

The sensations traveling through her body caused a restlessness, an urgency, but he didn't stop, he continued kissing her behind her ear, then her throat. Her body squirmed under his.

"Xavier," she whimpered, "don't make me wait."

"I need to taste all of you, Nicole."

His trail of kisses was driving her insane. Every touch was like a branding stick, searing his ownership. "You taste like honey." He kissed her hip, her thighs, her calves and her feet. But he wasn't finished. Flipping her over, he began from the bottom of her foot and worked his way up to her behind. There he lingered, massaging both globes, enjoying the feel of them in his hands. From behind, he slipped one long finger inside of her. She was so wet; he pulled out, put on a condom and entered her in one long smooth motion.

They both moaned. Placing his hands on her hips, he pulled her further back, sinking deeper inside her.

He kissed her behind. "Nicole." He pulled out, and eased back in. "You are so hot, slick, wet. He kneeled on the bed behind her, then pulled her up placing one hand over her breast, the other slithered to her nub, stroking with his thumb to the same rhythm of his movement inside of her.

Nicole's head laid back on his shoulder. Her hands covering his, as he stroked her, caressed her, loved her in a way no one ever had. She turned her face to his neck and kissed. "More Xavier," she moaned as his penis curved to the shape of her body, slowly moving in and out with determined stroke, after stroke, after stroke.

Xavier couldn't have imagined anything feeling so exquisite. Inside of her was like a cocoon, warm, soothing, so damn good. He could feel the racing of her heart he was so intimately connected to her. He no longer controlled the motion of his hand, it was her hand guiding his, moving his thumb over her nub, increasing to the speed of his movement. He snaked inside of her branding every inch his, slowly, methodically, letting her know; only he would do. "Do you feel it Nicole?" He increased his movement. "Do you feel the sweet sinergy flowing through our bodies?" He pushed up harder. "That's us babe, all us. No one else can do this." His breath hitched. "You feel it Nicole? I do," he kissed her lips. "I want you, all of you. Come for me Nicole, like you've never come before. Spill it all babe. There it is." He spoke against her lips as she released a high pitched moan, "Give it to me Nicole," he moved faster, pumping fiercely, holding her tighter as he felt the explosion, then her soft scream. The contraction of her walls around him, caused him to pump harder, deliberately into her, until he just couldn't hold back any longer. He pulled out slowly to the tip then slammed back in, causing her to explode again, this time with him.

They fell forward onto the bed. he was still lodged in her from behind, his finger still caressing her nub. Their breathing so fast, neither could speak. He gathered her in his arms, as they lay there spooning with each other eyes closed, allowing each to feel the wonder of their joining.

Their limbs were entwined, her head on his shoulder, his arms around her body with his hand resting on her hip, as they played with their fingers. They were so sated, neither had the strength to move even though it was only nine pm. The lights were low, there was no music, just the rhythm of their heartbeats serenading them as they held each other.

"I'm starving."

"All that sinergy you dispensed up in here," Nicole laughed.

He loved the way her laughter came from within and spilled over. "You must have been a very happy child."

"I was." She kissed his nipple. "I can only think of three times in my entire life that I was disappointed."

"Tell me about them and I'll fix them."

Nicole smiled. "You can't fix them, but my parents did. There was when Vernon got married. I was devastated. Oh, I thought my life was over. I cried for weeks and refused to be a part of the wedding."

Xavier laughed. "How old were you?"

"Six," she laughed. "I was six and my brother was leaving me for another woman. I did everything. I stomped, I slammed doors. I refused to speak to my father because he was allowing it to happen."

"What did your parents do?"

"You mean my mother. She pulled me in my room the day before the wedding and explained to me that

Vernon was not mine. He belonged to her and she could give him away if she wanted to. Then she said, if I didn't calm my little ass down she was going to give me away too."

"Sounds like Mrs. Lassiter."

"What about your mom? She doesn't appear to be someone you would mess around with."

"Whew, my mom? That's a long story."

Nicole sat up leaning on her elbow, running a finger across his chest, sensing this was not easy for him. "I have time."

"You sure you want to hear this? It's not a pretty story."

"It's your story, pretty or not. I want to know what made Xavier the man who creates words at will."

He smiled as he continued to play with her fingers. "My mom left when I was a baby. Zack says the street caught her and wouldn't let go. My dad would say, your mother needed to find her place on this earth and when she does, she will know it's right here with us."

Nicole smiled. "That's a beautiful way to look at things. Was your dad a poet?"

"Close, a musician."

"No way." Her eyes lit up. "What instrument did he play?"

"Sax, the instrument for lovers, he used to say."

"Can you play?"

"No, Zack can. I'm a keyboard kind of guy."

"Sounds like your dad loved your mother a lot."

Xavier nodded his head in agreement. "Until the day he died. I was sixteen and a handful." He tightened his hold on her. "Zack left college to take care of me. He gave up a very promising football career to take care of his brat of a brother. I would do things just to irk him. You know, he never got mad.

He would punish the hell out of me, but never once did he ever raise his voice or strike me."

"What did he do?"

"He made me go to that damn construction site with him every day after school. I hated it." He laughed. "Lifting heavy lumber and bricks. After I messed up enough times he took me from the field and put me in the trailer helping with the plans. That's where my love for designing homes came to light."

"Wow," she said softly. "So you two decided to form Davenport Industries?"

"Zack had started his own construction company while I was away in college. From time to time I would send him some of my drawings and he started sending me checks. He said I had the kind of talent people pay for."

"He was your first client?"

"Yep. I was the man." He laughed. "I was on campus studying and getting paid for doing something I love."

"That's how I feel about development. I love taking a piece of property, scanning all the surrounding areas and determining what would go in that space. What will prosper there? Should it be a school, a mall, a community? Once I decide then I pull all the pieces together and make it happen."

"When I return to one of the communities I designed and see people living there, children running around enjoying the outdoors, I get this sense of...accomplishment." They both said the word together.

"Like you've found your purpose."

"Exactly," he said in a low voice. He gazed into her eyes and loved the sparkle that reflected back. Reaching up, he ran his fingers through her curls, gently tugging them towards him, then he gently kissed her.

She sighed. "Okay, I heard about your dad and Zack. What about your mother? You said she was in the street. Was she involved with drugs or something?"

"From what I've been told by her and Zack, she was the queen of coke. It woke her up in the morning and put her to sleep at night. She did whatever it took to get the next high. Zack made her keep her distance from me. When she needed something, he helped, but if she ever came near me, he was there blocking her. He said she was to have no contact with me until she was clean and he meant it." He became solemn. "For a long time I thought she was dead. When she showed up at one of our construction sites I got to know her. I had no idea she was my mother until one day I knocked over some marbles that were sitting on Diamond's desk. I bent down to pick them up and she said, *'Let's get these back in the jar'*. A memory hit me so strong, because my mother used to say the exact same thing about Zack's' marbles."

"Wow, what did you do?"

"I left." He cleared his throat. "Before I walked out the door she stopped me and said, *'You're a good man, Xavier Prince Davenport. Find yourself a good woman and plant some seeds. You and Zack come from good stock. You should both be fruitful and multiply. Just make sure it's with the right woman.'*

"From the looks of things last night, you reconciled things with her. How did that happen?"

"I confronted Zack. He had no right to make the decision regarding my mother's role in my life. Since then we've worked it out. As for my mom, we take it one day at a time."

She touched the cleft in his chin. "Well, I beg to differ with you on that one. When your dad passed, it became Zack's responsibility to protect you. Keeping a drug-addicted mom away from you was the right thing to do. However, once she got her act together and was able to be a mother to you and you were old enough to handle the emotional toll, then he probably would have told you about her." She shrugged her shoulders. "You just happened to find her before he could do that. Now your mother seems fine. I wonder if she had that great sense of humor before or if it was drug induced?"

Xavier stared at her before he let out a soul-cleansing laugh. "Drug induced humor?"

"Yeah." She smiled. "If drugs can burn your brain cells, couldn't it impact your funny bone?"

"Do you find something pleasant in everything?"

"I try." His stomach growled. "Now, if I could find some food to fill your tummy."

"That's easy." He sat up, reached over to the nightstand, then clicked the remote. The television appeared from the center of the wall. He pushed another button and the monitor came on. The next button brought up a menu.

"You have a concierge service here?"

"I do." He smiled as she sat up and settled into his arms. She felt good in his home, his bedroom, and in his arms.

"So what's on the menu? Coffee, tea, you?"

"I'll have a special menu put in for your next visit."

She beamed up at him. "I get to come back?"

He shrugged his shoulders as he placed the order. "That depends on if I ever let you leave, you sweet sexy thang."

"Finished ordering?"

"Yes."

"Good." Nicole pushed the sheet aside, enclosed his erection within her hand, bent over and kissed it. "My appetite has changed." She slowly licked the top. "I have a taste for deep," she covered him with her mouth, squeezed at his base, then pulled upward, "deep," she repeated the action taking him deeper, "dark chocolate."

Xavier couldn't breathe. All he could do was run his fingers through her curls and guide her exquisite, determined movements. The warmth from her mouth was setting his body on fire. The tip of him touched the back of her throat just as her jaw contracted, sucking the life out of him. A low primitive growl escaped as he pulled Nicole from him, slammed her on her back, spread her legs and entered her in one swift movement.

Somewhere in her life she did right. That's the only reason God sent this man into her life. He knew what to say, how to hold her, how deep to go and oh did he have the most glorious, thick, long, sweet dick. She grabbed his arms that were braced at her sides as he plunged inside of her. They were strong. She could feel the power flowing through them every time his body slammed into hers. She raised her body to meet him stroke for stroke.

The heat was intense, yet he wanted, no needed, her closer. He wrapped his arm around her waist, sat back on his haunches and pulled her forward.

Nicole wrapped her legs around his waist and her arms around his neck. They were merged so tightly together you couldn't tell where her body ended and his began. She bit into his shoulder as he buried his face into her hair. What began as a raw, primitive need now manifested into something sensuous, loving and beautiful. It was the intimacy of the embrace that awakened something much deeper, more meaningful and unbreakable within them.

Their motions slowed as they savored the fullness of the joining. It became a delicate dance of mutual desire, as his hand held the small of her back, guiding her slow grinding motion, his other hand caressing her neck, his voice whispering in her hair. "My sweet Nicole." He felt her inner lips tighten. His fingers moved further into her hair. "Take me, baby," he moaned as the blood rushed to the tip of him. "Nicole," he growled. Her slow grinds were driving him to the brink. She was there with him. Her breath hitched, her body contracted and her sweet, sweet moan of release in his ear caused a ricochet of emotions. His heart filled, and his release spilled into her body.

They sat there, immobile as the telephone rang. Xavier laid her back covering her with his body. Afraid of the words forming in his mind, he kissed her, touching every corner of her mouth. He ended the kiss when the telephone rang again. Still unwilling to part from her, he kissed her eyelids, her cheeks, then her lips again. He gently rubbed her temples, then stared down into her face. This was the passion he'd been seeking. This beautiful, fascinating woman evoked from him emotions he never knew existed and in such a short period of time. "Don't you move."

"I don't have the strength even if I wanted to."

He smiled as he answered the call.

"Mr. Davenport, your dinner is on its way up."

"Thank you Joe."

"Sir, Ms. Hargrove is asking to be let up."

"Trish is here?"

"Yes, sir and she seems to be a bit agitated."

Xavier was still intimately connected inside of Nicole.

"We're going to have to face her sooner or later," Nicole sighed.

"Hold her for ten minutes, then send her up."

"Yes, sir."

Xavier gazed at her. "This is my fault. I promised to speak with her tonight."

"She's upset about the lawsuit."

"What lawsuit?"

"The one I don't want to discuss while you are growing inside of me...again. You, Mr. Davenport, have a lusty appetite."

"Only with you, Ms. Brooks, only with you."

"Then why is Trish here?"

"Why don't we find out?" He kissed her temple, then withdrew from her. They both moaned.

"Where's your shower?"

Xavier lifted her into his arms, carried her down the hallway and entered the bathroom.

"I can walk, you know."

"I'm not ready to let you out of my arms."

"You have another woman coming upstairs. She will not be happy if she sees me here."

"Two points." He keyed in the settings for the shower. "Trish is uninvited." He walked into the shower with her in his arms. "You, on the other hand, I want here." The water hit their bodies from all directions, as he literally walked through the shower with her in his arms. He stood her up against the marble shower wall, the main spray overhead, cascaded over them, as others pulsated around them.

"Hmmm, I may never leave this room," Nicole moaned as she held her head back enjoying the feel of his naked body against hers and the water massaging them all over.

He kissed her neck as he pushed the button for the shower gel dispenser. Rubbing the gel over her body started his blood to boil again. "You're going to smell like me for the rest of the night."

"Sounds like heaven to me." She pushed the button for the gel and returned the favor. "We keep at this and we will never eat."

He lifted his head from her shoulder. "Ah hell, I forgot about the food." He stepped under another spray to rinse off. "The food is probably in the kitchen by now."

"They have access to your apartment?"

"No, we have a dumbwaiter they send the food up on." Xavier stepped out of the shower and pushed the button for the dryer, which dispensed warm air all over his body.

Nicole smiled, more at the look of his body in front of the dryer, than at his reply. "I have to add that to my place."

"The dumbwaiter or the body dryer?" he asked as he pulled a robe from the closet. He reached in, pulled her to him and kissed her soundly on the lips. "I'll meet you in the kitchen."

"Give me five minutes."

Xavier walked into the kitchen, opened the cabinet door and as he thought, the trays of food were there waiting for him. The chime sounded indicating someone without an elevator code was requesting entrance into his apartment. He assumed it must be Trish. He walked back into the bedroom, pulled a t-shirt and a pair of sweats from the drawer, then gave Nicole one of his t-shirts as well. "I'm not ready for you to put your clothes back on yet. I'll take care of this situation with Trish and then you and I can replenish our energy for the next session."

Nicole watched as he walked from the bedroom, thinking, that was one hell of a sexy man. But he was naive to think Trish would be easy to dispose of.

However, she was going to stay in the bedroom to give him the room to try.

Xavier prepared himself, then pushed the button to unlock the elevator doors. Standing at the end of the foyer, he watched as Trish stepped off, marveling at the entrance.

"Trish," he spoke causing her attention to turn to him.

"Xavier." She rushed towards him, merging their bodies. "I called your cell phone several times and did not get an answer. When you didn't call I got worried and came right over." She now could see the living room and kitchen. "You have a beautiful place," she said with wonder in her voice. "May I?"

"Thank you. Why are you here?"

"I told you, I was worried." She walked over to the fireplace. "This is beautiful." She looked around and saw the view from the living room window. "Xavier, that is a magnificent view."

"Trish." He never moved from his spot near the entrance. "What do you want?"

She turned to face him just as her trench coat opened exposing the almost not there dress. It took everything in him not to laugh as Reese's words came to mind. Her look of wonder at his home changed quickly to one of despair.

"Xavier, I don't know what to do." She seductively walked back to where he stood near the kitchen, slouched on one of the bar stools and crossed her legs, exposing more thigh. "I can't believe the Brooks' are doing this to me."

Xavier's defenses went up. "That's between you and the Brooks'."

"Don't you even want to know what it is?"

"No."

"Xavier, you are the most sensitive person I know." Giving him the Sharon Stone move from Basic Instinct, uncrossing her legs, spreading them wide enough to tease then crossing them back. "I really need your help to sort through this mess."

The sigh was louder than Nicole meant for it to be, as she leaned against the fireplace watching the scene unfold. She shrugged her shoulders at Xavier and smiled as Trish turned.

She jumped off the stool. "What in the hell are you doing here?" Trish looked at Nicole from head to toe, then slowly turned evil eyes to Xavier. "You want to explain this." She pointed to Nicole as she spoke to Xavier.

"This is what happens when you come to someone's home uninvited." He walked over to stand in front of Nicole. "Have I ever invited you to my home?"

"No, but Xavier, we are in a relationship."

"No Trish, we're not and haven't been for months. I don't know how many ways I can say this to you."

"How many ways do I have to tell you, Nicole isn't interested in men. The heifer only placed a bid on you because I did. She has always wanted what I've had because she is a spoiled..."

"Enough." The bellow that came from Xavier was so loud Nicole jumped. "First you came to my place of employment with your drama. Now, you've brought it into my home." He walked slowly towards her. "This is my sanctuary. Nicole is an invited guest. You are not, allow me to show you the way out."

Trish was so stunned she couldn't move. It was the first time she had ever known Xavier to raise his voice. This was one time she didn't have to act. She was hurt.

Trish glared at Nicole. "You will pay for this." She pulled her coat together and tied it at the waist.

"Let's be clear, Trish, what is happening with you and I has nothing to do with Nicole. You and your mother disrespected me. Your actions today severed any ties you and I once had."

"Everything that has happened this week was because of her. If she had stayed in her lane you and I would be spending the weekend together."

"It would have been a very difficult two days."

She stepped onto the elevator with as much dignity as her pride would allow. "Five hundred and fifty million dollars, Nicole? Its menial compared to what's about to rain down on you. Enjoy your precious weekend, Xavier, for hell cometh in the morning."

The doors closed and neither spoke for a long moment. Xavier turned to Nicole.

His mind was having a conflict with his body. He wanted to forget the last fifteen minutes and go back to making love with the woman standing by his fireplace in his tee shirt. Caution signals in his body were telling him to get to the bottom of this issue with Trish and Nicole.

Nicole walked into the kitchen. She removed the tray tops then looked around. Xavier walked over to the cabinet, pulled down two plates, then opened the drawer for silverware. They settled next to each other at the breakfast bar and began to dine on rosemary shrimp scampi skewers, with rice and green beans, and a wonderful red wine.

"This is delicious," Nicole remarked. "You have a chef on staff?"

"We have several who work wonders in a kitchen. The residents have options from gourmet prepared meals to fried fish and potatoes that you would swear came from someone's grandmother's kitchen."

"What a wonderful amenity to have. This was your idea?"

"No, Diamond came up with that one."

"We offer amenities in some of our luxury residential buildings." She took a sip of her wine. "Trish and I went to high school together," she began.

"Nicole..."

"No," she stopped him. "Let me do this. One thing I've learned about relationships is secrets come back to bite you." She looked up at him. "I don't want that for us."

Xavier nodded.

They ate as she talked.

"The saga of Trish and Nicole began when she couldn't understand why she couldn't bully me. The Brooks' make up is a little different from most wealthy people. We don't value money above all else. We value people. My father always says, 'value your family and friends and you will always be wealthy'. We were raised to treat people as if they were the highest commodity in the world, because to us they are. If you think about it, our livelihood depends on people. It doesn't matter if they are rich, poor, green or yellow. For when all else is gone, if you have your family and friends you are wealthy beyond measure. Trish comes from a mother who placed value on status and wealth. They long to be in the upper echelon of society. Because my family is where she wants to be, she felt she had to tear me down. When one thing didn't work she would try another and another. She found out that I have dyslexia. The 'Nicole's a dummy' campaign began. My mother is very protective of her children. She threatened bodily harm to Mrs. Hargrove if she did not control Trish. Mrs. Hargrove informed her husband. Then my dad got involved, went to their home and followed through on the threat my mother had issued. We were sued for five million dollars. Because my dad was involved in a pivotal civil rights case at the time, we settled out of court. This ritual has gone on for over ten years. Trish provokes me in some way, I or my family reacts and we end up settling out of court."

Nicole put her fork down. "This time it's not my parents. It's me. I think it's time to hold Trish accountable for her actions. A multi-billion dollar deal is now in jeopardy because of Trish's statement at the auction. The development firm I was working with requested I make a public statement regarding my sexuality. I refused because what I do behind closed doors is my business. No one should be required to make a sexual declaration for a business deal." She looked up at Xavier. "When we met with Trish and her attorneys they requested a five million dollar settlement. Trish raised it to ten with an amendment that I stay away from you. I have searched through my short life looking for a man who evokes a natural passion in me. There was no way I could stay away from you. Therefore, I made the decision to counter sue for defamation of character. I have no idea how that is going to impact my life with the gay community, or my friend Alicia. But I know I have to stop this madness with Trish. I don't want to spend my life wondering when the Hargroves are going to strike again."

"Why five hundred and fifty million? You said it was a multi-billion dollar deal. Why not sue for that amount?"

"I've only invested that amount to date."

Xavier nodded. He placed his fork on the plate, then pulled Nicole onto his lap. "Your dad sounds like good people and your mother sounds like you." Their foreheads touched, as Xavier exhaled. "My apology for losing my temper in front of you." He squeezed her waist. "My life was simple until last week. But I asked for it. A few weeks ago I told my friend I wanted a woman who made me crazy with passion. Here you are. Gay, straight, bi, I don't care. I want you in my life. If you decide to follow through on this court case, Alicia is going to support you as will I. Trish is wounded. You know what they say about a wounded animal. She's going to come after you and she is not going to care who gets hurt."

Nicole listened as she gently pulled on his braids. It was calming to her. "I think we have a chance at something special. If you believe that Trish will interfere, I'll take the settlement and call it a day."

He kissed her throat. "No, you do what you have to do to protect yourself against Trish. But for now, I want our weekend." The kisses moved down between her breasts, his hands massaging her thighs.

Nicole kissed the top of his head. "I want that more than you know."

Chapter 12

Richmond, VA
Friday

The Richmond office of Persuasion was located in historic Shockoe Bottom. The cobble stone streets, the outdoor market and the brownstone like office fronts gave the area a blend of the old and new. The sedan pulled up in front of the building. Vernon stepped out.

"I'll send you a message when I'm ready," he said to his driver. He turned and looked at the double door entry with the address engraved on the glass. Stepping inside the building was transformed into an upscale modern office space. Vernon had only been to Nicolas' office twice and it seemed he had expanded. The entry was a wide, long foyer with burgundy and tan Persian carpeting, and white columns strategically placed throughout. On the wall to the right in an arch design was the name 'Brooks – Pendleton'. He smiled. His little brother had made it. Under the arch were framed pictures of their current clientele, from the ceiling to the floor. Across the hall was the same name pattern only smaller, Persuasion.

Vernon took the door on the left. Inside the office, there was a flurry of movement. The open floor plan had desks placed throughout the area with four offices against the wall, two on each side.

"Mr. Brooks."

Vernon turned, somewhat startled at the sound of the sensual voice. He never heard anyone walk up behind him. Bothered by being caught unaware, he was lost when he looked into the eyes of the woman standing before him. Words to describe the woman escaped him and that was not something that happened to him. Women came easy to Vernon. He'd had them in all shapes, colors and sizes. Not much about them struck him until this one. It was difficult for him to believe, but he was literally speechless. She was dressed in a long sleeved, pink, yes, pink off the shoulder band-aide dress which exposed the curves of her body with class. Her hair was in a side ponytail, which hung across her shoulder. Her face was free of makeup, yet her lips were coated in something, for nothing bare could be that tempting and smooth as a shot of Patron, and Vernon loved his Patron. He now wondered if it came in pink.

"Yes," he finally replied.

"Rene Naverone." She extended her hand. "Let's talk in my office."

He willed his hand to meet hers. The immediate rush of lust slammed into him so hard he withdrew his hand and took a step back. There was a flash of surprise in her eyes then it disappeared. The woman turned to walk away, expecting him to follow, but his legs wouldn't move. He stood there with his hands in his pants pockets, his over coat open, mesmerized by the sight of the woman's sensuous five-six, one hundred-thirty pound body and long sexy legs in four inch heels.

"Damn," he murmured under his breath.

"She takes your breath away, doesn't she?"

He looked over his shoulder to see his brother, Nick, standing behind him grinning. He turned back to the woman. "I think she just stripped me of my senses."

Nicolas hit him on the shoulder. "She can strip you of a lot more than that if you are not careful. Come on, let's get this started."

Rene Naverone's office was furnished with the high end clientele she serviced in mind. Rich dark mahogany glistened to the point that you could see your silhouette. The two chairs in front of her desk were plush, and burgundy in color. Pictures of her with athletes, celebrities and one or two dignitaries graced the wall. The office was almost as impressive as the lady...almost.

"Mr. Brooks, I understand there is a situation with your daughter you would like for Persuasion to investigate." She pointed to a chair. "Have a seat." She looked up at Nicolas and smiled. "Good morning Nick."

"Morning Naverone. You've met my brother Vernon?"

She nodded as she gracefully sat behind her desk and crossed her legs. "Briefly." She glanced at Vernon and smiled.

Damn, Vernon groaned the thought. She was having an effect on him in ways he couldn't explain even if he tried. Seeing the gold sparkle in her light brown eyes let him know she was very aware of her impact. "Remedy." He nodded. "Vernon Brooks, now we've completed the introduction." He held her gaze as he took a seat, feeling a little more in control of himself.

Nicolas looked from one to the other and only one word came to mind...explosive.

"I can leave, if you two need a moment. I'm beginning to feel like I'm intruding on a peek show or something."

While Vernon slowly turned to his baby brother, giving him an incredulous look, Naverone laughed.

"He's right, Mr. Brooks. We could sit here all day sending promising subliminal messages to each other or we can discuss your daughter." Naverone raised an eyebrow as she spoke.

A slow, lazy smile formed on Vernon's face. "I believe in flowing with the moment, Ms. Naverone, do you?"

"It's the spice of life-" she sat forward "-when the man isn't married."

Vernon touched his chest. "Schematics, Ms. Naverone, schematics."

"Do you two mind?"

"You can leave," Vernon strongly suggested to Nick.

"Not a chance," Nick chuckled. "I have to protect my team."

"From what I can see, Ms. Naverone is capable of taking care of herself."

"Very astute of you, Mr. Brooks. It's amazing you determined that in the short five minutes we've been aquatinted"

"I read people very well, Ms. Naverone. May I call you Rene?"

Nick groaned.

Vernon looked at Naverone. "Do you have little brothers?"

"Two younger, two older," Naverone replied as she sat back. "And yes, they are a pain." She opened a file on her computer. "Rene is fine. Now, tell me how I can assist you."

"I gave Naverone some information." Nicolas sat forward.

"My daughter Taylor Brooks' stage name is Lil Tay," Vernon explained.

"Multi-Platinum, Grammy-winning R&B singer signed with B7 Beats. A short sweet honey with a banging bod, according to one of my clients who sleeps, dreams and breathes Lil Tay."

"Who?" Vernon and Nick questioned.

Naverone smiled. "Privileged."

"Client attorney privilege consists of a client and an attorney," Vernon summarized.

"And me," Naverone advised. "Tell me about your daughter?"

Vernon shifted in his chair. "Something happened during a video shoot which caused her to walk off the set. Whatever happened was upsetting enough for her to want to stop the tour. In fact, she wants to stop performing and attend law school."

"That doesn't sound like such a bad thing."

"I'm thrilled," Vernon noted. "However, performing has been Taylor's dream from the age of five. If she's going to walk away from it, I want to ensure it's one, her choice and two, won't be detrimental to her career when she returns."

"As a father you want to know who did something to your baby so you can kill him or her."

"You understand completely," Vernon replied.

"No. However, I have a father who has done unthinkable things to boys who he believed hurt his only daughter. So let's say, I have a level of understanding. As such, I reached out to Tyrone Pendleton. His information indicates Taylor is working with Nigel "Nail" Lamont, a rapper out of St. Louis. He's a young a-hole who is topping the charts right now because of Taylor. He has a police record and a reputation that proves he's a 'wanna be' bad-ass. There are misdemeanor assault charges, here and there, nothing major," Naverone stated as she glanced through the file on her computer.

"Ty indicated the public is loving the good girl falls for the bad guy image the two have," Nicolas added. "The single hit platinum on the day it dropped and diamond within a week. There are plans in the works for a cross-country tour with Taylor as the lead act, Nail as the main draw, but the two of them closing out."

Vernon gave Nicolas a side-eye glance. "I deal in criminal not entertainment law. You want to break it down in laymen's terms?"

Nick grinned. "The CD sold over a million copies on the day the song was released to the public, over ten million within the first week. The two of them closing indicates Taylor is just as much of a draw as Nail."

"Taylor refusing to do the tour is like a smack in the face for Nail who's been in the business for years, yet hasn't reached the level he believes his talent is worthy of. This joint venture with Taylor will bring him an audience he hasn't been able to tap into." Naverone sighed. "This tour is expected to earn millions on the low end. If they take it international, the sky is the limit. If it doesn't happen, there goes Nail's chance at his claim to fame."

Vernon frowned. "If the single is doing well, and a tour is in the works that would benefit both Taylor and this Nail person, why would she walk away?"

"That seems to be the million dollar question." She hesitated. "You know, I'm not working on a case right now," Naverone stated. "My family hasn't seen me since I moved here last year. Seems like a trip home is in order. I know a few people. While I'm there, I'll ask a few questions, see what I can find out."

"Whatever the cost, your fee, expenses, bill me."

Naverone stood. "Nick's my boss. It's on the house."

"No, he pays." Nicolas stood. "He can afford you."

Vernon glared at his brother as he stood. "I'm telling Pop."

"James is right, you always run to Pop."

"Keeps both of you in line," Vernon smirked. "Rene." He extended his hand. "It was a pleasure. One I hope to experience again."

"You will, as soon as I have something to report."

Vernon started to say something more, when he was pulled away by Nicolas.

"It may be a good idea to call Connie, your wife, to inform her of the inquiries that may be coming her way."

He looked over his shoulder with his sexiest smile. "Until we meet again, Rene."

Once they were out of the office, Vernon cautioned Nicolas, "Don't say anything about this to the folks. My gut tells me Constance is involved or at the very least, trying to cover it up."

"Funny, according to Ty, Connie is close friends with a new owner at B7."

"Close?"

Nicolas nodded. "Close."

Vernon acknowledged his response. "You okay?"

With a slight tilt of his head, Vernon replied. "It's time. Constance and I have played this game long enough. I'm certain she has a lot riding on this situation with Taylor."

"As her manager, Constance stands to receive twenty percent of Taylor's contract. B7 is offering a twenty million dollar signing bonus for Taylor. " Nicolas opened the door to his office. "That's a healthy sum," he replied as Vernon stepped inside.

The setup in Nick's area was a stark difference from the openness at Persuasion. A receptionist sat at an oval shaped desk with the name of the agency engraved on the wall behind her. Nothing could be seen from the foyer. To the right there was a door with the name 'Pendleton' above the opening and to the left was a door with the name 'Brooks' above it. Each had a key-code bar for entry. They walked to the door to the left. Nicolas put in his code and they walked through. There were offices on both sides of the hallway, some occupied with staff and some not. They walked to the end of the hallway where a secretary sat in front of Nicolas' office. She stood when he approached.

"Mr. Brooks, Jarrett Bryson called. He wants to meet you in New York at the end of this month. Mr. Whitfield's mother called and would like to speak with you. Nicole left a message stating she will be out of reach until late Sunday, but not to worry. She is in good hands." The woman smiled as she delivered that piece of news.

"Thank you, Sylvia. No calls for now."

Vernon entered Nicolas' luxurious office, unbuttoned his suit jacket and took a seat in front of the desk.

"Constance is positioning herself for a divorce. I'm certain she has a nest egg somewhere waiting for the right moment," Vernon summarized.

"Would you grant it to her?" Nick asked.

"Yes, and I'll make certain she has a home comparable to ours wherever she wants it."

"You would think after all this time Connie would know how we operate," Nicolas stated, his mind still on the message from Nicole. He sat back in his chair. "What do you know about this Davenport character?"

"My marriage is over and you want to discuss Nicole and Davenport."

"Your marriage was over the day you slept with Katherine. Did you check him out?"

"Make one mistake and this family never lets you forget it." Vernon sighed. "Of course I did. He's clean."

"Nikki likes this guy, Vernon. I need to know more."

Vernon was on the verge of laughter when he caught himself. This was the exact conversation he had with Nicole about Nicholas' last girlfriend. He warned her to stay out of Nick's business and she didn't listen. She interfered causing a rift between herself and Nick for months. Now here he was about to do the exact same thing. The two had this weird twin psycho thing going on, always had.

"I'm going to tell you the same thing I told Nikki when she approached me about you. Nikki is a grown woman. She is very insightful when it comes to people. Hell, she was right about what's her name. You still haven't told her how much the woman took you for have you?"

"She didn't take me, she took one of my clients."

"Which you ended up putting back into his account, same difference." Vernon sat up. "Look if you are that concerned about Nikki talk to your boy Grant Hutchinson. He and Davenport are tight. Before you do that, know that Davenport does not need Nikki's money. Hell, if anything, her wealth is her biggest problem with him. He's a simple guy. Other than the thing with Trish his taste isn't bad."

Nicolas nodded. "I'll give Grant a call anyway, as a precaution."

"Suit yourself. What's the deal with Naverone?"

Nicolas dropped his head and shook it. "You are a married man. There is nothing you can do for her."

"All I'm asking is, what's her story?"

After a deep sigh and a stern look at his brother, Nicolas gave in. "Ex-Secret Service. Ex-Ty Pendleton and one hell of a woman."

"Secret Service? Hmmm, I wonder if she knows Genesis?"

"She's one of her associates."

"Genesis left the agency?"

"I think she does jobs for them here and there, but she works across the hallway. They're four of the finest damn women you ever laid your eyes on who can whip your ass before you blink. Half of my players are scared to death of them."

Vernon laughed. "I know Genesis can. I've seen her in action."

"They all bow to Naverone."

Vernon raised an eyebrow, intrigued. "Rene Naverone, I'll have to remember that."

"Vernon, she is not to be played with."

Vernon stood. "My playing days ended years ago." He walked towards the door. "Stay out of Nikki's business."

"You stay out of Naverone's panties."

Vernon laughed as he walked out the door. He sent a message to his driver, then dialed another number. He stood on the sidewalk waiting for the call to go through.

"Hello, you beautiful sexy woman. How the hell are you Genesis?"

**

She was in his bed, with the scent of her hair on his pillow and he liked it. Their lovemaking filled the air and he liked that too. Hell it was turning him on. Three times during the night they took showers together with the intention of going to sleep. He sat on the edge of the bed watching her sleep and smiling about how they laughed and finally gave up on sleep.

He moved away from her about an hour ago because he wanted her again. Closing his eyes with his head tilted back, he wondered what would happen on Sunday when they had to go their separate ways. Would he be strong enough to let her go? He released a deep sigh, opened his eyes and looked into her beautiful light brown eyes and the sensuous smile on her face. "Good morning," he said fearful to move any closer to her.

"Good morning." She sat up on one elbow. "I was wondering. What are we going to do come Sunday? I live in New York, have a business there. You live here with a business. It's going to be hard to leave you."

"Schematics," Xavier replied as his long, sleek body covered hers. "Whether you are here or in New York, I'll have a part of you with me. I do know, I am nowhere near ready to think about you being anywhere other than with me. For the next two days I want to discover all your darkest secrets. Your every nook and cranny, then I want to kiss you from head to toe. For now, we are going to get this weekend started." He took her hand and pulled her from the bed. "You shower and dress while I prepare breakfast, then we are out of here."

She kissed his chest. "We have to take a moment to say good morning properly." She placed a trail of kisses down his chest, stomach, then kissed his manhood.

It jumped to attention before Xavier could think. He pulled her up as she giggled, and settled her legs around his waist. He entered her in one powerful thrust. They moaned.

"Sinergy," he whispered as he walked her into the shower.

Two hours later they were fulfilled, fed and on the road to their weekend get-a-way.

Chapter 13

Charlottesville, VA
Friday

The playlist in Xavier's SUV was a collection of old-school, jazz and R&B. Every song that came on, they sang along as if they were two kids in the back of their parents' SUV on a road trip. An hour and twenty minutes later they pulled off the highway onto a road where there was nothing but winding roads and trees, as if they had turned into a forest.

"Seems like we have left civilization," Nicole stated as they continued down the road. "Oh look, there's a deer, and three baby deer."

Xavier laughed at the sheer amazement on her face. "You've been in the city too long." The trees seemed to part the further up the mountain they traveled. Coming into view was a magnificent scene of cottages, and a beautiful brick building. They pulled into the circular driveway, where two men were waiting. They each opened their doors.

"Welcome to Paradise Inn."

"Thank you." Xavier gave the man the keys to the vehicle then joined Nicole on the other side.

They walked into the building and were greeted by a brunette, dressed in a navy blue suit, trimmed in tan, a white blouse and heels.

"Mr. Davenport, welcome to Paradise where the mountain tops touch heaven." The woman shook his hand as she gave him a package. "Your cottage is ready, and has been stocked per your request." She walked over to a desk nestled in the corner of the room, which appeared to be a large foyer. There was a fireplace in the center, tables throughout, with place settings. "It seems a number of news media have contacted us regarding your stay. I took the liberty of gathering their names, however, it is our policy not to divulge guest information. Due to the number of calls, I moved your cottage to the far end of the grounds. If anyone were to trespass, there are a number of check points they would have to clear before reaching you."

"Thank you, Ms..."

"Mrs. Leigh." She handed him a card. "This is my number. I am available to you around the clock during your stay. If you need anything at all, please don't think twice, give me a call."

"Thank you, Mrs. Leigh."

"It's my pleasure. If you would follow me, we can get your weekend started." Mrs. Leigh walked out of the building through the back. It appeared as though they were walking right into a mountain. "You picked a perfect time of year to visit," she said as she walked onto the deck. "The trees are turning to the fall colors and the view of the Blue Ridge Mountains is breathtaking, wouldn't you agree, Ms. Brooks?"

The comment took Nicole by surprise. It was the first time the woman had addressed her directly. "I do."

Mrs. Leigh smiled. "It's a beautiful location for a wedding, if one so chooses to take that step." She walked down steps to the wood deck leading to an extended walk way. There was a waterfall under it, a clear view of the mountains, and small walkways on the right leading to cabins.

Nicole wished she had thought to bring a camera when Xavier bent down and whispered, "I have a photographic memory. I'll draw it for you."

"How did you know what I was thinking?"

"Everyone thinks it when they take this walk," Mrs. Leigh replied as they came to the end of the walkway. They turned and walked the short ramp that led to the door of the cottage. Mrs. Leigh put in the code and opened both doors, then stood back. "Welcome to the Paradise."

Xavier and Nicole stepped inside. The cottage was exquisite, from the floor to ceiling windows, which captured the view of the mountains brilliantly, to the fireplace in the center of a curving staircase, leading to the loft, to the cozy kitchen with just about every amenity they could want.

"Your luggage is upstairs in the loft. Enjoy your stay," Mrs. Leigh said as she backed out and closed the double doors behind her.

"I think I want to take her back to New York with me."

Xavier smiled. "She has been indispensable over the last week." They walked around admiring the scenery, from the foyer to the great room to the dining area.

"Cookies," Xavier picked up a macadamia nut cookie and bit into it. "Hmmm, warm and delicious. Almost as good as you."

She turned, walked over and bit his cookie.

"You eat my cookies, I'll eat yours."

"You already did."

He kissed her. "I want more." The kiss deepened until they were both trembling. Breaking away, Xavier stared down into her eyes. "If we don't leave now, we will spend the entire weekend in this room."

"And the problem would be..." She trailed off with a side ward glance.

Giving her a crooked grin he took her hand as they walked out the door. "I want to show you a few things while you don't have my mind scrambled. You are a very sexually charged woman." He closed the door behind them.

They walked hand in hand in the opposite direction from the main house, toward a wooded trail. "I didn't used to be. My last boyfriend said I was a prude. All I ever did was work."

Xavier stopped.

Nicole had taken a step further when she turned to look up curiously. He was so fine, standing there dressed in jeans, a rust colored V-neck sweater with a crisp gold collar shirt against his mahogany dark skin. The expression on his face indicated he was thinking something through. "What is it?"

His thumb caressed the silky smooth fingers beneath it. "Boyfriends come and go." He looked at their entwined fingers. "I don't want to be a boyfriend. I want more. He pulled her to him, wrapped a hand around her waist, the other he used to gently touch her brow. "I want to be your lover, your friend. The man you think of when you open your eyes each morning and when you close your eyes at night. I want to be the man creeping through your dreams. I want to be the man on the receiving end of your adorable little gasp every time you come. I want to be the only man enjoying that sweet, salty, unique taste of you." He stopped as if cautioning himself. "I don't want to be your boyfriend. I want to be your man. The one you can't do without." He took a step back breaking all contact with her. "Cards on the table."

"Good card players don't show their hand."

"Never been good at playing games."

She wanted to let the emotions inside go, but if she did, there would be tears so she took a step back. "It's not a gasp, it's an exhale. A release of tension that has been building up inside of me since we saw each other across that room." She stepped back again. "As for taste, I haven't experienced the full taste of you, but I will before we leave here. As to the creeping, well..." A teasing smile appeared in her eyes. "Your body must be tired cause you been creeping through my mind ALL night long."

Xavier smiled as he took a step toward her. "That was a weak line."

She stepped backwards again. "I know and now that I have a man in my life, I don't have to hear the sad come on lines anymore." She looked away then back to him. "I'm a simple woman, contrary to what the media writes. Money doesn't stop the hurt or bleeding. There's no walking away when things get dicey." He took another step closer. "Being the man in my life isn't going to be easy. There will be my family, the money, the media and Nick."

He stopped in front of her. "None of that matters." He took her hand then kissed her knuckles. "Know why?"

"Why?"

He put her hand in the crook of his arm and began strolling again. "Because we have Sinergy."

Her smile brightened. "That may work on me Mr. Davenport. But you'd better come up with something better by Sunday."

"What's happening on Sunday?"

"Since you are now the man in my life, it's time you meet the family."

***

Trish walked off the plane into Hartford International Airport in Atlanta at 11:58. The first class plane ride was combined with a driver and car waiting to whisk her off to a two o'clock appointment with her new benefactor and attorney. Now that Xavier had made his position clear, she had no problem doing what was needed to secure her desired lifestyle. Thirty minutes later, the car was pulling into the underground parking at the executive offices of B7 Beats studios. Her curiosity peaked a little, but she really didn't care what the person's motives were, if it lined her pockets and brought Nicole Brooks down a notch or two, she was in.

The car stopped at a door marked 'Private'. A woman stood there. She was dressed in a canary yellow body dress, a pair of heels she would kill for and had a tablet in her hand stood to meet her.

"Good afternoon Ms. Hargrove. Your meeting is scheduled for two, however Mr. Cannon would like a few moments with you before the others come in. I'll take you to his office."

Scanning the hallways as they walked, Trish was impressed by the plush office surroundings. "Who exactly is Mr. Cannon?"

The woman stopped so abruptly, Trish almost ran into her. The woman grinned. "He's the man who makes everything happen." She pushed open the door to their left with her hip, knocked lightly, then stepped aside.

Trish walked into the office.

"Cannon, Ms. Hargrove." The woman left closing the door behind her.

A man, the size of a linebacker in the NFL stood behind the desk. He buttoned his suit jacket, the quality of which she knew was in the thousands, as he walked toward her with his hand extended.

"Ms. Hargrove, it's a pleasure to meet you in person." He shook her hand as he directed her to a chair. "Have a seat, please."

For a big man his voice was tender, his manner gracious and his smile genuine. "Mr. Cannon."

"Just Cannon," he said as he rounded the desk to reclaim his seat. "Thank you for seeing us on such short notice. The project we need you on is time sensitive. Once you agreed to assist us, I saw no reason to delay our meeting."

"Would you explain the project, my role and the compensation?"

He picked up a contract and gave it to her. "This is a confidentiality agreement. It's fairly clear cut," he said as she read. "You are not to discuss any information regarding this assignment. In return for your satisfactory cooperation, you will be compensated in the sum of two million dollars. If the desired outcome is reached, that figure will be doubled."

Trish read over the agreement. "All you want from me is information."

Cannon nodded. "We would like to also represent you in the pending case against Nicole Brooks, at our expense, of course."

"Very well." Trish signed the document. "What do you need to know?"

Cannon picked up the document, reviewed the signature, then handed her a cashier's check for one million dollars. "Tell me everything you know about Xavier Davenport."

"I thought this was about Nicole."

"Since your efforts to cause issues between the two seemed to have backfired, we now have to prepare a defense against her would be protector."

"That would be her family, Xavier barely knows her."

"You are defending a man who according to you, put you out of his home for that lesbian heifer? Hmmm. Shall we rethink this assignment?"

"No," Trish quickly replied. "No issue."

"Good. Shall we continue?"

Manhattan, New York
Friday Afternoon

Vernon had never enjoyed a plane ride as much as he enjoyed the one to New York with Taylor. The short forty-five minute trip was filled with his daughter's music. Not any of the songs she'd released or even had on paper. Just music in her mind and he loved every bit of it. Taylor was not only beautiful she was talented. With her intelligence she was going to give some man a fit.

He put the luggage in Nicole's first spare bedroom and began to unpack.

Taylor walked in eating ice cream. "What are you doing?"

"Unpacking."

"We never unpack ourselves, Mother always hires someone to do that."

Vernon eyed his daughter. He was not going to have a pampered princess as a daughter. He reached down, picked up her bag. "Come with me." Taylor followed him to the second bedroom. He placed the bag on the bed. "There are certain things you learn to do for yourself. Unpacking your own underwear is one."

Taylor looked appalled. "Daddy."

Vernon stopped at the door. "Taylor." He smiled as he left the room. Constance may have a sense of entitlement, but the Brooks' worked for a living. He shook his head. The last thing he wanted was his daughter to think the world owed her something she hadn't earned. The house phone rang.

"Brooks residence."

"You have a visitor, Mr. Brooks."

"We'll be right down," Vernon replied, then called out. "Taylor, time to go."

Taylor peeked out of the door. "Daddy do I have to fold these before they go into the dresser drawer?" The incredulous look on her father's face caused her to huff. "Hey, I've never done this before, what do you expect."

Vernon walked into the room, taking the top from her as he walked by. With patience she did not know her father possessed, he folded the top then placed it neatly in the drawer.

"You try it."

Taylor took another top, emulated what she'd seen, then smiled up at her father.

To him she looked like a little girl waiting for her father's approval. "Not bad." He kissed her temple, put his arm over her shoulder then walked out of the room. "When we come back I'm going to teach you how to wash clothes."

Taylor paused. "You are not serious."

Vernon stepped onto the elevator. "Are you serious about Columbia?"

"Yes, but what does that have to do with washing clothes?"

The elevator doors closed. "College students have to wash clothes at some point."

"Mother just sends them out."

"Clothes that have to go to the cleaners, yes, but not your underwear."

"Yes, the underwear too."

The look on Vernon's face must have been hilarious, for the moment Genesis Williams saw him she burst into laughter. "Having a father daughter moment?"

"Daddy, we have maids at the house. We don't wash clothes at the house."

"You are not going to have maids at Columbia."

"Why not?"

Genesis laughed again as they walked out of the building to the waiting sedan and driver. "Why not, Daddy?"

The driver opened the door allowing the threesome to climb inside. "You are not helping." He quickly glanced at Genesis."

"I don't understand why you raised me one way and now because I want to go to college you expect me to be somebody different. If you had wanted me to grow up knowing how to do laundry, you should have taught me."

Everyone was quiet for a moment. "Point taken," Vernon replied.

"I have no objections to learning, however, this is not going to be an overnight change. It took you twenty years to make me this way, it should take at least that long for me to break the habit." For the first time Taylor looked up at Genesis. "Hi, I'm Taylor, daughter to the father with no heart, who is throwing his daughter into battle unprepared."

"Forgive my child." Vernon turned to Genesis. "She's not usually this unruly."

"She's a mini you. Has an argument for everything a person has to say. I take it the trip to Columbia means you are going to law school?"

"That's the plan unless father dearest is planning to ship me somewhere to milk a cow or something." Taylor smirked and looked out the window.

"Driver, pull the car over."

The driver did as requested.

Taylor began to laugh. "Daddy, what are you doing?"

Vernon tipped the driver, as Taylor and Genesis stepped out of the vehicle.

"Daddy is going to prepare you for the battle."

Being off the job didn't diminish the skills used to detect trouble. Being with the FBI for the past five years, Genesis had learned to see what normal eyes missed. Such as the taxi that suddenly stopped when they pulled over. Or the man who casually stepped out of the taxi, who was now acting preoccupied, but keeping an eye on them. The question in Genesis' mind was, which one of them was he following? Vernon? Taylor? Or, her?

"We're going to walk to the campus. No time like the present to learn to walk with the common folk, princess." Vernon tilted his head.

Taylor did the same, but she had no retort. She took her father's hand and smiled like a kid in a candy store.

"Do you mind?" Vernon looked over his shoulder as Taylor pulled him along.

"Not at all. I prefer it," she said. In her mind Genesis was thinking it gave her an opportunity to determine what or who the man was after.

An hour later, Vernon and Genesis sat on the steps outside a building on campus as Taylor browsed the bookstore. They each had a bottle of water as they talked.

"Why did you leave the agency after fighting so hard to get in?" Vernon asked.

"The plan wasn't to stay at the agency forever."

"Yeah, but five years, I would have expected at least ten."

Genesis shrugged. "You get burned out."

"Not you, Genesis. It's in your blood."

"You asked me to meet you here to discuss my career choices?"

"No. You keep your own counsel, you always have."

"Thank you, I think. So, what's up?"

"I met someone. She sparked my interest in a way..." He shook his head unable to explain. "It felt like a bolt of lightning."

"The great untouchable Vernon Brooks, you are blushing." Genesis laughed. "Must be a hell of a woman to capture that brain of yours."

"You captured me."

Genesis looked away as she replied, "I was a hell of a woman."

"You still are." They held each other's gaze for a long moment.

"That was a long time ago." She broke the contact. "Why are you traveling backwards?"

"It was fun. I was full of life then. I haven't felt that free in years. Until yesterday."

"You've been rather tense since you married Connie," Genesis smirked.

"She was carrying my child. I wasn't going to give that up for anything."

"I'm the person you don't have to remind." Genesis exhaled. "She's a beautiful young woman. I love the way she handles you."

"I can't be handled."

Genesis laughed. "You are delusional."

Vernon laughed. "Yeah, she got me." He hesitated. "I'm going to divorce her."

Genesis did not reply.

"I look at my parents and all they have endured, especially with me. I used to wonder how they made it through. Then I see James and his wife and the answer finally hit me. They married for love. That gave them that foundation to make it through the hard times."

"I'm not sure that's the right conclusion."

"Because we didn't make it?"

"No," she replied a little too quickly, but recovered just as fast. "We were young, had no idea what in the hell we were doing. You were with Connie, I was with butthole."

They both laughed. "Have you ever called that man by his right name?"

"You mean his birth name? No." She smiled, then sobered. "Vernon, life is a funny thing. You have to grab the moments. Few people get do-overs." She held his eyes. "If you found someone who makes you tingle inside, grab her and don't let go."

"Getting sentimental in your old age?"

"No." Genesis grinned. "Realistic."

He hesitated. "She's someone you know."

"I know. She called me yesterday inquiring about you."

Vernon sat up from his slouching position. "What did she say?"

Genesis grinned. "Look at you acting like a high school teenager, all inquisitive and everything."

"Don't play with me, Genesis. What did she ask? Did you tell her about us?"

"No. Rene wouldn't give you the time of day if she thought it would cause a rift in our team. I have to say, until this moment, I was debating on my response to the thought of you and Naverone."

"And."

"I love both of you. If any woman could tame you, it's Naverone. I'm cool with it. At some point you are going to have to tell her about us. If you don't, I will. Clear?"

"Clear."

Genesis turned to see Taylor walking toward them with a bag in her hand. She smiled. "Question, before your daughter reaches us."

"Sure."

"Why is she being followed?"

Charlottesville, VA
Friday Evening

They had barely made it through the first course of dinner when the urge to touch her consumed him. They left the restaurant and returned to the cottage before the main course was served. Mrs. Leigh had the meal wrapped and sent to them.

Hours later, Xavier stood at the window of the cottage taking in the majestic view of the mountains at night. It did seem the top touched heaven. If he were a rich man, he would buy property in the area and build a private retreat for him and Nicole to visit every year. The thought caused him a moment's pause. He was thinking in future terms with a woman he only met a week ago. He ran his hands through his braids as he exhaled. There was no reason he couldn't do exactly what he was thinking. Thanks to his uncles, Royce and Grayson Davenport, he had invested well. Following their leads had made him comfortable financially. Not to Nicole's level, but then few people were. Building a retreat for them was well within his means. The question was whether he was ready for the long-term commitment.

Unlike Nicole's parents, his could not provide him with an example of how to do long term. His parents were not the model for long-term relationships. Zack and Diamond were only two years in. Less for his Uncle Royce and Shelly, who married a little over a year ago. His Uncle Grayson was still playing the field. There was his friend Grant's parents, who were the weirdest of them all. They had been separated for as long as he had known Grant, but neither had filed for divorce. Anytime they needed something, the other was right there helping. Whenever Mr. Hutchinson had events at his home, Mrs. Hutchinson acted as hostess and he did the same for her. It seemed to be one of the happiest relationships he had ever witnessed. Yet they slept under different roofs. Hell he couldn't even imagine not having Nicole in his bed after the last two nights. He glanced up at the loft where she was asleep. His body was yearning to be with her now, but after two nights of round the clock lovemaking, he knew she needed to sleep. What in the hell had gotten into him? He had just concluded he'd officially lost his mind, when from the corner of his eye he saw a movement outside.

Not moving, he kept his eyes on the area. After a few seconds he started to turn away thinking it was his imagination, but then he saw it again. There was someone outside their cottage. It was three o'clock in the morning. There was no reason anyone would be in the area. Their cottage was the only one down that end. It startled him for a second, then he thought, the media. They must have found their cottage. As long as they kept their distance he didn't care. He turned, walked back up the stairs to the loft, gathered Nicole in his arms, closed his eyes and prayed his erection would not wake her up.

Chapter 14

Charlottesville, VA
Saturday

Nicole stretched enjoying the warmth of the comforter over her. Something was missing. Her hands spread over the area next to her. It was empty. She sat up and inhaled the wonderful aroma coming from downstairs. Standing, she ran her fingers through her hair as she walked over to the railing.

"This is what I call enticing, a man cooking early in the morning."

"Good morning, beautiful," Xavier beamed from the kitchen. "Coffee's hot." He took a sip.

"I'll be right down." Nicole quickly jumped in the shower, washed her face and brushed her teeth. When she entered the kitchen area, the table was covered with fresh fruit, waffles, and bacon. Xavier was at the counter top cracking eggs into a bowl.

Dressed in a tee-shirt, she walked up behind him, wrapped her arms around his waist and let her hands splay across his chest. She planted a kiss between his shoulder blades, then rested her head there. "What are you cooking now?"

"Omelets with a little salsa for the spicy woman who shared the bed with me last night."

"How spicy was she?"

He reached back and pulled her in front of him, her back to the counter and kissed her. "So spicy, I'm still sizzling." He rocked against her as he whipped all the ingredients in the bowl.

"How can I help?"

"You can cook tomorrow. This one is on me."

She slipped under his arm, as he poured the mixture into the pan. "I'll get some juice to cool you off."

"Juice will help, darling, but it will not douse the heat you generate."

"Smooth talker." She smiled as she poured juice into the glasses on the table.

"Where did you learn how to cook?" she asked after taking a seat at the table and biting into a slice of bacon.

"Zack. Survival was paramount in our house. So everyone had to learn to fend for themselves. Zack made sure I knew the basics so I wouldn't burn down the house." He added a generous amount of cheese to the omelet, then neatly folded it in half. After a few moments the omelet slid easily from the pan onto a plate. He then cut it in half, sharing it with her.

"Smells delicious," she said as he filled their plates.

"I have to keep your stamina up, we have another night to explore."

The crooked smile he sent her way caused involuntary reactions from her body. "You keep looking at me like that and we're not going to make it through breakfast."

"Eat." He winked at her. "There is a method to my madness. I feed you, then wear you out. It keeps you healthy and happy."

"If all the men in my life would be as thoughtful, I'd be a happy woman."

"Hmmm." He watched her take a bite into the omelet and savored the expression on her face. "Tell me about this London deal that has you stressed out."

"Whew, I don't want to talk business. Especially that deal. I can't believe I screwed it up."

"From the little I know about it, I don't see where it's screwed. You want to design a community in London with all the amenities of city living. The designer is not cooperating in the manner you'd like. It's your project, why not take control?"

"It's not quite that simple. See the rule of thumb is never use your own money for business deals. I broke that rule. I allowed emotions to cloud my judgment."

"How so?"

She stopped eating and looked up at him. "It was petty. I wanted to show Hayward Ellington that I could play with the big boys."

"The real estate mogul of the world and you wanted to show him up." He grinned. "Ambitious."

"Go big or stay home." She smiled. "Brooks' has properties all over the world, however, we have never developed any of it from beginning to end. I wanted to put the Brooks name in that international category."

"Have you done it here, in the United States?"

"No." She began eating again.

"Why not? Is there some significance to establishing Brooks in development internationally?"

"Not really."

"You wanted to go big." She nodded. "Your mistake wasn't emotions. There is nothing wrong with having a goal, even a big one. Your mistake was allowing Ellington to take you out of your game. Rethink your position. You own the land designated for the London deal, right?"

"Yes."

"Well, they can't do the project without the land."

"Ellington is trying to." She shrugged her shoulders. "In reality, he would have to purchase the land from me or find another property."

"This was your concept, right."

She nodded. "Yes."

"It seems one of the reasons Ellington is fighting this project with vigor is because you are pushing it so hard. What do you think Ellington's reaction will be if you step back and stop pushing this plan?"

"Let the project sit?"

"Work on something else. Do a development project here, in the United States. I know for a fact there are abandoned properties all over the city of Richmond that could stand for a good revitalization. A completed project here will put you in a better position for an international deal next year."

She thought about that for a moment. "A lot comes along with the name Ellington on a project."

"Are you saying it doesn't with the Brooks' name? If that's the case this could be an opportunity for you to change that. Are you saying a project would not succeed without Ellington's name on it?"

"No, it just brings in top level investors." She shrugged her shoulders. "It would take finding property, assessing the area's needs, determining if the land can get the proper zoning."

"Minor obstacles," he shrugged. "I kind of like the idea of seeing Nicole Brooks on a building. NB all the way, from beginning to end."

Xavier pushed his plate aside, took her hand and walked to the overstuffed chair next to the fireplace. He grabbed his pad along the way and pulled her onto his lap. "Tell me your vision."

She snuggled next to him.

"Who do you imagine living there?"

"Newly married couples who still want to enjoy the night life. Singles who want a safe environment to live. Young couples with one or two children."

"Sounds like you need a combination of one, two, and three bedroom condos. You need daycare, a play area for the children." He began drawing. "Shopping, both grocery and boutiques for the women, maybe a sports complex of some kind for the men, restaurants, night clubs, a bistro or two and a church for those single, or living in sin couples who want to tie the knot?" He looked down at her and grinned. "You will need schools, elementary, middle and high school. Maybe even a small community college that offers workforce development."

"It would take substantial land to do all of this."

Xavier thought for a moment, looking out at the mountain top. "You know, I have this property near the waterfront, a little distance from the city. Grant, that's a friend of mine, talked about doing something with the property that will build up that area of the city."

"How much land is it?"

"About forty acres with a stream running through it that connects to the river." He turned back to her. "It could be a perfect location for this. Or we could check out locations in Brooklyn."

"Or the Bronx near Yankee stadium."

"You like baseball?"

"It's the American way. Baseball and apple pie, right."

"You are the weirdest rich woman I have ever met." He kissed her nose and continued drawing. They stayed in that position for hours making plans for the project and subconsciously for themselves too.

The scene was magical, with the fireplace lit in the background. The couple curled up in a single chair oblivious to their surroundings. Outside a light trickle of snow began to fall. The only contrast to the romantic scene was the man behind a tree with a long lens camera invading their private moment.

Atlanta, GA
Saturday

Most executives worked Monday through Friday and spent their Saturdays on a golf course making more deals. Not Cannon, this was a working day for him. He'd held meetings for several hours straight. Now, in the late hours of the evening, he sat at his desk reviewing all the reports submitted by his team. A decision had to be made and it was his job to deliver the best option for success to Mr. Singleton.

One lesson Cannon learned early was never let the right hand know what the left hand was doing. With this in mind, none of the people involved in this project were privy to each other or the ultimate goal. Monday, he had to meet with the man, one on one, to determine the best course of action to take.

His meeting with Trish Hargrove revealed interesting tidbits on Nicole. He believed a lively public court case against the legendary family of lawyers would be the easiest way to sensationalize. Money and sex always peaked the media's curiosity. They would use the 'public has a right to know' angle and the media would feed on the case day to day. That would keep the Brooks name in the paper in a somewhat negative light.

Another option was to go at Nicole Brooks with the land deal in London. With Ellington's help they could plant evidence that the funds from her purchase of the property were connected to terrorism. That area was a hot spot for that type of activity and it would be easy to get the rumor started. Hence keeping the Brooks name negatively in the news cycle for days. This option would pull in James Brooks and his connection to the White House. That could bring in a level of investigation from the FBI he did not want his employer to endure. Using Nicole Brooks brought in the unknown entity, Xavier Davenport. Could the man be brought?

Vernon Brooks brought another element of danger to the table. He was volatile, unpredictable when riled. The man should know this better than anyone. Messing with the man's wife was one thing, bringing his daughter into the mix was a colossal mistake, in Cannon's opinion. Using Nail was dangerous. The man was a two bit punk with no boundaries. They could only pray he hadn't done something stupid with Taylor Brooks that would bring the wrath of Vernon Brooks on them all.

From what he'd learned about this family, they were sophisticated, but ruthless as hell when it came to their own. Why Singleton had targeted them, Cannon wasn't sure, all he could do was pray like hell Singleton knew what he was doing.

"When they told me Lawrence Cannonball McNally was the exec at B7 Beats, I said nooooo, not my Cannonball. I walk through the doors and who do I see? Cannon."

Cannon sat back from his desk to appreciate the unique combination of beauty, brains and balls of Rene Naverone leaning against the entrance to his office.

"I've died and gone to heaven." He placed his hand over his heart. "Be still my heart."

The stride she took to his desk was meant to mystify and it did. Cannon watched every step those spike heel boots, with the long shapely legs took, until they reached his desk, sat and crossed within his reach. "You're killing me, Naverone." He kissed her knee. "Whatever you want is yours."

"There's no challenge in that Cannon. I haven't even begged you yet."

"I'm cutting my losses early," he said as he moved some papers from under her nice behind.

Naverone looked back over her shoulder as she sat forward to allow him to pull the papers from under her. She caught the name Brooks, but it wasn't Taylor. It was Nicole. She made a mental note of the information, as he put the papers away.

"Since you are the man here at B7-" she played with his tie, "-would you give me an intro to Nail?"

"Nail?" The request caught him off guard.

"Yes, Nail," she said with a bit of sassiness.

"You are way out of his league. You know it and so do I. So what gives?"

"I need a meet for a client. One of my boys wants to meet some chick named Lil Tay. Said if something's happening with her and Nail he wants to know before he goes that way."

Cannon hesitated, then moved away from his desk, standing with his legs braced and arms folded. "Who's your client?"

Naverone stood. "You taking a battle stance with me, Cannon?"

"Never, you know that."

"Looks like it to me." She shrugged taking a step towards the door. "You can't help, okay. I'll find another way. I always do."

"I can't give you this one, Naverone."

"Yes, you can, Cannon. Connections are our business. You know that. Clients, they come and go. Our bond is in blood, man, that's forever." She stood there in a purple thigh high dress that held her body so tight you would think it was a glove.

"Who's your client?"

"A basketball player. He ran into her at some club here in Atlanta the last time he was there. Got the hots for her. So after you get me in with Nail I might need an invite to her for my client."

They stared at each other a long hard moment, before Cannon pulled a card from his pocket, wrote something on the back then gave it to her. Naverone looked at the address on the back of the card, smiled, then kissed him on the cheek. "Thank you, Cannon." She turned and walked out.

He watched the doorway for a long time after she left and knew without a doubt his client's plans were in trouble.

Charlottesville, VA
Saturday Night

They were enjoying the nightlife in Charlottesville at a club that had line dancing, with cowboy hats and all. They were doing the country western thing and loving every minute of it. Xavier looked good with his braids hanging beneath the hat, his polo shirt, and jeans hugging his behind. Nicole was doing all she could to keep up with the two-step everyone was doing. But not Xavier, he took to it as if it was second nature. He was doing the dosey-doeing and swinging her around like he had lost his mind. And she must be just as crazy, because she was laughing and enjoying every minute of it. A slow song hit the speakers and without skipping a beat, Xavier eased her into his arms and began swaying to the rhythm of the music. She heard him exhale and it felt good. He felt good. He felt right.

"I'm keeping you, Nicole Brooks." He whispered in her ear.

"Is that right?"

"Yes," he replied as they listened to the Whispers sing, '*I'm going to make you my wife, you're my everything, all my hopes and dreams come true. I can spend my life with you.*'

He held her tight as they listened to the words of the song while moving to the rhythm. Each allowing the reality of what was happening to them to sink in.

When the song ended, Xavier sat Nicole at a table then went to the bar to get drinks. There were a few couples at the bar. At the end was a man sitting alone drinking. Xavier stood between the last set of couples, putting the man on his left. He placed his order with the bartender and put two twenties on the bar.

"Refill my man here." He nodded, then turned to the man when the bartender walked away. "Is there something I can help you with?"

The man looked around as if to see who he was talking to. Xavier grinned. "You've been following us for two days. You're either with the media, a blogger, or what, I don't know. I really don't care. Keep your distance from me and the lady and you and I will not have a problem."

"Man, I'm just sitting here having a drink."

The bartender returned with the drinks. Xavier picked his drinks up. "Come near us and it will be the last drink you will have. Have a good evening." He nodded and walked away.

He placed the drinks on the table as Nicole spoke. "Do you know that man?"

Xavier looked over his shoulder. "No."

"Your feathers seem to be a little ruffled."

He had to smile at the realization that she was that in-tune with him. He kissed her lips. "My feathers are always ruffled when I'm around you."

"That was smooth, Mr. Davenport. Now, take me back to the cottage and make love to me until I can't move."

That crooked grin appeared, as he took her hand to stand. "Your wish is my command." As they left the club, the crowd, a mixture of college students from the university and young adults, dancing, drinking and enjoying the weekend, was growing. He looked around and did not see the man who had been following them. There was something about the man that did not register media. Maybe it was the outline of the gun under his jacket.

It was late October. The air was cold in the mountains, but neither of them seemed to mind. Hand in hand they were in their own world strolling to the cottage, anticipation building to the moment when they could once again bring the other to an heightened awareness of that feeling they called sinergy.

"Do you believe what we are experiencing is normal?"

Xavier smiled as he entwined his fingers with hers. "No and yes. People refer to it as love at first sight, finding your soul mate. It's that feeling you get when words aren't necessary. That gut feeling we got when we first saw each other, you knew and so did I. We saw each other across the room and knew what we each wanted. Even when we were at odds the other day, neither of us pushed the other away. The calmness we felt when we touched, it was instant." They walked a few moments in silence.

"I can work from anywhere." Nicole tilted her head towards the sky. "I will have to keep an office in New

York, but I can move the northern Virginia office to Fredericksburg or Richmond."

He brought her hand up to his lips, opened her palm and kissed it. "You would do that for me?"

They stopped. "I would move heaven and earth for you."

The sincerity in her eyes cut through to his heart. This was the woman, the one who tilted the axis of his universe. He felt it rocking back and forth on the edge. Either way it rolled they were going to win. What did he ever do to deserve this...to deserve her? He ran his fingers through her hair, cupped her neck, then bent until his lips touched hers. "Sinergy."

"Sinergy," she giggled.

The kiss was sweet, sensuous and branding, as tongues swirled, touching every corner, doing the tango their bodies had perfected. His hands cupped her face between them, as his thumbs caressed her cheeks. "I'm keeping you." He kissed her nose. How do you think your parents will react to all of this?"

They began walking again, swinging arms, smiling like children. "The suddenness of it will throw them for a moment. Then they will see how elated I am and won't care. What about your mother?"

Xavier laughed. "As long as you are not Trish she won't care."

Nicole stopped. "What are we going to do about Trish?"

He pulled her forward. "Be happy, she is out of our lives."

"But she's not." Nicole stopped before entering the cottage. "People like Trish don't stop until you make her. What you did the other night, believe me, it only energized her to do something else. That's how she operates."

Xavier opened the door, picked Nicole up in his arms and walked her over the threshold. He kicked the door closed behind him as Nicole giggled. "The drama of Trish ended when that door closed. She's outside, we're in here. Now, what are you going to do to make up for the last five minutes you took from my weekend to discuss another woman?"

With her arms wrapped around his neck, she kissed his cheek. "I guess I have to find a way to make you forget."

"It's going to take a lot more than a kiss on the cheek," Xavier warned.

"Really?" She kissed him behind the ear, then nibbled on his earlobe. "What if I undress you with my mouth, kiss every inch of your body, then ravish you until you scream?"

He carried her over by the fireplace, which was lit, putting a glow on the room. "I have another idea." He peeled her leather jacket off, dropping it to the floor. "To show you how forgiving I am-" he pulled off her boots, "-I'm treating you tonight." Next he pulled her sweater over her head, leaving her standing there in tight jeans and a black lace bra. Xavier dropped to his knees, then pulled her to him. The first kiss landed on her navel, as his hand unzipped her jeans. His tongue dipped into the crevice of her navel. His hands traveled inside the back of the jeans, then down the back of her thighs as the material uncovered her, revealing black lace panties.

He sat back on his haunches and slowly took in her body from head to toe. He pulled the blanket from the back of the chair, and spread it out on the floor in front of the fire, which crackled in the background. He placed one arm around her waist and the other under her knees, then placed her gently on the blanket. Standing above her he slowly began to undress. The jacket was thrown to the side. His sweater was next, revealing each ripple of his six-pack, one at a time. The sweater was thrown to the side pulling his braids, causing them to cascade around his broad shoulders. Then he unzipped his jeans, stepped out leaving his arousal standing proud and erect. His dreamy brown eyes held hers as he took a single red rose from the vase above the fireplace. "Welcome into my dream Nicole Brooks."

With the bud of the rose, he drew a straight line from the tip of her nose, down her cheek, between her breasts, down her stomach, between her legs, down her thighs, then tickled the bottoms of her feet. "Allow me to introduce you to my fantasy."

Taking the rose petals from the stem, one by one, he dropped them onto her body, until the sweet fragrance filled his nostrils. He knelt between her legs and was overwhelmed by the mixture of her scent and the roses. He stretched out on the floor between her legs. "You know, one of the most sensuous things about a woman is her unique scent." He pulled her pants down her legs. "Your scent sends my testosterone into overdrive." He licked his fore finger then touched her bud. Her body jerked. "Sensitive. I like that." His long, thick finger dipped inside of her. He pulled it out, then sucked it. "You are so sweet." Spreading her legs, he held her thighs down, licked her from top to bottom then dove in. His hand massaged her inner thigh as he gave her the tongue lashing, he hoped, of her life.

Nicole couldn't believe the sensations the rose petals were having against her skin. It felt as if she had been blanketed with silk. As each petal dropped Xavier's eyes darkened. Was it the feel of the petals or the look of pure desire in his eyes that was causing her body to react as if she had been caressed? She didn't know. Then his wet finger touched her and the blood began to pump furiously throughout her body. When he replaced his finger with his tongue, lavishing her, all senses flared to attention, relieving her of all control. Blood whooshed through her mind as if she were in a wind tunnel. Everything went blank for seconds, then slowly returned.

Xavier lay there on his elbows watching her body react to his assault. He decided then and there, nothing was more beautiful than Nicole when her body exploded...nothing.

Reaching for his jeans, he pulled out a condom, slid it on then braced his arms on both sides of her easing into her pulsating inner lips. No other part of their bodies touched as he withdrew, then eased in again. Looking down at her, he knew there would never be anyone else for him.

Chapter 15

McLean, VA
Sunday

"So, you are the man who has turned Nicole's life upside down." Gwen smiled as she hugged Xavier. "My, your picture does you no justice."

"Guilty," Xavier replied with a smile, "and thank you, Mrs. Brooks."

"I see it a little differently from my wife, Davenport." Avery shook his hand as they stood in the foyer of the Brooks' home. "You're the person who is causing havoc at Brooks International."

"More than you know, Daddy." Nicole kissed her father on his cheek.

Avery gave his daughter a side-ways glance. He had never seen her blush so. "Yeah, well, you're welcome to dinner anyway."

"Pay Daddy no mind." Nicole took Xavier by the hand. "This is my brother, James and his wife Ashley."

"Hello, James, Ashley, it's good to see you again."

"Hello Xavier." James shook his hand. "Please tell the Lassiters hello from us."

"I'd be happy to."

"This beautiful creature is..."

"Lil Tay, I'm a fan."

"Taylor, and I'm a bigger fan now that I've seen you in person."

"Hey, pop star, back off this one." Nicole walked between the two pulling Xavier along laughing.

"You've already met Vernon," Nicole said as she whisked by him and stopped at her twin brother. "This is my other half, Nick. Nick, meet Xavier." She watched as the two assessed each other. For her, this was the test. Not her father or her mother. Nick was the test Xavier had to pass. In so many ways Xavier reminded her of her brother. They were both very intelligent. However, neither of them flaunted it. They did what came naturally, never taking their place at the mic to talk about their accomplishments. Nicole loved her brother so much there were times she felt as if she could not breathe without him in her life. Xavier was quickly surpassing that benchmark.

"I've heard a lot about you, Nick."

"Same here, Xavier," Nick shook his hand. "We should make it a point to get to know each other."

"I agree."

Gwen held on to her husband's arm as they watched Nicole parade Xavier around the family. "Look at her," Gwen said to her husband. "She is beaming."

"Davenport's smile isn't too dull either, my dear." Avery patted his wife's hand. "I have a feeling this is going to be an interesting night."

Nicole's smile could have lit the entire room as she introduced Xavier to her family. "Let's have a seat until dinner is ready." The couple sat on the sofa. Xavier placed his arm around Nicole's shoulders as she crossed her legs and snuggled next to him.

Gwen and Avery glanced at each other, observing the unusual behavior of their daughter. "Tell us about yourself, Davenport."

"Not much to tell. My brother and I have a development company in Richmond. We build communities for low income families."

"The homes are beautiful," Ashley stated. "We attended the ground breaking ceremony for Davenport Estates."

"Very impressive," James added. "Just about every home site was sold at that event."

"Davenport Estates." Avery thought for a moment. "Was it selected as the best designed community a few years ago?"

"Yes, sir. It was," Xavier replied.

"You should see the plans Xavier is designing for a community center in a low income area of Richmond. It looks like a country club we would pay thousands to be a member of," Nicole boasted.

Xavier smiled down at her. "We want to ensure the families who have to use the center know their children are in a well maintained, safe environment."

"That's not all, Poppa. You should see what he designed for the London project."

"The London project? What happened to Allen and Allen?"

"They tabled the project since I refused to declare my sexual preference publicly."

"When did this happen?" Avery sat up.

"Thursday at the board meeting," Nicole explained. "If they want to jeopardize a billion dollar deal, let them. I have a perfect design ready to present to the partners in London. And-" she smiled at Xavier, "-we have a design for a project state side as well. I want to get your take on it before we present it to the board."

"I would think so," Vernon stated. "Nothing against you, Davenport, but we can't have a project of this magnitude riding on your talent as a good lay."

"Vernon," Gwen exclaimed.

"Mother, that's about all we have to go on at this point."

"How did he know I was a good lay?" Xavier asked Nicole with a grin.

"I don't know." Nicole looked. "Vernon?"

Nick and James laughed.

"At least you have your lawsuit against Trish won," Taylor said.

"How so?" Nicole asked.

"You just spent the weekend with a man," Vernon declared as he took a drink.

"It will come up in court."

"Is that why you slept with him Nicole?" Constance asked.

"Dinner is ready, Mr. Brooks." The cook said from the doorway.

"Thank goodness," Gwen said as they stood.

"We have an interesting family, Mr. Davenport," Avery stated. "We would like to be graceful hosts. However, every now and then we slip." He gave Constance a stern look as they walked by.

"I'm sure there will be many questions before the evening ends, Mr. Brooks. I welcome them." Xavier winked at Nicole as they followed the family into the dining room, walking hand in hand.

Once seated, and grace was said, Vernon took over the conversation.

"Tell us about your relationship with Trish Hargrove." Vernon sat back with a smirk.

James and Ashley glanced at each other and began laughing. Years ago it was Ashley who was in the hot seat being interrogated by Vernon.

"I fail to see the humor in my inquiry." Vernon raised an eyebrow.

"You would," James laughed. "Haven't you learned, once a Brooks decides who is going to be in their life, your tactics are not going to change their minds."

"Honey." Ashley touched James' arm. "I want to hear Xavier put Vernon in his place. Hush." She pointed her fork. "Go ahead, Xavier, give it to him."

Xavier held Vernon's glare. "My personal life is shared on a need to know basis. As Nicole's brother, you may need to know about her life. As for me, I have no intentions of sleeping with you, therefore I see no need to share my sex life with you."

"Hmmm." Nick nodded his head. "A point for X-man over here. What you got, Vernon?" He grinned at his oldest brother.

"It's what do you have, Vernon," Gwen corrected.

"No, Mother. This is a street fight. It's what you got."

"Street or not," Avery chimed in. "You don't have to answer those types of questions unless I ask them." Avery sat up. "The Hargrove girl is the least of my concerns. Although I pray you have no plans to sleep with Vernon. We've had enough of that in this family." Several occupants of the table choked on that statement.

Even Vernon ducked his head to laugh. "Am I the only person who takes new members to this family seriously?"

Gwen patted his hand. "No, darling, we all care. We just don't ask asinine questions like you. I have one daughter." Gwen looked at Xavier. "What I need to know is, what are your intentions? Before you answer I want to qualify my question. This is the first time Nicole has ever brought anyone to this table. It is clear to us you have captured her interest in a short period of time. You don't have to answer my question at this moment. At some point, I expect an answer."

"Mrs. Brooks." Xavier put his fork down. "At some point tonight I would like to speak with you and Mr. Brooks on that very topic."

"We're all family." Nick grinned. "You can talk to all of us now."

Vernon's cell phone chimed.

Nick laughed. "Saved by the bell."

"Vernon, you know we don't take calls at the dinner table."

Vernon was looking at the message he'd received. "I have to take this, excuse me."

"As you were saying, X-man." Nick nodded with a bit of teasing in his grin.

Xavier had to grin, he knew the game Nick was playing. "Why do you call me X-man?"

Nick thought for a moment, then shrugged his shoulder. "I have no idea, it seemed to fit."

Xavier nodded acknowledging the reason. "My plan is to get your parents' permission to see Nicole. If they agree, in a reasonable amount of time, I plan to ask for her hand in marriage. If they don't agree, I'm going to give them six months to get over it and then marry her anyway. If she'll have me." He grinned looking at Nick. "Which she already has."

Avery and Gwen shared a glance with each other. "Well, now," Avery replied. "I'll have to see what you have to say before I give you my only daughter."

"Oh, Poppa," Taylor laughed. "You might as well give your blessing here and now. The heat between these two is so hot they are sizzling over here."

Nicole touched Xavier's arm with her finger. "Ouch, hot, sizzling." She laughed as he kissed the tip of her nose.

Vernon returned to the table, attitude apparent. "Connie, Taylor, I need to speak with you in private."

"We're in the middle of dinner," Gwen stated. "Surely it can wait."

"No, Mother, it can't. Constance, Taylor." Vernon walked towards the stairs.

Taylor glanced at her grandfather. He nodded. "Go ahead. It'll be all right." He patted his granddaughter's hand.

"What did you tell your father?" Constance snapped at Taylor.

"I did not tell him anything, Mother. Maybe it's time one of us did." Taylor turned following her father.

"Constance," Avery called as she began to walk away. "Don't fight him on this."

"I have no idea what you are talking about, Avery."

"You will."

Constance held his glare then turned and walked away.

"What's the problem Pop?" James asked.

"Vernon will have to share that with you." Avery replied then looked down the table at his daughter. She was in love. It was evident in the glances the two shared, the way they touched and finished each other's sentences. They were oblivious to everything else going on in the room. He looked up at his wife and saw her smiling at the couple as they chatted away.

While one couple was reveling in their new relationship, another couple upstairs was coming to the end of one. "I want to know exactly what happened with Nail," Vernon demanded.

"It was nothing more than a misunderstanding," Constance replied as she gave Taylor a warning glare.

"I'm asking Taylor."

"Taylor." Constance held her daughter's gaze. "Tell your father it was nothing."

This was what Taylor was trying to avoid. She did not want to tell her father about Nail or that her mother did nothing when she told her what happened. Their marriage was fragile. She did not want to be the cause of the divide growing.

"Taylor, nothing you say will change things between your mother and me." Vernon could see the indecision in his daughter's eyes. "I want to know what that man did to you."

"Vernon, you are making it sound like he raped her or something. It wasn't anything like that."

The lethal, cool voice combined with the ice cold stare from Vernon chilled the room. "I will have your body disassembled and distributed across the Potomac River if you speak one more time."

"Do you see how your father is, Taylor? He just threatened me, did you hear that?"

"Daddy, please," Taylor cried out, torn between her mother and her father. "It wasn't bad, not really."

Vernon gathered his daughter in his arms. Kissed her temple. "It's all right, baby." He held her tight. "Did he touch you?"

"Yes."

"Taylor," Constance called out in warning.

"Mother, please, stop." Taylor broke away from her father. "I can't keep doing this with you and Daddy. I love both of you. But what Nail did was wrong. It was wrong and I think somewhere deep down you know it was to." She wiped a tear from her cheek. "Daddy, we were on set doing a love scene. I was dressed in a sexy outfit. He got carried away and began fingering me during the scene. I tried to get up, but they were still filming and his body was heavy. He knew what he was doing. He kept saying 'the camera is on, baby girl, we got to make it look real.' Even when the director said cut, he kept doing it." She looked at her father, ashamed. "I tried to get up Daddy, I did. I didn't want him doing that. I don't even like him like that. I told mother" Taylor wiped a tear away. "She said it was no big deal. Things like that happen when a man gets excited. Like I didn't have the sense to know when a man has crossed the line."

It took every ounce of his will to keep his expression soft, not murderous like he was feeling on the inside. He walked over to his daughter, and allowed her to cry on his shoulder. As he held and comforted her, his deadly glare landed and held on Constance. "Don't ever take my daughter around that man again." He didn't say anything more as Constance stood, then walked into the bedroom.

Hours later, Avery was in bed with this wife in his arms. The day had indeed been eventful. "We're going to be giving her away one day soon."

Gwen smiled against his chest. "I like him. He's good for her."

"Well, the real test is going to come when the media gets wind of their relationship. Constance's question is going to come up again, you better believe that."

"Don't mention her right now. I'm so angry I could shoot her myself."

"It's hard enough trying to keep Vernon from killing her, don't you add to the mix."

"How could she stand by and allow that man to violate her daughter in that way? How could she? I have a mind to show her how a real mother would act."

"She's going to have enough on her hands dealing with Vernon." Avery sighed. "As for our daughter, you know I have to have the man investigated."

Gwen sat up. "You will do no such thing, Avery Brooks. You let those children be and I mean that. If there is something out there on him, let Nicole find out on her own."

"It's my job to protect her. But I have to say, he is an impressive young man. Did you see the details in that design for the London project? Hell, if Nicole decides to go with the plan he just saved a billion dollar project."

Gwen settled back into her husband's arms. "Hell, next the blogger will say Nicole is with him for his designs.

Chapter 16

Richmond, VA
Monday

The morning began with him making love to Nicole then saying good bye as she flew to New York. Once at the office he made remarkable progress on the designs for the recreation center. Now that the funding was in place, he could design the center he wanted for that community. He held several meetings with clients and was in the process of returning calls when Diamond stepped into his office.

"Okay." She sat in the chair in front of his desk and crossed her legs. "I don't want to be nosy or anything, but...."

Xavier grinned. "Yes, we had a great time. And yes, you should get used to seeing Nicole around."

Diamond pulled her cell phone from her pocket. "Did you hear that?"

"You owe me twenty dollars," Ann's voice boasted through the speakers. "I told you she was the one."

"Yeah, yeah. I owe you." Diamond smiled. "This is worth it. You should see the look of contentment on your son's face right now."

"You and my mother took bets on me?"

"Yes, along with your brother and that Reese boy," Ann laughed. "I'm hanging up now." Diamond disconnected the call. "Well, Mr. Davenport. What do you have to say for yourself?"

In the past, when Diamond asked that question, Xavier usually had to explain why a particular girl wasn't worth his time. This time he had no problem expressing his thoughts. "I could make love to the woman twenty-four hours a day and it would not be enough. It will never be enough."

"Awe, Xavier, I'm so happy for you. I could feel the heat between the two of you. So what are you going to do about Trish?"

"She knows where she stands."

"There's knowing and accepting," Diamond warned. "By the way, did you check out the latest blog on Nicole?"

"No, what now?"

"Oh nothing special, just something about her sexual preference being declared over the weekend." Diamond stood. "You may not enjoy the picture as much as the female public."

Against his better judgment, Xavier pulled up the blog once Diamond left.

Rumor Has It

> *Rumor Has It Nicole Davenport's sexual preference is no longer in question. Check it out, ladies. Xavier Davenport has a body to match those good looks. I give ten points on position, but a full twenty on form.*

The one thing Xavier had never been ashamed of was his body. However, it angered him to know that he had been photographed during a private moment. He stepped out of the office to ask their staff attorney a few questions concerning steps he could take to ensure their privacy.

Upon his return to his office he paused in the doorway. "May I help you with something?"

"Mr. Davenport. It appears our businesses have crossed paths. I've come to see if we could reach a compromise."

Xavier turned slowly to the man sitting in his office, behind his desk. "There are several chairs on this side of the desk."

Cannon nodded. "I thought I'd see what this seat felt like. I may be in it one day."

Xavier walked over to the man, stood before him and looked down. Xavier shrugged his shoulders. "Vacate the chair."

Canon hesitated, then slowly stood and walked around the desk.

Xavier stood behind his desk. "What can I do for you, Mr...?"

"Cannon, just Cannon."

"Cannon," Xavier said as he sat in his chair.

"There's been what I'm certain was an unintentional interference in my business dealings. I'm a generous business man, therefore, I'm here to give you an opportunity to correct your error."

"Mr. Cannon, I rarely make errors. Is there a problem with a property or something?"

"Or something," Cannon acknowledged as he sat forward. "You and your brother have a nice business here. What would happen if business stopped coming your way? For example, those bids you have in with the city, to design and build the sports complex, is worth what, a few million?" He sat back then crossed his legs. "What do you think would happen if that disappeared?"

"There will be another project and to cut this short if there wasn't I would create one. My brother and I are self-made. We don't depend on others for our livelihood."

"Research on your company has proven that to be true. And as you say, let's keep this short and to the point. It has come to our attention that you have supplied Nicole Brooks with a design for her London project. We would like you to withdraw the offer."

"Why would I?"

"We would like to make an offer for the design."

"Sight unseen."

"Sight unseen." Cannon nodded.

Xavier studied the man for a long moment. "I would simply design another for her."

"We will offer for that as well."

Xavier nodded in understanding.

With his finger propped on his chin, Xavier stared at the man for a long while. "It's time for you to leave, Mr. Cannon."

Cannon gave a smooth smile as he stood. "Thanks for your time, Mr. Davenport. I would suggest you call your people in city hall. You will find the decision on the sports complex is on hold, indefinitely." He reached into his suit jacket, pulled out a card and placed it on the desk. "You have a good day, sir." He nodded then walked out.

It took a moment for Xavier's temper to calm. He picked up the phone. "Diamond, have we heard any word on the bid for the city's proposed sports complex?"

"I'm told we are in line to receive that contract."

"Give someone a call, see what the status is and let me know." He hung up then pulled out his cell. The voice on the other end had a calming effect so powerful for a moment, he had no idea what he was angry about.

"Tell me something sweet and sexy," Nicole answered.

He could hear the smile in her voice, and he smiled in return. "Have you ever been kissed from head to toe?"

"Last night, as a matter of fact. However, I'm up for a replay."

"I have something different in mind tonight," Xavier teased. "Am I flying to New York or are you coming to Richmond?"

"I'm coming to you. The sooner I finish going through the information from my IT folks I'll be on a plane."

"How did the meeting with the board go this morning?"

"As I suspected, Ellington was pissed that I went with another architect. Warren was thrilled that the project was no longer on hold. The design has been sent to the London partners. When it's approved, we will contact Allen and Allen, and of course, Davenport Industries."

"No need to contact us. That is your design free and clear. It's my gift to you."

"Xavier, this design is worth millions. Davenport Industries' name is going on it."

"You're a stubborn woman. Can't wait to see you tonight. Question." He fought to keep his voice calm. "Does the name Cannon mean anything to you?"

"Cannon? Cannon?" She held the phone. "No. I'm afraid the only Cannon I know is Mike Cannon from the Las Vegas TV show."

Xavier grinned. "I used to watch that show."

"I did too," Nicole laughed. "You have good taste in women and TV shows. I have to go. Wait up for me."

"I'm always up for you."

She growled, "You are too much. Check you later."

Xavier hung up the phone just as Diamond walked into his office. "Why did you ask about the sports complex bid?"

"Curious," he replied as he looked up at her.

"According to my source, the project has a temporary hold on it."

"By who?"

"The Mayor."

"Thanks, Diamond, keep me posted."

"Is something wrong?"

"No, establishing priorities."

Diamond nodded, then hesitantly walked away.

Xavier pulled out his cell. "Grant, are you free?"

"I can be. What's up?"

"Who do you know at City Hall?"

"I'm about to take the Mayor's job. I know everyone."

"I'll be at your office in an hour."

A threat to him, he could ignore. A threat to his brother he could not. Once he secured the bid on the Sports Complex, he was going to have to explain a few things to Mr. Cannon.

Twenty minutes later, Xavier was at the construction site speaking to Zack and Reese. "I had an interesting visitor today. It seems Nicole has an enemy out there."

Zack sat up. "What do you mean, enemy?"

"You mean other than Trish," Reese joked.

"Unlike Trish this one just threatened to block our sports complex bid if I did not withdraw the plans I designed for Nicole's London project."

"What?" both men echoed.

Xavier only raised an eyebrow.

"Who is he?"

"Name is Cannon," he explained. "Just Cannon."

Zack stood. "Let's go." He said to Reese.

"Hold up, Zack. This is my situation. You needed to be aware of it, but I need you to trust that I will handle this."

"This is something that can impact our business, X-man." Zack's temper was getting the better of him. "If someone is threatening this company, we all need to be involved."

"I brought this to you because I understand we all need to be involved at some point. What I'm asking you at this time is to have a little faith in me."

Zack believed in Xavier's abilities as a designer. He hadn't been involved in situations like corporate takeovers. Zack had. However, his little brother asked him to have faith in him and he would. "Let us know if you need us."

"Will do." Xavier didn't think it was possible but Zack had shown him again how much he believed in him. He would not disappoint his brother.

Grant was pacing the front lobby when Xavier arrived. "My office," he said with a touch of urgency. "This is why I'm running for office. It seems one of the councilmen has requested a hold be put on the vote on the sports complex project. I spoke with him after you called. He gave me the run around. I spoke with one of his secretaries. She indicated he was for the project going forward until a messenger arrived with a package earlier today."

"A package from whom?"

"Someone named Cannon."

"The same person who paid me a visit this morning."

"What did he want?"

Xavier shared the details of the visit with Grant. "I have no intention of doing what he asked. However, I can't ignore the situation because it could impact Zack."

"What do you want to do?"

"First, I want to ensure the sports complex project is not impacted by this. How much power does this councilman have?"

Grant grinned. "Not as much as I do. The only thing is I don't want to influence the vote on the project either. What I can do is put the vote back on the table and make sure it stays there, but I will not sway the vote."

"All I'm asking is things go as normal."

"That I can do." Grant made a call as Xavier paced and considered his next move. Checking his watch it was now after five. Nicole should be wrapping up. The last thing he wanted was for this issue to cloud their first day at home together. When Diamond married Zack, the Davenports became honorary Lassiters. As a result, he was given a get out of jail free card of sorts. His gut was telling him, Cannon was not the mastermind behind this conspiracy with Nicole. Someone else was pulling the strings. Trish crossed his mind. But she would have had no way of knowing about the design. That was the one thing that was bugging him. He gave Nicole the design over the weekend. She called a meeting with her staff and then with the partners to present the design. Within hours Cannon was in his office. How did he know about the design and that it came from him? Did Nicole have someone in her office sharing in-house information with Cannon? If so, who and why?

"Done," Grant stated, pulling Xavier from his thoughts. "The vote on the design is back on for later this week. I requested the decision not be announced until Thursday. Therefore whoever is behind this will think the plot is working."

"I appreciate that."

"Now what are you going to do about this Cannon person?"

"Cannon isn't the mastermind behind this. I'm going to gather some information, then I'm going after the mystery man."

***

The elevator door opened to Xavier waiting with a hot cup of chamomile tea. The kiss they shared was long, lingering, meant to make up for all the hours they were apart.

"Hmm, how was your day?" he asked as he ran his hands down her back.

"Too long," she replied as the warmth of his long fingers penetrated her senses.

"Well..." He took her case, containing her tablet, and her purse from her, placing them on the table in the hallway. "I have a hot dinner and a glass of wine waiting for you. I thought you would enjoy a nice bath and a cup of tea, while I put the bread in the oven."

"Bread? Oven? A fine, sexy man filled with sinergy. I must have died and gone to heaven." Taking the cup of tea she looked over her shoulder and smiled as she entered the bedroom.

"If you did, I'm right there with you." Xavier watched as she walked away and could not believe she was here with him. Walking into the living room, he turned the fireplace on, then looked out his window. He loved the view. Anger touched him as the thought that someone might be out there with a camera came to him. His first reaction was to close the blinds, but that would be allowing whoever was behind the pictures in the blog to have control over his life. That was something he would not allow.

While in the kitchen thoughts of Cannon's visit continued to plague him. The thought of his involvement with Nicole interfering with his business had never occurred to him. It was hard to imagine what type of issues people with money had to deal with. He and Zack had worked all their lives for a living. They did not have the kind of money that would cause someone to target them. Nicole did.

He was thinking of the impact of that fact when she walked up behind him, and put her arms around his waist. All thoughts and concerns about her money and the impact it might have on their lives vanished. Her touch, her presence, her being was worth anything he would have to endure. He stopped buttering the biscuits and turned to her.

"Not long ago I asked for a woman who would make me forget who I was with her passion and beauty. God sent you. I enjoy the passion and beauty, but find myself falling in love with the person known as Nicole... What's your middle name?"

Kissing his throat, she replied, "Cheyenne."

"Nicole Cheyenne Brooks. We should name our first child Cheyenne."

"We're having children?" Nicole asked as she pushed his sweater up to kiss his chest.

"Yes." He pulled the sweater over his head and dropped it to the floor. "At least five."

"Three boys, two girls," she replied as she unzipped his pants which joined the sweater.

"Three girls, two boys." He ran his fingers through her hair then lost his train of thought as she took him into her mouth. His head fell back as the sensations surged through his body. "Hungry, are you?"

She squeezed his testicles then released him, wrapped her arms around his neck and her legs around his waist. He was prepped and ready to take her and he did, easing into her creating a perfect union of their bodies.

"I love you, Xavier Davenport," she moaned into his ear.

He braced her against the refrigerator, held her hands above her head with one hand, the other hand held one thigh a little higher than the other. He kissed her, slow and sweet, moving in and out in rhythm with his tongue. He raised her thigh a little higher, allowing him to go deeper into her. She moaned. He lifted it higher, then slowly went deeper. She broke the kiss as her voice hitched. "Xavier." He pushed deeper, and deeper hitting that spot that made her sing. Each time she moaned his urgency increased, soaring until neither could fight the explosion.

The kiss continued as their bodies handled the aftermath of their lovemaking. Xavier kissed her neck, her collar bone, her breasts, as he lowered her back to her feet.

They held each other until their bodies began to relax. "Dinner's ready."

Nicole began laughing. "Good, I'm starving."

"Shall we eat...some food?

Chapter 17

Atlanta, GA
Tuesday

Xavier made a trip to Atlanta, since that was the location listed on Cannon's card. He wasn't sure where he would have to go, but he had patience. Sitting in a downtown hotel, he scribbled, designing the home he and Nicole had talked about. As he sketched the bedrooms, a question popped into his head. Smiling, he sent a message to Nicole. *How many children are we going to have?*

His cell buzzed with a reply. *As many as my body can pump out and your wallet can take care of.*

Xavier smiled. *We'll be making babies for years.* His cell buzzed, a call was coming through. He answered the call, it was the one he was waiting for from Reese. "You have a location for me?"

"According to my friend with the FBI, he's using the same tower as you for his call. He's less than ten miles away. We have a name for you." There was hesitation.

"Today, Reese."

"Lawrence Cannonball McNally."

Xavier's brow creased. "The football player?"

"The one and only," Reese replied.

"Thanks for the info, Reese. One more thing. Can we get a list of calls made from his line?" Xavier was still frowning as he disconnected the call.

"What could he have against Nicole?" Using his cell phone he looked up the location and telephone number for B7 Beats. He then dialed the number.

"Hello is Mr. McNally available?"

"Mr. McNally isn't available until after four this afternoon. May I assist you?"

"No, thank you. I'll have to catch him another day."

"If you are interested in an audition open sessions are held on Thursday evenings from seven to nine. It gives you ten minutes to demonstrate your talents."

"Thank you for the information. I may do that."

An hour later Xavier sat outside the building where B7 Beats was located. He worked from a bench across the street from the parking entrance. He made notes as cars entered and left the facility, taking down license plates of those he thought might belong to Cannon.

"X-man? I thought that was you. What are you doing in Atlanta?"

Xavier looked behind him, shook his head and grinned then broke out into a full-fledged laugh. "All Diamond knew was a project was put on hold. What more could she have told you?"

"My surprised to see you act didn't work, huh?"

"Atlanta is a big city. There was no way you of all people would just happen to be where I am."

"You told me and Diamond where you were going." Adam Lassiter, Diamond's brother, came around to sit next to Xavier on the bench. He smiled at the look on Xavier's face questioning his statement. "Your secretary made the reservations using your credit card to purchase your plane ticket, book your room and rent the car. If you don't want anyone to know where you are going always use cash, it can't be traced." He looked around. "So, what are you doing?"

"Waiting for someone to come out of that building."

"Who?"

"A man named Cannon."

"You need his license plate number?" Adam pulled out his computer. "You know his full name?"

"Lawrence McNally," A curious Xavier looked on.

"The ex-football player? He's a new executive at B7." He began typing. "I have this new program I'm developing for the government with a tracking element." He turned his computer screen to Xavier. "Here you go."

Xavier stared at him amazed at how quickly he'd retrieved the information. "Are you able to trace calls on there?"

"Sure." Adam shrugged.

Xavier pulled up the list Reese had sent him of the numbers from Cannon's phone. "Can you tell me who he was calling?"

"Tell me what's going on and I'll tell you how I can help."

Xavier looked around wondering if he should involve anyone else in this situation. He had to admit, his plan could take days or weeks to find the information he needed while Adam took a matter of minutes. "I think Cannon is working for someone who is out to hurt my lady's business in some way. He paid me a visit yesterday threatening to put a bid we placed on hold. I was able to get a friend to counter act the move so Davenport Industries will not be impacted. Now, I want to know who is behind this scheme and why."

"I read about you and Nicole Brooks. Not bad. If it was me, I'd want to know not only who and why. I'd want to know what's their end game." He began keying. "Let's see who he's been talking to."

The entrance to the building no longer held any interest for Xavier. His mind and his eyes were on Adam's computer screen, where it seemed to be filtering through the list, giving each number a ranking.

"Most of his calls are random, no significance for they lasted a few minutes at most. However, this number." He pointed to the screen. "This number has less calls, but the minutes spent on each is significant."

"Who does that number belong to?"

Adam keyed a few more strokes, then waited. "Hmmm. Good privacy program." He opened another program, keyed a few strokes, then went back to the original, hit enter and a name appeared.

"Isaac Singleton."

The two men looked at each other. "I have no idea," Adam replied to the look Xavier gave. "Let's run the name."

"Did the name Trish Hargrove appear in the list of numbers?"

"Yes," Adam replied without checking. "Is she involved in this...whatever it is?"

Xavier shook his head. "I'm not sure if she is involved or what this is. What we do know is Cannon is leading the charge and I think Isaac Singleton is the mastermind."

"If that's true we may have a bit of a challenge ahead." He turned the screen around. "Meet Isaac Singleton. Self-made Billionaire."

"Money doesn't appear to be his motivator. So what's his connection to the Brooks'?" Xavier wondered out loud.

"All of this is speculative," Adam cautioned. "We have no proof this Singleton guy has any connection or is involved in this scheme, as you call it."

Xavier gathered his things. "Let's get some proof. Did you drive," he asked as he stood. Adam nodded. "We'll drop your car off at your place. I'll drive to Singleton's while you key. I want every piece of information you can find on Singleton and Cannon. Before it's over with I'm going to know the last time their mothers had a period. "

"I can do that, if they are still alive. Adam nodded eager to help."

Xavier stopped walking and stared at Adam. "You have a little Joshua in you, don't you?"

"All the Lassiters do."

"Good, we might have to blow up a building or two before this is over with."

"I can put together a few explosives."

Xavier stopped again. "You're not excited are you? I thought you were the quiet one?"

"Those are the ones you have to keep your eyes on. I mean, look at you. This is the first time you've said more than five words at a time. This is me." He pointed to a vehicle, then opened the door. "I'll drop you off at your car. You can follow me home and we'll be on our way."

An hour later they were parked outside a sprawling mansion surrounded by a black iron gates, with a double-gated entrance, leading to a driveway.

"This is the part of town where you will be arrested for parking here too long." Adam explained.

"It's just a little after one in the afternoon." Xavier replied after checking his watch.

"Doesn't matter." Adam shrugged his shoulder. "You don't come here unless you belong."

"Okay, any suggestions on how we can surveillance this place?"

"Hire a professional to take pictures of people coming and going. They have more liberties than what we have."

"Let me think on that," Xavier stated as a vehicle drove past them and pulled up to the gate. The woman pushed a button on the stand outside the gate. She gave her name and the gates opened. "What in the hell is she doing here?"

"Who?" Adam looked around to see who Xavier was talking about.

Xavier was too shocked to reply. If he wasn't sure before, he now knew Isaac Singleton was the man behind whatever was happening with Nicole and the man had help. "Let's go Adam."

"Who was in the car?"

"I can't say right now. When all this unfolds I'll tell you."

They pulled away. "So, what's our next move?"

Xavier's mind was on what he'd just seen. But he couldn't dwell on it. It had to be put away for now, his first priority was Nicole. "As a business man I keep all of my appointments on my calendar so I can access it at any time. Do you think Cannon has an electronic calendar?"

Adam keyed then turned the computer to Xavier. "Which date are you interested in?"

Xavier smiled. "You work for our government— right?"

"I'm deciding if I want to take them up on their offer."

"We haven't broken any laws here, have we?"

"Oh hell yeah, but it's cool. This is my prototype. They wanted me to test it and that's what I'm doing."

"They?"

"One of those agency's with three initials, you don't want to know which one."

"I agree, I don't." Xavier checked his watch. "Can you tell me where Cannon is right now?"

"At his office."

"Can you get us in the building?"

"Of course. What do you want to do once we are inside, is the question?"

***

"Daddy, you don't have to watch me twenty-four seven. I've been dealing with this for over a month now."

"I'm not watching over you." Vernon continued to review the case on his desk. "I thought you would like to see how a law office is run."

"You don't run this office. Mrs. Morgan does."

"And you better believe it. Been doing it for fifteen years." Geraldine Morgan winked at Taylor as she walked over to the television monitor in Vernon's office. "You need to see this." She clicked the monitor on.

"Since the District Attorney doesn't see fit to file charges against the mighty Brooks', my client has no recourse but to seek monetary damages for the physical and mental damage done to her. Have you seen these photographs, or the video? The total humiliation my client suffered at the hands of Nicole Brooks alone should raise a few eyebrows. We have documented evidence of a history of this behavior against my client's family. And we say enough is enough. Someone has to send a message to the mighty Brooks' that they cannot go around throwing their money at people to get away with criminal activity. "

Vernon stood. "Valarie Russum is taking over the Hargrove case."

Mrs. Morgan nodded. "Ish just got interesting."

Taylor laughed. "Mrs. Morgan, where did you get that from?"

"I have children."

Vernon snorted. "You're kidding me."

Mrs. Morgan grinned. "I'm afraid not."

"Now why do you think a high profile attorney would take a defamation case," Mrs. Morgan asked.

"She's going to try the case in the media," Taylor stated.

"Exactly," Vernon agreed. "Mrs. Morgan, pull our PR and Investigative team together. Meeting in the conference room in fifteen. Looks like we are going to court sooner than anticipated." He picked up the telephone. "We're going to nip this before it gets started."

"Daddy, how can I help?"

"Stand back and watch your daddy work."

She smiled. "Well all right. Let me see how you work."

"Nicole, there's been a development on your case."

"What is Trish up to now?"

"The District Attorney's office is not filing charges against you. Trish is now filing a personal injury claim against you."

"What does that mean?"

"One, there is no jail time on the table. Second, you can drop your suit and have the platform you want for the privacy issue. But I have another suggestion that I believe will win this case. You trust me?"

"Of course I do."

Vernon smiled. "Good. I'll be in touch." He hung up the telephone just as Mrs. Morgan walked back into his office. "Mr. Brooks, a Rene Naverone is here to see you. She doesn't have an appointment."

Vernon hesitated as he glanced at Taylor. "Send her in."

Naverone walked into the office dressed in a gold dress, black blazer and stilettos that extended those beautiful long legs of her more. He never considered ponytails sexy, but damn if she didn't put sexy in them. "My lord."

Taylor had never seen her dad at a loss for words until now. She looked from him to the woman in the doorway, then back to him. "Daddy, are you okay?"

Naverone extended her hand. "Hello, Mr. Brooks."

It took Vernon a moment. He looked at her hand and remembered how the touch affected him the last time. *Man up*, he thought to himself. He took her hand. Bam, there it was again. "Rene." He played it off the best he could.

"There's some information I think you need to hear. Do you have time to talk?"

"I have an emergency meeting I have to attend. Are you able to stay for a while?"

"It's important. I'll hang around."

"Good." He saw Mrs. Morgan come to his desk to pick up his folder.

"I'll see to it this is waiting for you in the meeting."

"Thank you," Vernon replied and was thankful, her interruption cleared his mind. He turned to Taylor. "Taylor, this is Rene Naverone. Would you keep her company while I'm in the meeting?"

"Sure." Taylor stood and extended her hand to Naverone. "It's nice to meet you Ms. Naverone."

"Thank you. It's just Naverone. It's nice meeting you Taylor. I have a client who thinks you're a taste of heaven on earth. His words, not mine."

"Really? A client? What type of work do you do?"

"I do investigative work for your Uncle Nick."

"Wow. Do you know his client named Jason Whitfield?"

Naverone looked from Taylor to Vernon and back. "I do. He's the client."

Vernon was about to walk out of the office when he stopped. "Maybe I should stay."

"Daddy, go to your meeting. Naverone and I will be fine. So tell me." Taylor turned from her father to Naverone. "What's he like for real. I mean I met him once after a show, but we didn't really get to talk."

Vernon watched Naverone cross her legs as she took a seat next to Taylor. The movement caused him to groan.

"Everything all right, Daddy?"

Vernon cleared his throat. "Yes, everything is good." He walked out of the office closing the door behind him. He liked seeing Rene with Taylor. It felt all right.

***

Cannon walked into his office and stopped. He stood in the doorway and chuckled. "Mr. Davenport." He shook his head as he walked in. "This I did not expect." He took a seat not bothering to ask Xavier to get out of his chair. "How did you accomplish this?"

"Wasn't hard." Xavier turned in the chair to face him. "It's amazing what people can do when provoked."

"Oh, I've just gotten started Mr. Davenport." Cannon sneered. "You don't want to take me on. You're the clean cut, local kid that made good. I'm the down and dirty street kid who made good. Which one of us do you think will win a dirty fight?"

"The one with the stronger motivation, know what motivates me?"

"Let me guess, Nicole Brooks?"

"No." Xavier stood, walked around the front of the desk and leaned against the edge in front of Cannon, then crossed his legs at the ankles. "Nicole Brooks' love motivates me. Her happiness is paramount to mine."

"Makes a man weak."

"It gives me strength to take you out if you continue down this path."

"Huh, that's cute Davenport." Cannon stood. "You had your say, now get the hell out of my office. And know, next time, I won't be so polite."

Xavier uncrossed his legs and stood. "As you wish." He started towards the door just as Cannon reached his chair.

"What the hell is this?"

Xavier stepped back and peeked over the desk. "Oh, that." I forgot to tell you. I paid a visit to your home earlier." He reached across the desk pointing at the picture. That is your bedroom, living room, pool house oh and yes, that's your kitchen with your lovable pets, Bruno and Buster. That's cute. This piece of paper is the combination to your home safe. You would be surprised what people keep in a safe." He held Cannon's eyes when he looked up. He pulled a disc from his pocket. "This is a copy, you know what's on it." Xavier put it away. "Don't fuck with me or mine." Xavier tapped on the desk and smiled. "See you next time. Oh, and please, give Mr. Singleton my regards." The smile was replaced with a glare.

Cannon heaved with fire in his eyes. "What are you going to do with that?"

"Nothing, I don't condone invading another person's privacy. I do wonder how what's on this drive could impact your clients."

"I could break your ass in two before you reach that door."

"You could, but then you would have to deal with me." A dark figure stepped from the corner of the room.

Cannon stood. "Who in the hell are you?"

"A man you don't want no parts of." Spoken in a chilling voice.

Xavier glanced at the figure, turned and they walked out of the door.

Cannon picked up the documents off the desk and threw them across the room.

Adam removed his hat, dark shades and trench coat. "He's pissed."

"Yes." Xavier exhaled. "Let's get out of here, I have a plane to catch."

"He threaten you? We could have him arrested for that."

Xavier looked exasperated. "We just broke into the man's house and you want to have him arrested?"

"Let's be clear, Xavier, we did not break into his house. The house was unlocked by some force of nature."

"Yes, your computer program."

"It was being tested."

"And the dogs you hypnotized?"

"I did not hypnotize them. I used sound to control them."

"Un huh. And the safe?"

"A few combinations here and there." He shrugged his shoulder.

Xavier laughed and Adam joined in. "Your brother would be proud of you."

"Joshua, yes—Samuel would be kicking my ass across town if he ever found out."

"Your illegal activities are safe with me." Xavier laughed. "You can hang out with me anytime."

"That was cool what you did. Nicole will never know how you put yourself out there for her. You realize you have an enemy now."

"He became my enemy the moment he targeted Nicole. Her enemies are my enemies."

"That's a good thing to love that deep. I pray to have that one day."

Xavier laughed thinking about how he'd had that same prayer.

***

Naverone and Taylor were still talking when Vernon returned from the meeting. "You two seem to be hitting it off."

"Girl talk." Taylor smiled. "Do you think Naverone can join us for dinner?"

"If she's free."

"I am." Naverone smiled.

Vernon almost lost his composure again, but held fast. "Taylor, would you give Rene and me a few minutes to handle business."

"Sure, I'll wait for you at Mrs. Morgan's desk."

Vernon waited until Taylor was out of the room. "So." He took a seat and pointed to one in front of his desk. "What do you have for me, Rene?"

"I met with Nail and his crew at the B7 studios. I believe it would be in Taylor's best interest to stay away from Nail. She should fire her mother as manager and move on."

"What does her mother have to do with this?"

Naverone hesitated.

"Mr. Brooks, the last thing I want to do is interfere in your marriage."

Vernon held up his hand. "First, it's Vernon. We are beyond the formal stage, you know it as well as I do. Second, my marriage was over years ago when I made the mistake of sleeping with my brother's wife. My brother and I moved on. Connie never did." He held her eyes for a brief moment. "My first priority is to my daughter. Do not hold anything back. I want to know everything."

"Very well. Your wife is sleeping with the new owner of B7 Beats. His name is Isaac Singleton. If it is any consolation she was targeted, as well as Taylor. According to the crew, Nail was told to make Taylor look bad to the staff, the crew and especially the media. Nail's attempts to disgrace her during performances, or rehearsals failed. Taylor did not fall for or respond to any of his abusive tirades. She stayed professional." She adjusted her position. "On the day in question no one knows exactly what happened except Taylor and Nail. However, everyone knows it was of a sexual nature."

"It was," Vernon interjected in an impatient tone. "What role did Connie play in this?"

Naverone tilted her head. "She took her lover's word over her daughter's. She reported what Taylor told her to Singleton. He said he would look into it. He claimed Nail's accounting of what took place was a little different than Taylor's. There was touching and rubbing, to make the scene look real, but nothing more. Connie took it as Taylor overreacting because of her virginal state."

The pen in Vernon's hand snapped in two.

"I know the feeling." Naverone nodded. "So you know, Singleton never spoke with Nail and according to the crew, they get a bonus for Taylor running off the shoot and refusing to come back. Every day the shoot is delayed is a mark against Taylor's reputation.

In the industry she'll be seen as a difficult person to work with. Your top producers do not want to work with someone who will cause delays. Time is money." She sat forward. "Between you and me, if Taylor were my child, every person in the crew would lose their life."

There was silence in the room for a long time. Vernon got up, walked around the desk, pulled Naverone from her seat and proceeded to kiss her with the vigor of a man possessed. He brought the kiss to an end, then stared down into her eyes. Using his thumb he wiped the moisture from her lips. "I want the name of every person who was in that room."

She pulled a disc from her pocket. "I have video."

Vernon smirked, as he caressed her neck. "You're a woman after my heart."

Naverone pulled away then walked toward the door. "I am, but not until the divorce papers are signed." She opened the door. "Shall we go to dinner?"

***

Sunday dinner at the Brooks' with all the family in attendance was like a holiday. It reminded Xavier of holiday feasts at the Lassiter's home. This was what he wanted his family meals to be, lively, loving and full of laughter.

Vernon's cell phone chimed and Gwen gave him a look. The family laughed and pointed at him. He looked at his mother with pleading eyes. "I have to take this." He gave a knowing laugh, stood and kissed his mother on the cheek as he stepped way.

He returned to the table a few moments later angry. He motioned to Nick. "We need to take a quick trip."

Nick and James stood, wiping their mouths. "Let's roll," James said.

"No," Vernon said to James. "We need you on the outside." A stare passed between the brothers. James nodded in understanding. "Call when you need me."

Nick patted Xavier on the shoulder. "Take a ride with us."

Xavier looked to Nicole, then back to Nick. He wiped his mouth, kissed Nicole. "I'll be back in a minute." He followed Vernon out the dining room.

Nick kissed Nicole on the cheek. "Umm, you better make that a few hours." He ran from the room.

"Butchie." Gwen looked down the table at James "What is going on?"

James looked around the table at all the eyes on him.

"Brooks family initiation." He shrugged with indifference.

"Daddy," Nicole shouted.

Avery laughed. "You brought him to the dinner table. Did you think your brothers weren't going to put him to the test?

***

"What's the damn hold up?" Nail yelled from the console in studio D at B7.

"Yo, someone here to see you, Nail."

"Who is it?" he yelled to one of his boys who had gone to the door when the bell chimed.

"Time is money," Nail huffed.

Vernon, Nick and Xavier walked into the room to see four men in various positions in the studio.

"This better be good. You are messing with my money."

Vernon looked around the room at the entourage surrounding the man, and he used the term loosely.

Nick and Xavier stood in front of the door as it closed. Before anyone knew what was happening, Vernon had a gun at Nail's head.

"Whoa, whoa, whoa," echoed around the room as the men jumped to get out of the line of fire.

"First cell phone I see gets shot. Understood?" Vernon looked at the men. He looked down at Nail with a wicked grin. "Your boys don't seem too interested in changing places with you, Nail. Is that your name?" He pushed the barrel of the gun to the front of Nail's head. "What, cat got your tongue? I thought that might happen. Here's what we are going to do. Gentlemen, if you would all step into the sound booth. Mr. Lamont and I need a private, uninterrupted conversation." The men did not move. "Now, gentlemen."

The men filed into the sound proof room.

"Nick."

Nick walked over and locked the door, then stood in front of it.

"Look, man. I don't have no beef with you."

Vernon gave his gun to Xavier. Before Nail could move, Vernon had him by the throat pulling him from the chair. He threw the man against the wall with a flick of his wrist. Nail bounced off the wall back towards Vernon and collided with his fist. The expressions on the men in the sound booth were animated, as Nail attempted to get up. Their hands were signaling for him to stay down. Vernon picked Nail up, placed him against the wall, then used his foot to kick the man in the balls. The men in the room all bent over, covering their balls, with their mouths forming an 'ouch'.

Vernon stood over the man, who had fallen to the floor. "If you ever come within five hundred feet of my daughter again, I will cut every finger from your hands then I will kill you." Vernon stood, wiped the blood from his hands on the man's jacket, then nodded to Nick.

Xavier walked over and stood over Nail. He bent down next to the man on the floor. "Tell me something. Does the name Singleton ring a bell?" Vernon's attention heightened as he listened. Xavier tapped Nail with the butt of the gun.

"Nah man," Nail cried out. "I mean I know he owns the studio."

"What's his connection to all of this? Now, I want you to think before you answer. My reflexes are bad and my finger might pull something if I get angry."

"Man, look." Nail wiped the blood from his nose with the back of his hand. "All I know is the man paid me to put Tay in a compromising position."

"How much did he pay you?"

"Fifty grand."

"Take a look around." Xavier waved the gun. "I'm Taylor's uncle-to-be." He pointed to Nick. "That's her uncle. That's Taylor's father. There's this thing about daughters I learned a few years back. If you don't want your balls cut off, don't mess with them." He stood. "The next time you touch anyone else's daughter, think about this." He pointed to Vernon. "He's the nice one." Xavier stood, then pulled the cock back on the gun. Nick and Vernon eyes threw quick glances at each other not knowing what Xavier was about to do. He put the gun between Nail's legs and pulled the trigger. Nail's face turned red. Xavier held up the magazine he had removed from the gun. "It's that simple." He stepped over the man and walked back to the door where Vernon stood.

Nick unlocked the booth door, as Xavier opened the outer door. The men in the booth did not move.

Nick looked back over his shoulder. "You can come out now."

"No, man, we'll wait. You're good."

Ty Pendleton walked in looking backwards at the men exiting the room. "You picked the wrong father to screw with." He looked down at Nail, shaking his head.

"Man, never underestimate the anger of a father." One of the men from the booth choked out.

"Whoa, I ain't going nowhere near Lil Tay," another exclaimed. "Her Daddy ain't no joke."

"Yeah," a third man replied, laughing.

Ty stood, shaking his head at the man on the floor. "He's lucky. I would have killed him."

"It's still early, gentlemen." They all turned to the woman standing in the doorway with a briefcase. She walked over, placed the briefcase on the console, and extracted paper work. "One way or another, I'm here to persuade Mr. Lamont to release Taylor Brooks from this contract." She smiled. "How we accomplish that is totally up to you."

"Who the hell are you?" Nail moaned from the floor.

The woman stood a good five-ten in her four-inch stiletto boots, with a red dress that caressed every curve on her body. She stood over Nail, legs spread for battle. "Why, Mr. Lamont, I'm The Persuader."

Nick and Xavier were in the back seat of the vehicle when Vernon got into the front seat. No one said a word for a good fifteen minutes. Vernon turned to the back and looked at Xavier. The conservative, mild-mannered slip of a man simply raised an eyebrow at him as if to say, 'and.'

"You got a little gangsta in you."

Without cracking a smile, Xavier replied, "I'm a Davenport."

Vernon stared at him for a moment then all he could do was start laughing. Nick joined in, asking. "What in the hell does that mean?"

Xavier stared him straight in the eyes. "It means don't mess with me or mine."

"Welcome to the Brooks family, Davenport."

Vernon turned back in his seat and laughed.

Chapter 18

Richmond, VA
Court Day

Weeks later Xavier had not revealed his findings while in Atlanta. He and Nicole had been so busy putting the presentation together for the London team, they had not had the opportunity to have dinner with her family. There was no way he wanted to be the one to tell Vernon, his wife was involved with Isaac Singleton without giving Constance the chance to come clean on her own.

Unfortunately, the court case with Trish soon took on a life of its own. Whenever Xavier and Nicole ventured into the public cameras and reporters asking question after question surrounded them. It was a relief when the court date finally arrived. The plaintiff's attorneys had rested their case and Vernon was presenting. It was Xavier's day on the stand. He prayed all would go according to plan.

Rumor Has It

The courtroom is packed and yours truly has a front row seat to what may be the final chapter of the Nicole Brooks, Trish Hargrove chapter. We heard the heart wrenching claims of Trish, who describes a life of living under the fear of The Brooks' tyranny. Today the defense takes center stage. We will hear from the man at the forefront of this battle, the sexy Xavier Davenport and the defendant, Nicole Brooks, who by the way has won the man. The only question remaining is who will win on the financial end, the lovely Trish or the wealthy Nicole?

A hush came over the courtroom as Xavier Davenport took the stand and was sworn in. All eyes turned to Vernon as he approached the stand. "Good morning, Xavier. For the benefit of the jury let's establish our relationship."

Xavier nodded.

"We met through my sister, Nicole, on the night of the incident, correct."

"Yes."

"Do you like me?"

"Not particularly, but you're growing on me."

Vernon laughed along with the courtroom. "I can be a difficult man to like. We've had several meals together. Correct?"

"Yes."

"When and where was the first time?"

"A week after the altercation, at your parents' home."

"Why were you there?"

"To meet Nicole's parents."

"Why?"

"Objection," Valarie stood. "Relevance, Your Honor?"

"Establishing the depth of the relationship between the witness and my client."

"Again I ask, relevance?"

"Your Honor, a portion of damages requested by Ms. Russum claims my client interfered with the affection of Mr. Davenport for her client. We intend to show that was not the case."

"I'll allow it. Mr. Davenport, you may answer the question."

"I was there to meet Nicole's parents."

"Was there some significance to that meeting?"

"Yes. I found myself falling in love with Nicole and I wanted her parents to know my intentions."

Trish gasped. "Xavier we were still involved at that time." Tears began to flow down her cheeks.

The judge hit his gavel on the stand. "Ms. Russum, control your client."

Valarie put her hand on Trish's arm, willing her to be seated.

"That's not true," Xavier replied.

"You do not have to respond to that outburst, Mr. Davenport," the judge stated. "You may continue, Mr. Brooks."

"Thank you, Your Honor," Vernon replied as he placed a box of tissues in front of Trish. "Xavier, will you tell the court when you stopped seeing Ms. Hargrove?"

"Approximately two months prior to the auction."

"Would you mind telling the court why?"

"Your Honor." Valarie interrupted the testimony again.

"I want to know Ms. Russum. Have a seat."

"We weren't compatible." Xavier replied as the attorney took her seat.

"It had nothing to do with Nicole?"

"Nicole and I had not met at that time."

Vernon stared at the jury. "You had not met." He nodded, then turned from the jury, back to Xavier. "Okay, on the night in question you were one of the businessmen being auctioned for charity? In fact you were the man on stage at the time of the incident?"

"Yes."

Vernon nodded. "Xavier, in your own words, could you share with the court exactly what you witnessed after the bid was won by Nicole?

Xavier looked at the jury. "The crowd erupted." He shrugged. "It was a significant bid. After the moderator confirmed the bid, Trish and her friends made their way down the row to Nicole. Trish made the statement 'how dare you come in here spending your daddy's money'. She then looked over her shoulder at me and smiled. Then turned back to Nicole and said, 'you don't even like men, you're gay'."

Vernon pointed to his sister. "She indicated that Nicole Brooks, my client, was gay. What was Nicole's reaction?"

"She seemed a little embarrassed at first, then she shrugged her shoulders and said, 'I like this one.'"

"What happened then?"

"Nicole turned to walk away and Trish yelled at her. 'Are you still a dummy?' She turned to her friends laughing, then said 'can you read yet?' Nicole stopped walking then slowly turned back to Trish. That's when I saw the look of humiliation in her eyes as Trish and her friends continued to laugh. Nicole gave her purse to her friend Alicia, grabbed Trish, and punched her."

Vernon watched the reaction of the jury. "What were your thoughts as this scene unfolded before you?"

He looked at Trish when he answered. "I thought of the high school bullies who always belittled others to make themselves look good."

"A high school bully," Vernon replied as he walked back to his desk. "Thank you, Mr. Davenport. Your witness, Ms. Russum."

"Mr. Davenport isn't it true you're a bought man?"

"No."

"Ms. Brooks paid $50,000 for your services, did she not?"

"No, she did not."

"There's a check in that amount."

"Is there a question?"

Ms. Russum gave Xavier the side eye. "Was there a check written in that amount?"

"Yes."

"And Ms. Brooks received the benefits of your services for the weekend because of that check, is that correct?"

"She received the benefit of my company for the weekend."

Ms. Russum walked over to her table. "What did you do that weekend, Mr. Davenport?"

"We enjoyed each other's company."

She held up pictures. "I'd like to place theses into evidence. Are these pictures of you providing your brand of services?" She put the pictures in front of Xavier.

He looked at the pictures and smiled. "These are pictures of us enjoying ourselves. This one was particularly enjoyable." He held it up for the jury to see as the courtroom laughed.

"Your Honor, would you instruct the witness not to address the jury?"

"Ms. Russum, you put the pictures into evidence. If you did not want them seen you should not have placed them into evidence. Move on."

"Very well. Mr. Davenport, did Davenport Industries receive a grant from Brooks International?"

"Yes."

"What's the amount of the grant?"

"It has not been determined yet."

"Waiting on the outcome of the trial?"

"Objection." Vernon stood smoothly. "Leading the witness and appearing snide while doing so."

"The objection is sustained, the comment is not, Mr. Brooks. Watch yourself."

"Mr. Davenport." Ms. Russum stood close to the stand. "Isn't it true you are a man bought and paid for by Nicole Brooks, who has always used her money to walk over people who don't have as many zeros at the end of their bank account? Don't answer that question." She slowly looked the jury over. "I think we know the answer." She turned and walked back to the table.

Vernon stood. "Redirect, Your Honor."

The judge nodded.

Vernon almost laughed, but instead smiled as he approached the stand. "I'm tempted to let the jury keep the picture of you painted by Ms. Russum. But my honor will not allow that."

"Objection, Your Honor. Mr. Brooks doesn't have any honor."

"Touché Ms. Russum."

"Order in my court, Counselor," the judge warned.

"Xavier, have you ever taken a dime from Nicole for any reason?"

"No."

Vernon nodded. "What was the $50,000 check for?"

"A donation to the building of a community center."

"And the grant mentioned is for what?"

"The building of the same community center."

"Thank you. One last question. What are your feelings for my client?"

"To say I love her would be trivial. Nicole is my sinergy. We are two forces brought together by human means and divine grace. I don't believe we would bring the same energy to life apart from each other. That's why I'm asking her to marry me, have my babies and give my life the fullness God intended."

The courtroom was silent as all eyes went to Nicole.

"Objection, I think Your Honor."

"What is your objection, Ms. Russum?"

"Sensationalism, I think."

"I think it's love. Overruled."

"No further questions, Your Honor."

"In that case, you may step down, sir, and I'm granting a fifteen minute recess for you to receive an answer to your question." He hit the gavel.

Xavier stepped down and met Nicole half way. No one had left the courtroom, as the two embraced.

"Yes," Nicole replied, as Trish screamed 'no'.

Even her own attorney turned and gave her an incredulous look.

The Davenports and the Brooks' were in the courtroom. They all surrounded the couple with hugs and congratulations. Vernon stood back basking in his sister's happiness. In a corner of the courtroom, he noticed Trish and her parents. The attorney was giving them a summary of where their case stood. Yes, they were in danger of losing the case after Vernon's interrogation of Trish. Vernon knew Nicole wanted to use the privacy platform and Vernon did touch on it. However he used a different tactic.

"Ms. Hargrove, in your earlier testimony you indicated you and Nicole were friends. Would you share some of the things the two of you did together during high school?

"We attended social events and classes together all throughout high school."

"So did 534 other students in your class. Did you visit our home?"

"No."

"Did she visit your home?"

"No."

"Went to the movies together?"

"No."

"Skating, bowling clubbing?"

"Badgering the witness." Russum stood.

"Sustained. You made your point, Mr. Brooks, move on."

"The truth of the matter is you two were only in the same places as dictated by school boundaries. During classes and events. Would that be more accurate?"

Trish scowled at him. "We were together frequently," she hissed back.

"Let's examine that claim. Nicole was a math tutor. She worked with several students, were you one?"

"No, I did not need tutors."

"Nor were you a tutor. Nicole was a member of Future Leaders of America. Were you a member of that club?"

"No. My parents couldn't afford the fees associated with that organization."

"Shame. Nicole was the Student Association Treasurer. Were you a part of the student government?"

"No."

"Would you tell the court what organizations you were a member of?"

"Certainly." She perked up. "I was a cheerleader from ninth through twelfth grade"

"Did you practice a lot?"

"Yes, we did," she proudly replied. "We won several competitions."

Vernon stared at her. "Congratulations." He frowned. "When did you have occasions to hang out with Nicole?"

"We had classes together every day. We talked just about every day."

"I'm happy you brought that up. How many times did you call my sister a dummy?"

"I don't think I ever did."

Vernon laughed. "In your earlier testimony you mentioned my mother Gwendolyn Brooks threatened your mother. Would you tell the court why?"

"That was between my mother and Mrs. Brooks."

"Weren't you the cause of the dissension? Wasn't the argument due to your treatment of Nicole during class? Weren't you the leader of the mean girl pack and your number one target was Nicole Brooks?"

"Objection Your Honor, Mr. Brooks is badgering the witness. Which question would he like her to answer?"

"I'll withdraw all of them." Vernon waved off Trish as if he was done with her then walked back to his table. "One last question, Ms. Hargrove. What is the total amount of money you and your family have received from extorting The Brooks'?" He glared at her.

"Objection. Relevance Your Honor?"

The judge took a moment before he answered. "I think I'm going to allow this one, Ms. Russum. The witness may answer the question."

"I haven't extorted anything from the Brooks'."

"Allow me to rephrase the question." Vernon picked up a sheet of paper from his table. "I'd like to place this bank statement into evidence."

"Objection, may we approach," Ms. Russum demanded.

"Approach."

"Your Honor," she began. "I want it on the record, again, that I believe this document to be prejudicial to my client. She cannot control her parent's actions."

"We discussed this in chambers Ms. Russum. It will be allowed."

"Thank you, Your Honor." Vernon nodded.

"How much money has your family received from the Brooks' in the last ten years, Ms. Hargrove?"

"I...I can't say."

"I can. How does the total of 3.7 million dollars sound? Am I close?"

"Each time the Brooks' broke the law. They stepped on our rights. You claim to be these upstanding righteous people, but you go around acting like your shit don't stink. Well it does. And when you do wrong you should be made to pay. Every time one of you precious Brooks stepped across the line, yes, we were there to make sure you paid the price. Your mother hit mine, yes, she is going to pay. Your father hit mine, yes, he is going to pay. Nicole hit me. She is going to pay. It's the way of the world, Mr. Brooks."

The rant was the turning point of the case. He made her look like the bully she was. Now, it was up to Nicole to bring this case to a successful conclusion. At the moment she was in bliss, it was the only way he could describe it. Vernon interrupted the group.

"Nicole, it's your turn to take the stand. Are you ready?"

"Yes," a beaming Nicole replied.

"Please be seated. Court is back in session," the bailiff called out.

Everyone took their seats.

"Mr. Brooks call your next witness," the judge ordered.

"Your Honor, the defense calls Nicole Brooks to the stand."

Nicole took the stand and was sworn in. Vernon walked over to his sister and smiled. "Hey Nikki."

Nicole smiled back at her brother. "Hi Vernie."

Vernon laughed. "How you doing?"

The members of the jury were smiling. They could feel the affection between the brother and sister and that was exactly what Vernon wanted them to see. He leaned against the witness box. "I have to say that was a first. I have never seen any one proposed to in a courtroom."

"Objection, Your Honor," Valarie stood disgusted. "Where is the question?"

"She's right, Mr. Brooks. Sustained."

"Are you happy?"

"Your Honor," Valarie jumped up again.

"It is a question," Vernon stated as he looked over his shoulder at Valarie.

"Make it relevant, Mr. Brooks," the judge stated.

"Yes, I'm very happy," Nicole rushed in.

"Then I'm happy, too." Vernon let that sit for a moment. He looked at the jury as he asked his question. "Ms. Brooks, this case was never about money for you was it?"

"No."

"In fact, you dropped your law suit against Ms. Hargrove, did you not?"

"Yes, I did."

"What was the amount of that suit?"

"Five hundred and fifty million dollars."

The jury gasped.

"Why that amount?"

"It was the amount I stood to lose when one of my partners pulled out of an international deal."

"Why did your partner pull out?"

"Because I would not declare my sexual preference in public."

"Why did they require you to do that?"

"Because Ms. Hargrove made the statement that I was gay. The partner will not work with anyone they believe to be homosexual."

"Are you a homosexual, Ms. Brooks?"

The courtroom laughed.

"No."

"Therefore, Ms. Hargrove's statement was false, and detrimental to a deal your company was involved with, true?"

"Yes, that is correct."

"Why didn't you comply with your partner's request? It would have solved the problem."

"I don't believe anyone should ever have to answer questions about their sexual preference to seal a business deal, much less be forced to declare it to the public. What I do behind closed doors is my business."

"Ms. Hargrove's statement caused a financial problem for you. Yet according to Mr. Davenport, you turned to walk away. Why?"

"The statement embarrassed me because it was made in front of Xavier. I was trying to be the better person and walk away without causing another confrontation with Ms. Hargrove."

"But you hit her. Why?"

Nicole sighed as she looked at the jury. "I don't know if any of you have experienced being bullied. So you may not understand my actions. I struggled in school with reading. In a house full of lawyers, reading is fundamental, as my father always says. I never felt I could measure up to his expectations because my reading and comprehension levels were much lower than my brothers. Vernon, you used to tease me and say my twin brother Nick got all the brains, and I got the beauty. You meant it as a compliment, but I internalized it as me not measuring up in a family of over achievers. In high school Trish...Ms. Hargrove, recognized my weakness and she preyed on it. Every chance she got, she would call me a dummy. Whenever a boy paid me any attention, Trish would find a way to bring up my disability by asking in front of him, can you read the menu? Or Nicole, let me help you read that. I know how difficult it is for you to read. I went through my two years of high school hiding from Trish and her friends because I knew she would try to embarrass me. When I was in the tenth grade this guy asked me to the prom. I was so excited. I liked him a lot." She smiled. "Trish told me later that the guy was her boyfriend and if she saw me talking to him again I would be sorry. The next day my report card was posted in the main hallway. Trish was showing everyone the D I received in English and History. When she saw me, she yelled, here comes the dummy now. I reacted poorly." Nicole shrugged. "I hit her." She shook her head. "I was wrong then and I was wrong the night of the auction. Violence is not the solution to problems. But...that night, when she said, 'are you still a dummy, can you read yet,' in front of

Xavier, I lost my temper again. I just felt like enough was enough. I dealt with her and her cruelty all through high school and I just could not take it again. I'm not sorry that I hit her, she deserved it. People say all the time words can't hurt you. I disagree. A cut with a knife will heal. The wound will close and the skin will return to normal. Words cut deep and they cannot be taken back." She hesitated, then looked up at Xavier sitting in the courtroom. "I wanted this case to come to court just to take a stand against a person I consider to be a mean, insecure bully. But what I discovered was it was my own insecurities that gave her the power over me. Today, I'm taking that power away from her."

There was a hush over the courtroom.

Vernon looked at the jury, then at the judge, then at Valarie Russum. "Your witness." He smirked then took a seat.

Valarie Russum stood at her table, she did not approach the stand. "Ms. Brooks, did you strike my client?"

"Yes."

"No further questions."

***

The verdict had come through loud and clear, but it was Nicole's graciousness that proved to be the media darling. After leaving the courtroom, the Brooks family was bombarded by the media. Everyone was eager to see their reaction to Nicole's plea to the judge. "This case was never about money," Vernon declared. "The root of the case was about bullies, for that is what Trish Hargrove is. This court case started back in high school where Ms. Hargrove made my sister's life unbearable. Nicole conquered her disability and is now a very successful businesswoman. She's reached a point where her self-esteem is in her control. The physical action she took felt good, but she knows it was wrong. The jury heard her story and understood her frustration. You never know how something you say can impact another person's life. It is our hope that people will begin to think before they slander another person's reputation. My sister has again demonstrated how the Brooks' carry themselves with dignity and grace."

Just then a man from the crowd spoke. "Dignity and grace is a bit of a stretch for a man being hit with a paternity suit, don't you think, Mr. Brooks?"

Vernon laughed. "I'm afraid you are mistaken, sir. My child is twenty years old and well provided for."

"That may be, but can your father say the same?"

The cameras turned to Avery and Gwen Brooks. "Excuse you." Gwen raised an eyebrow.

The man handed Avery a court order. "You've been served, Mr. Brooks."

Avery opened the document. Gwen looked on, shocked.

"Pop, what is it?" Vernon asked as Nicole, Xavier, Nick and James looked on.

"Stacy Crane claims I'm the father of her son."

Naverone and Genesis pushed through the crowd pulling the family from the courtroom steps.

"No comment," Xavier stated as the media began shooting questions one after another. He stood between the cameras and the family as they were directed to the sedans waiting for them.

Nicole looked back as Xavier spoke to the reporters. "This seems convenient and contrived, don't you think. The gentlemen who served the papers, he pretended to be one of you. Do any of you know him? Ever seen him before? I find that very suspicious."

"Is there any truth to the claim?"

"I don't know. It appears we are once again faced with the right to privacy issue. The claim, true or false should be discussed between Mr. and Mrs. Brooks, not through the media. No further comments for now. I am certain Vernon Brooks will have a statement for you soon." Xavier turned and entered the last sedan.

Nicole was there, waiting with tears in her eyes. He gathered her into his arms and kissed her forehead.

"What is all of this really about, Xavier?"

"I don't know, sweetheart. We savor this victory and move on to the next battle until we bring our enemies down."

"Whoever is doing this is not after you. They want to destroy the Brooks'."

"You are a Brooks. Your enemy is my enemy. We don't take prisoners."

The vehicles pulled up to the mansion as the family poured out and gathered in the family room.

"Gwen, I have never touched that woman. We shared some long hours at Brooks International and we had some moments, but I never even looked at her in that way."

Gwen walked over to her husband, put her arms around his neck and proceeded to kiss him until all doubt of her belief in him was gone.

"You two need to get a room, or something," Taylor joked.

It eased the tension in the room.

Avery kissed his wife on the nose. "I don't know what this is about."

"I have an idea." Naverone stepped into the room.

"Of course you do," Constance smirked. "The apple doesn't fall far from the tree."

"You know one of the first things a dog learns?" Naverone stepped to Constance. "Never bite the hand that feeds you."

"Advice coming from one of Vernon's whores."

Naverone kicked Constance's feet from under her, then placed her booted foot at her throat when she fell to the floor. "I'm a lot of things, Mrs. Brooks. But I'm nobody's whore."

"Whoa." Nick ran over. "Naverone, let her up." The woman hesitated. "Let her up, now," Nick ordered.

Naverone slowly stepped back. She put her tablet on the table then pushed play. "I'm not married to anyone," she said to Constance, "but you are." She stepped back as photo after photo of Constance and a man played across the screen.

"You are involved with a dangerous man. What he might do to you pales in comparison to what I will do if you ever attempt to use our daughter again. You have 24 hours to file divorce papers. If you do not, I will. If I file, you will not receive a dime."

"Vernon."

"Don't." Vernon shook his head once. "I'm five minutes from putting a contract on you and your man. 24 hours." He turned his back and looked at his watch. "The clock is ticking."

Gwen stepped around to see the photos. She gasped.

"Who is he, Mother?" Vernon asked.

Gwen looked at the picture again, shocked at the sight of the man. She glanced over at Avery. "I don't believe this?"

Avery looked at the picture then stared back at Constance and sighed. He knew in that moment, who was targeting his family and why. He took his wife into his arms.

"One of you needs to answer my question." Vernon's calm demeanor was deadly.

"His name is Isaac Singleton," Xavier stated as he walked into the room with Nicole. "Cannon was the man who approached me about the London project, however, I believe Singleton is the mastermind behind the threat."

"He is also the man who hired Trish's new attorney," Nicole added.

"Mr. Singleton is the new owner of B7 Beats." Taylor looked at her mother.

"Okay, everyone calm down for a moment," James attempted to diffuse the possible explosion. He looked at his parents, who were now clutching hands. "This man seems to have a vendetta against this family. Nick and I are the only two he has not contacted."

"That we are aware of," Nick stated. "He seems to be working in a clandestine fashion."

Naverone placed the other pictures on the table. "Mrs. Brooks." She looked up at Constance. "You are being used to get revenge on the Brooks'."

"I don't believe that," Constance proclaimed. "Isaac loves me."

"He loves your connection to the Brooks'," Naverone stated. "Everything this man has done in the last five years has been directed at bringing the Brooks' down from grace, from the scandal with Nicole to the contract dispute with Taylor and now this paternity claim against your father-in-law. I have proof that this Stacy Crane has been working with Singleton's people for a few years now. He's Hayworth's new partner in the London project Nicole is involved with. It's all a scheme of some type to disgrace the Brooks'."

"Why?" Nicole asked. "I don't know this man. Why would he want to destroy my reputation?"

Xavier took her hand. "It's not about you, sweetheart." He looked at Vernon. Looking at the picture, he could see why. But, it wasn't his place to say.

"Mother?" Vernon asked as he glared at his parents. "Who is this man?"

Gwen looked around at her family. Her answer would impact them no matter how it was said.

Avery squeezed her hand as she took a step toward Vernon. A moment ago, she was letting him know she loved and supported him no matter what the court document stated. Now it was him letting her know he was supporting her, for what she had to do now was not going to be easy.

Gwen reached for Vernon's face with a gentle touch to his cheek. "Isaac Singleton is your biological father."

The room was silent. No one moved or said a word.

Suddenly, Taylor's voice hitched as she turned to glare at her mother. "You've been sleeping with my grandfather?"

Epilogue

Atlanta, GA

"I wondered when you would show up," Isaac turned slowly in his chair to face the man who'd walked into his home uninvited.

Vernon stood in the doorway, legs braced apart, with his hands in his pockets, dressed as if he'd stepped off the pages of Men Weekly. "Disagreements are handled among men. You targeted my family. I call that a coward." He took a seat in front of the desk, crossed one leg over his knee and stared at the man behind the desk. "Allow me to demonstrate." The intensity in his eyes turned deadly. "The wife you can have, my siblings can take care of themselves. My Pop will wipe the floor with you. Mess with my daughter and I will kill you, your family and any remnants of your existence."

Isaac grinned, "Idle threats are beneath you Vernon, after all, you are a Singleton."

"Brooks," Vernon coolly corrected him. "Never issue threats." He stood. "We advise you of our intentions. He buttoned his suit jacket. "You've been warned." He turned to walk out.

Isaac stood. "You should know what this is about before you leave."

Vernon stopped and looked at the man. "When you dared to involve my daughter your reasons ceased to have merit."

"Funny you don't feel the same about your son."

Vernon watched as the man's features turned dark. "I don't have a son."

Isaac stepped to the front of the desk. "Come now Vernon. You can't believe you could sleep with your brother's wife and there would be no consequences." He leaned against the desk, folding his arms across his chest and grinning.

Vernon held the eyes that looked so much like his and raised an eyebrow. A cynical laugh escaped from Isaac as he stood, bracing his legs a part. "The devil is always found in the details, son. Check James Jr.'s birthday, then count backwards."

Vernon stepped over to Isaac. "Stay away from my family."

"You are allowing another man to raise your son. Like father like son"

The punch landed before Vernon knew his intention. As he stood over the man responsible for his creation he growled. "Stay away from my brother and his son. Defy me and I promise you will not like the consequences." He stepped away from the man. "Oh, the men you have stationed around your house, they're not dead, just immobilized for an hour or two. Your goons cannot protect you from me."

Vernon closed the door behind him as he entered the vehicle.

"Do you want me to kill him?" The man behind the wheel asked.

Vernon hesitated. After a moment he replied. "No, not yet. But keep your people on him. If he goes anywhere near my daughter...handle your business."

***

"The damn check bounced!" Trish yelled into the phone.

Cannon wanted to laugh. He had to give it to Isaac. He may be an asshole, but he was one with a wicked sense of humor.

"Ms. Hargrove, I can only conclude, my superior was not satisfied with your performance. However, the million you received upfront will have to sustain you."

"How in the hell am I supposed to live off of this?"

"A job might be a good start."

"This was not the agreement."

"You can always sue us," Cannon grinned. "How much did you get from Nicole Brooks? I believe the judge awarded you one dollar." He couldn't hold back, he laughed, then he sobered. "Be satisfied with the million, Ms. Hargrove. Trust me on this." He disconnected the call.

Cannon stood, looked out of his office window and shook his head. "Round one to the Brooks'. Now what?"

Richmond, VA

Trish slammed the telephone down. What in the hell was she going to do? Her father cut her off. The money in her trust fund plus the million from Cannon would not last forever. "I will get you for this Cannon. I will."

Trish pulled a bottle of wine from the cooler, then turned to the television that was on in the kitchen. She poured wine into the glass just as Grant Hutchinson appeared on the screen. She picked up the remote and turned up the volume.

"It is because of this type of corruption that I stand before you today announcing my candidacy for Mayor of the great city of Richmond."

A smile began to form on Trish's lips. She picked up her cell phone, pulled up the Internet. Once she found what she was looking for she dialed a number.

"Hello, I would like to volunteer to work on Mr. Hutchinson's campaign."

Manhattan, NY

It was well after midnight and neither was ready to call it a night. Xavier sat on the balcony, wrapped in a blanket, with Nicole in his lap. They were enjoying the view of the Manhattan skyline. It was a crisp night, but the heat between them was electric.

"I can't believe Ellington is trying to get in on the new deal in London," Xavier shook his head at the news.

Nicole pulled his arms tighter around her. "That's not all that came out of the conference call with Steven. He liked the idea of doing a project like London here in the United States. In fact, he thinks Washington DC would be a good place to start."

"I think it would be a good place to start. It will put you near your parents while they deal with the situation Isaac Singleton has created."

Nicole nodded. "I want to be there to support them and Vernon in any way I can."

"Yes, well with any luck, Vernon will not have to deal with Constance."

"She's not going away that easily. I'll just settle for her being out of Taylor's life." She smiled at him. "I know this will sound crazy, but I feel bad for Connie and Trish."

Xavier frowned. "Why?"

"They want what we have, but don't have a clue how to get it."

"Exactly what is it that we have?"

"Love," she sent him a sexy glance as she wiggled against him, "and other things."

"Other things, hmm."

He lifted then penetrated her from behind, her back lying on his chest. Her head resting against his shoulder as his fingers gently stroked her nub as his other hand massaging her breast. The sensations flowing through them were at the brink of combustion.

Xavier kissed her neck. "You know what I'm feeling?"

Unable to speak, Nicole shook her head.

"I'm feeling the merging of sin and sensuous energy."

She released a small gasp of laughter as fingers increased the pace.

"You, Nicole Brooks, breathe life into every moment of my existence," he laughed with her. "You have me creating words, for there are none in the English dictionary to describe what I feel when I'm with you. I love you just isn't enough." He moved his body beneath her to the slow rhythm of his thumb against her nub. "Say it with me Nicole. Say what I need to hear."

The slow movement of him inside of her and his thumb was too much to bear. The blood rushed through her body, her head fell back and the word he wanted to hear escaped her lips. "Sinergy."